Roses Round the Door

Christine Marion Fraser lives in Argyll with her husband and teenage daughter. A keen reader and storyteller, she first started writing at the age of five. *Blue Above the Chimneys*, the first part of her autobiography, is also available in Fontana, together with her novels in the 'Rhanna' series and *King's Croft*.

Shirley

Roses Round the Door

Christine Marion Fraser

Fontana/Collins

First published in 1986 by Fontana Paperbacks, London
8 Grafton Street, London W1X 3LA

Copyright © Christine Marion Fraser 1986

Set in Linotron Plantin
Made and printed in Great Britain by
William Collins Sons & Co. Ltd, Glasgow

To the memory of
Smokey Joe; Sunshine;
and Shona, the smiling Samoyed

Contents

1. Hitler's Big Mate

'Sunday pa-pers! Sunday pa-pers!'

With thudding heart I wakened, my dreams as torn apart as the Sabbath morning by the newspaper vendor's uncaring yells. Blearily I opened my eyes to face another 'day of unrest' in the concrete jungle of the housing scheme. It was fast becoming a tough area where thuggery and vandalism abounded. Our terrace was known as 'the goldfish bowl'. Everybody saw your comings and goings, therefore gossip, real or imagined, abounded.

Calum, my brother-in-law, had tried valiantly to create a garden at the front of our flat and had put a fence around it. In came the hooligans, ripped out the flowers and the fences and for good measure threw stones at the window.

Gangs played rough games of football in the road and if the ball came into the garden and crushed the replanted plants, woe betide you if you dared to open your mouth in protest. The louts simply made faces and warmed your ears with strings of oaths and quite often a window would be thrown open and the louts' parents would give you a good tongue-lashing into the bargain.

If it was known that a possession was one that was particularly prized, then an all-out effort was made to ensure that it soon became fit only for the scrapheap. Bertha, my little three-wheeler invalid car, was the most prized possession of my life so the thugs battered balls into her bright blue paintwork and also fiddled with the engine and the spark plug, causing me many a morning of heartache at not being able to get my little car started. Worst of all, they climbed on top of Bertha to dance all over her with fiendish enjoyment and my vigil at the window was so constant I suffered badly from nervous anxiety.

Noise was another nuisance, from the vulgar blaring of the ice-cream van to the indelicate bellowing of the Sunday morning newspaper vendors. Govan had been a rural village in comparison and I now hated and feared the housing scheme, as did Callum and my sister Kirsty though at that time they had to make the best of it.

It was little wonder that I escaped it as often as I could. I rarely spent much time in the house where I lived, or more accurately lodged, with Kirsty, Callum and Sarah, my baby niece.

I went my own way a lot, partly to escape the housing scheme, partly to indulge in the kind of freedom I had never tasted before the advent of Bertha Buggy into my life. I loved every last rattling bolt in the uncomfortable little machine and would happily have driven to Timbuctoo if I could.

A lot of my young life had been spent in enforced inactivity after I contracted a rare bone disease at the age of ten. In those days I had lived in Govan with Mam and Da and a big family of brothers and sisters. Now it was just my younger sister Margaret and me living with Kirsty and Callum.

In the days of my disabled childhood I owed a great deal to the Girl Guides when outings and camps had helped me over many hurdles, both physical and emotional. Now I was a member of the Disabled Drivers' Association and it was through this establishment that I had made many friendships, both of disabled and able-bodied people. It was a fascinating den where courage and fortitude went hand in hand and where the younger set ignored the conventions and prejudices that had surrounded the disabled since the year dot.

I was one of that mob, shining-eyed, laughing at rules, always ready for any adventure that chanced along. I lived on impulse, taking each day as it came, uncaring about tomorrow and what it held.

That Sunday morning of June 1962 I lay in bed, the yells of the street vendor rattling my eardrums, watching the dismal sheets of rain streaming down the window, blotting out the drabness of grey concrete and grey skies.

'Aye be thankful for small mercies.' Da had preached us that on countless occasions and just then I was thankful that the miserable day outside made the prospect of another half hour in bed all the more cosy and would allow me to indulge in my favourite occupation of daydreaming.

My thoughts travelled with luxurious tranquillity back to Friday evening when I had trundled into the club with my friend Marie. It was a night I would always cherish in my mind because for the first time a young man called Kenneth Cameron had spoken to me.

Marie and I were discussing the forthcoming September weekend with enthusiasm as we had arranged to spend it in a caravan. It was to be a foursome, with Sadie McRae, a tiny person with a deep booming voice, and Nellie Brown, a tall, fair woman with dimples and crutches. I always relate these two things to Nellie because whenever I remember her I think of her swinging crutches and her laughing dimples.

We were all sitting in the games room talking, unaware that Bobby Meredith, a big red-haired man who used wheelchair leg supports like battering rams, was sitting nearby taking in everything we said.

'Come on, girls,' he had chuckled wickedly. 'How about letting me come? You'll need a man to look after you.'

'Listen tae him,' smirked Nellie. 'He canny even look efter himself.'

But after a few minutes of persuasive argument Bobby got his way and disappeared out of the room in red-faced delight.

'We'll be crushed in a wee van together,' protested Sadie vigorously. 'It means we'll have to try and get another van.'

Nellie giggled as she wondered aloud how Bobby would manage in a caravan.

'We'll help him,' said the unflappable Marie.

'Ay, but he'll likely need help tae get undressed and that,' persisted Nellie gleefully. 'And knowing him he'll be wanting somebody to powder his backside.'

Later in the evening Bobby came whizzing back to tell us that he wanted us to hear a funny story from Ken Cameron who was a student at the Glasgow School of Art.

Marie frowned and asked, 'Who's Ken Cameron?'

'Och, for heaven's sake!' cried Bobby lustily. 'The chap with the red hair and moustache, the one who runs about daft after us poor souls.'

I remained silent, trying to compose my features into a look of complete disinterest. For long I had driven Marie to distraction with my romantic hankerings after the elusive KC who was an able-bodied associate member of the club. At last I was going to get the chance of meeting him properly.

He was in a corner, piling chairs on top of tables, when we surrounded him. Bobby introduced us in his usual boisterous fashion. We exchanged polite greetings while the blushing Ken handed round cigarettes, obviously put about by our noisy intrusion. Bobby pressed him to tell his funny story and after a few minutes of humming and hawing he launched forth, his blue eyes shining. As a naive seventeen-year-old he had gone to study at the art school and part of the curriculum entailed life classes. At first he had been rather shocked to see people clad in nothing more than their birthday suits but gradually he got used to it and even became rather bored with the whole thing, preferring design work to anything else.

One day he was sketching a female model who was seated on a raised dais in the centre of the room, her back to the window which was above street level. Ken's attention strayed a little, his eyes wandering to the window. A little head attached to a man on a telescopic platform was slowly hoving into view, his objective being to paint a lamp standard. For a few minutes he worked away diligently, then glanced casually through the window.

Paint brush suspended in mid-air he gaped with complete and utter joy at the scene within before slowly disappearing below. In seconds he was back with several workmates who settled on the platform to eat their morning 'pieces' while enjoying the free nude show, huge grins of delight splitting their faces from ear to ear. By this time the class was snorting with fiendish joy while the model snorted with rage and demanded to know what the hell was going on.

The story broke the ice. We plied Ken with questions and learned he was in his final year at the art school.

'What about you lot?' The question was for everybody but his blue eyes smiled at me.

Marie laughed. 'Enjoy ourselves mostly but we do work as well — though if Christine Fraser could have her way she would spend her life in a tent or caravan.'

'Here, why don't you ask Ken to the caravan?' broke in an eager-faced Bobby. 'He could help me off with my calipers.'

Marie shot him a dark look. 'Thinking of yourself as usual?'

'No I'm not, I bet Ken would love to come.'

'It seems an awful intrusion.' Ken's tones were polite but hopeful.

'Oh, all right,' decided Marie briskly, 'though I don't envy poor Ken being saddled with you.'

I looked at Ken, he looked at me, and in those few moments real love for him was born in my heart, a steady thing that burned like a bright flame, not the flickering uncertain feeling that previous infatuations had instilled in me, but something good, and warm and lasting . . .

'Chris, are you not up yet?' Kirsty's voice at my door brought me out of my lovely reverie and reality came flooding back. The rain was still hissing outside, the Sunday paper man had departed the sodden streets but other voices were taking over, un-Sundayish voices, hotting up nicely. Soon the closes would be full of damp children, kicking balls at the wall and throwing abuse at one another and at anybody else who got in their way. In days gone by I too had bounced balls against close walls — never on a Sunday though. Neither Mam nor Da would have allowed it but values like that were fast disappearing in the alien environments of drab concrete blocks that looked like prisons.

When I duly presented myself at the breakfast table both Kirsty and Callum looked at me suspiciously. They always did that after I had crept into the house at one or two a.m. on a Sunday morning. It was no use me telling them I had indulged in nothing more wicked than a good going sing-song at a friend's house. I knew they both imagined I was 'going to the dogs' and nothing short of a miracle would check my headlong flight to total destruction.

To them I was wild, headstrong, and entirely without self-control. They had known me in my days of terrible loneliness when reading, knitting and solitary writings had been my only outlets and the big highs in my life were the outings with the guides. The complete contrast of that with my present life style floored my family completely and my times spent at home were fraught with tension on both sides. In their minds a young girl staying out till the wee sma' hours could mean only one thing and I was too resentful of their attitudes to even try to explain away my nocturnal wanderings.

Kirsty and I clashed continually. There was a lot of Da in her but there was also a lot of our warmhearted, caring Ma. Sometimes I caught her looking at me in a puzzled, unhappy way and I knew inside myself that she worried about me but wasn't sure how to handle the situation. It was a vicious circle really. My life as a disabled child, then as a teenager, had alienated me from my own family to a certain degree. Being disabled was something that was not socially acceptable in the fifties and sixties. There was nothing at home to help me enjoy my life as it was and so I sought my pleasures outside of the family circle. It's very difficult to explain. I only know that with the loss of our Da just two months ago and Mam fourteen months before that the bonds that had tied us all together had become a little frayed. Now, of course, they are stronger than they ever were but in those days we lived in different worlds and when we bumped into each other in the course of day-to-day living we often hurt one another in the process.

'I'm going away for the September weekend,' I announced nonchalantly as I ate my breakfast and made faces at little Sarah sitting in her high chair.

'Who with?' Callum shot the question at me.

'Some of the crowd,' I hedged, adding boldly, 'both sexes.'

'In the same caravan?' Kirsty's question came out in a squeak.

If I had been truly wicked I would have enjoyed it if I could have answered in the affirmative, but I wasn't truly wicked and I was also a peace-loving sort, so I reassured my big sister that I wasn't hellbent on a weekend of carnal pleasure and that my bedmate would be no one more dangerous than bossy little Marie.

A few minutes later Kirsty looked at Callum then at me. 'Chris,' she began hesitantly, 'Callum and me were wondering — well we were wondering if you would like to bring some of your friends up for a visit sometime. We never know who you go out with.' I looked at her earnest dear face and chose to ignore the veiled implications of her last words. In actual fact I think I was too pleasantly surprised to feel any sort of anger. I had often longed to introduce my motley assortment of friends to Kirsty and Callum but they had never indicated their desire for such a meeting, and I had never pursued the subject simply because I was afraid of their reactions to the various disabilities of such people.

'I'll ask them,' I said carelessly.

'Right,' smiled Kirsty. 'We'll have a party for them — after the September weekend.' The mention of such a notable event in my calendar brought Ken dancing into my

15

mind, but I didn't mention him to Kirsty — it was much too early in the day for that.

On the holiday Thursday I sat impatiently at my machine in the government-subsidised factory where I was a trainee overlocker. The whistle blew, my neighbour uttered a heartfelt 'Thank God' and I got down from my seat and into my wheelchair.

'Freedom at last!' I cried as I whizzed to the door, excitement daring me to blow a kiss at the boss who was skulking among the big knitting machines as if loath to put them out of action for three whole working days.

Jeannie the presser looked at me in surprise. 'Ye're daft,' she said with conviction. 'The boss doesny like familiarity — no even wi' his wife — no in public anyway. Ye must be mad.'

That holiday weekend was a memorable one for me, both for its hilarity and for the opportunity it provided of getting to know Kenneth Cameron. At first he must have wondered what he had let himself in for. We were a weird collection of wheelchairs, crutches and sticks and all we seemed to do that first evening in the close confines of the caravan was trip each other up, trip Ken up, and generally get in each other's way. Ken was endearingly courteous to us all and had a busy time running back and forward to the buggies to unload bedding and boxes of food. His rather serious façade lasted for as long as it took to get a meal going. Over it we discussed Nellie's ability to get lost, no matter how short or how easy the journey. She had somehow managed to take the wrong road on the way to the caravan and one of us had had to go and find her to bring her back. Sadie had been amazed at her friend's airy-fairy attitude about the affair. She was always being amazed at Nellie though they had known each other for years.

Nellie was forever incurring her wrath and Sadie's opinion of her friend had worsened after the night Nellie had nearly blown the two of them to kingdom come.

Nellie's buggy had broken down and they had been fiddling around with the engine to try and get it started when, without warning, Nellie struck a match to peer into the petrol tank to see if she had run out of fuel. Whoosh! Flames spurted out of the tank, singeing Nellie's eyebrows and hair, Sadie's head went up in a blue light, robbing her of much of her thick, curly hair. It had taken a long time for it to grow back in again and from then on she never completely trusted her best friend.

Marie brought steaming bowls of soup to the table and we tucked in hungrily. Bobby had decided to have his on his tray to save him moving from his seat. Despite his light-hearted attitude to many things he was a very fastidious type and before tackling his soup he tucked a huge white hanky cornerwise in at his neck. That was when Nellie christened him with a name that was to stick for many a long day.

'My God,' she intoned laughingly. 'Would ye look at Hitler's Big Mate!' There was no peace after that. Nellie kept up such a flow of nonsense we could hardly finish the meal. Bobby slowly slid off his seat and the rest of the evening passed in a shambles of merriment.

After the dishes were washed Ken and Bobby departed for their van which was situated a few yards away from ours. Once hauled to his feet Bobby could get about reasonably well on crutches and we watched them going over the grass, Ken hovering by Bobby's side with a torch, Bobby chuckling as usual. Nothing ever seemed to get him down which could often be a bit wearing for those left with the responsibility of his welfare.

Marie and I were sharing a bed under the window while Nellie and Sadie were to sleep in the double bed which came down from the wall near the door. It seemed very quiet without Bobby's boisterous presence and we were content to sit around preparing for bed, Marie with her rollers and cleansing lotion, Nellie with a few sorry-looking sponge curlers which she wound carelessly into her Pansy Potter-sort of hair.

Sadie eyed Marie's cleansing lotion with interest and asked for some. In seconds she was mopping away industriously, spreading her thickly pencilled eyebrows all over her face till she resembled a coalman.

I snorted but didn't dare make comment. Nellie however had none of my reserve. She had gone outside for a breather but was no sooner back over the threshold before she burst out, 'My God! Whit next! Ye go oot the door for five minutes and when ye get back yer white pal has turned black! Ye'd be a knockoot for the "Black and White Minstrels"!' Sadie was not amused. She scowled through her black eyes which only served to make Nellie laugh louder.

We were finally settled in bed, Marie last in because she was the most active and got the job of turning off the Calor gas lights. Once she was settled we lay talking, discussing everyone, for my part dwelling mostly on Ken till Marie groaned in my ear. The talk then turned to other topics, Sadie's temper in particular.

'She's a scream,' hissed Marie. 'It's the way her eyebrows disappear into her hair and she swears away like a trooper for the least thing.' I buried my head under the blankets to muffle my laughter. 'That's what I find so funny, and she's so serious about it all. My God! She's priceless and doesn't know it.'

Sadie's voice boomed suddenly from the other end of the van. 'What are you two loonies laughing at? Tell us the joke and we'll all have a bloody good time!'

I grabbed Marie's arm and tried to choke back my mirth but it was useless. We both let out a roar of ecstasy.

'Whit the hell's a' the noise?' came in Nellie's sleepy voice.

'God knows,' came in Sadie's rich tones.

'Whit's the matter wi' that two?' demanded Nellie. 'I wis jist droppin' into a nice sleep — noo I think I'll need to get up to the bog.'

'Oh no,' groand Sadie. 'That means ye'll have to climb over me and ye're like an elephant! Watch ye don't break my leg.'

I clutched Marie in agony as I listened to Sadie's groans

18

and Nellie's grunts. A muffled 'bugger it' came from Nellie who was bumping around in the dark. Shortly afterwards there came a loud drumming from the little chemical toilet. Being the old-fashioned metal type the acoustics were tremendous. The sides plunged straight downwards making the camouflage of noise well nigh impossible. For this reason I hated using it, and had opted to go outside to the bushes before turning in.

Nellie had no such modesty. The sounds from the 'bog' echoed loudly through the caravan.

'Would ye listen!' burst out Sadie. 'It's like the bloody Niagara Falls! Make sure ye don't flood the place.'

Nellie's uncaring giggles rent the night while Marie and I almost smothered under the blankets as we tried to muffle our laughter. After all that I thought I would never get to sleep but it had been a long day, the bed was warm and cosy and despite the tremendous snores coming from Nellie I was soon drifting off into the land of dreams, blissfully aware of the peace and the silence of the countryside all around.

The next three days were filled with the delights of that lovely spot by the deep, dark waters of Loch Eck, with laughter and singing, with the increasing awareness of my growing feelings for Kenneth Cameron. I gave no thought to the morrow, the housing scheme, the aching boredom of my job in a clothing factory. There's a lot to be said for living for the moment, for taking each thing as it came. I took all my moments and enjoyed them right well. I pulled time back, at least I pretended to. I achieved this notion quite successfully by filling each second with pleasure, the pleasure of the purpled hills, the bronze of the bracken, the gold of the birches. Unless called to attention I could sit for hours just staring at a particular scene, not measuring time by the hands of a clock but by the slow drifting of fluffy clouds, the tranquil ambling of the sun across the sky. Hours go quickly by when you rush about not taking time to really notice things, but out in the open countryside everything goes at its own pace. You are lulled by a sense of timelessness and are inclined to sit back and let the peace wash over you. I had noticed that Ken was apt to rush about, hardly pausing for breath, and I had wondered if he ever noticed his surroundings. The day before we went home I was delighted to discover that he did, and that he, like me, could sit for a long time drinking in beautiful things.

We were lying on the shores of Lock Eck, lying quite close together, now that I remember, though at first he seemed some distance away.

'There's a feeling of magic here,' he confided eventually as he looked at the hills mirrored in the green loch. 'I've spent a lot of holidays in different places but none of them had the kind of quality I can feel here.'

'It is a magic place,' I agreed softly, all at once remembering my days as a little Glasgow urchin when my mind had fed on fantasies of fairy castles with spires reaching into the sky to pierce the clouds. In those days my reality had been the looming grey tenements of Govan with their endless chimney towers thrusting into the sky. My stories of fairy castles had in some measure blanked out the grey streets, the squalor of the back courts. Now there was Bertha Buggy, taking me to places full of heavenly peace and heart-rending beauty. My castles now were the rearing pinnacles of mountains jostling shoulder to shoulder towards the sky. And it didn't matter if the sky was grey or blue, I loved it no matter what the weather.

'I'm glad you like it,' I told Ken. 'I saw it first with my mother and knew I'd one day come back to it.'

His steady blue eyes smiled at me. 'You're different from other girls,' he said shyly.

I laughed carelessly. 'I hope so. The world would be in a terrible state if there were a lot of people like me in it. Can you imagine us all? Bumping into each other? Getting our wheels all tangled together.'

'I don't even think of you as disabled,' he said earnestly. 'You're so full of life you put me to shame.'

I smiled. 'My kind of activity only comes in short bursts. I'm really quite a lazy person. I love just sitting back and daydreaming.'

'I suppose . . . there are lots of boyfriends?' he fished nonchalantly.

'Hundreds,' I teased, then seeing his crestfallen look added quickly, 'Only one at the moment.'

'Are you going steady?'

I hastened to reassure him I wasn't, adding, 'What about you? That girl you told me about yesterday?'

'I've hardly given her a thought since meeting you — I don't know why I even mentioned her to you.'

With a shout of joy I threw a pebble in the water. It plopped beautifully. Ken looked at me and we both smiled. Da would have said we were making sheep's eyes at one another.

Hitler's Big Mate was watching us. 'You two are helluva quiet. All that whispering and nudging. Can anyone join in or is it all top secret?'

Ken winked at me. 'Yes, Bobby, it is, just you go away and keep the others company. Nellie's just dying to talk to you.'

A roar of derision came from Bobby's able lungs to be thrown back at him from the encircling hills. Hitler's Big Mate didn't like to be left out of anything. Ken's hand crept to mine. The warmth of it embraced my heart and I tried not to think of the next day when we would all go our separate ways and these precious moments would become only memories.

2. Glasgow Knights

The time had come for me to leave my job in the little factory in the industrial estate. I was now considered to be competent enough as an overlocking machinist to spread my unwilling wings in the direction of the big hosiery factories.

The director of my own cosy little factory fixed me up with a job in a busy clothing firm in Glasgow. I was assured that I was very lucky to be accepted by this firm. A lot of people in my position never got such a wonderful opportunity to expand their horizons and had to be content to stay in small factories like the one I worked in now.

I did not want to go. I would have been perfectly happy to have stayed in a place where people were people, not robots who hung over machines all day, churning out garments as if their lives depended on it. I had had a trial run at the bigger factory and had witnessed these robots at work, sweating, pounding every last ounce of speed out of their machines. And I had heard the throb of other machines, a constant throb of enormous knitting machines clacking out bales of material, of pressing machines that hissed and steamed all day . . . and over all this bedlam the radio played through speakers. It was a mad, chaotic hell and I wanted none of it but of course I smiled gratefully at the director and thanked him for giving me such an opportunity. After all, he was doing it for my own good but then he simply couldn't know what was really good for me because he had never spent enough time with the real me, the restless me who hated repetitive work and who knew deep inside that there had to be something else.

But I went to my new job, feeling an accustomed pang of dread as I wheeled myself through the unfamiliar doors. Because there were steps at the front entrance I had to come in by the side doors. This meant that I had to wheel myself down the length of the factory in order to reach the time clock. Clocking-in was an entirely new experience in my life. It was a merciless beast and I grew to despise its accurate detailing of every second of my time. Being a machine it did not take into account that I had to trek through half the factory to get to it, a fact which often made me a few minutes late. The bosses did not take this into account either. Excuses about buggy punctures and wheel-chair punctures were met with sour acclaim. Often I limped into the factory with a deflated tyre threatening to pull me round in circles. It made no difference. I was in a world of able-bods and that meant keeping up or getting out.

Although there were several other disabled people in the factory they could all get about reasonably well on their legs. I was the only one in the entire place with a wheel-chair, which made me very self-conscious. But gradually I melted in and became part of the austere scenery. Like all the other machinists I was on piecework. In the beginning I felt I wouldn't make enough money to fill a thimble, let alone a pay poke. Gradually I got faster but I knew I would never become like the demented automatons that surrounded me. I dreaded a visit from the 'Time and Motion man' but I needn't have worried. They went for the fastest robots. Prices were fixed on how long they took to rip through a dozen garments. Pretty early on I realized I would never make my fortune at piecework but doggedly I plodded on, joining seams, making all the bits fit together, over and over from morning till night, all the while dreaming things inside my head in order to keep myself sane.

When the robots left their machines they turned into warm, laughing, often wonderfully funny human beings. I heard stories and jokes that made me shriek with glee. I made friends with many of them. Yet I was often lonely, especially at dinner time when everyone disappeared into the canteen which was in another building and had steps up to it. The steps effectively cut me off from the lunch-time mob. I missed the ways of my little factory where there was no canteen, only sociable little groups, companionably eating pieces and talking. I missed the little garden I had created out of a patch of waste ground. In this tiny, scented paradise we ate our pieces on sunny days and lifted our faces to the warmth, forgetting for a while the mundane things of everyday life.

At the big factory there wasn't so much as a blade of grass, only dismal grey concrete and the morose chirping of sparrows trying to be heard above the din of the boilerhouse.

Often I went to visit Marie whose work lay only a few streets away. Sometimes she buzzed round to see me but mostly I sat at my machine, eating my pieces in solitary isolation, throwing the odd crust at the mice which sometimes lurked among the mounds of boxes and bags just behind my machine. The 'ratman' paid regular visits to the factory, poking his poison baits into all the available cracks under the walls. His diligence ensured a strictly controlled rodent population and my crusts ensured that the remaining families were well enough fed. On one memorable day a particularly courageous little mouse came out of its hidey hole while all the machines were clacking away like mad. It sat on the floor beside me on its little hind legs, looking for all the world like a tiny dog begging. Carefully I raked in my piece box and threw the trusting little soul a crumb of bread. With an excited twitching of its whiskers it nibbled eagerly, while I watched entranced.

An unholy shriek rent the air. My little friend had been spotted. In panic it took to its heels, straight down the passage and in among machine pedals and feet.

'A mouse! A mouse!'

The agonized yells filled the air. Scuttles, screams, moans. Hell could not be as bad as that pathetic uproar brought about by one tiny frightened mouse looking for an escape route. Its presence brought the overlocking section to a standstill. Wailing girls scrambled on top of their machines to clutch at skirt hems and wind them tightly round their legs. Is there a belief among females that little mice are put into the world with the sole ambition of climbing up human legs? Especially feminine legs? During all the screaming I remained at my machine, stolidly working away.

'Chris, there's a mouse near you!' cried my nearest neighbour, just in case I was oblivious to the fact. The overlocking supervisor was valiantly trying to keep her cool but now she too succumbed to her fears. Climbing on to the highest machine of all she yelled, 'Send for Wullie! Somebody send for Wullie!' Wullie was the boilerman, an unflappable sort who could always be relied on to deal with unusual emergencies.

A girl came from the buttonhole section, brandishing a brush, her face full of scorn at the sight of all the overlockers perched atop their machines.

'It's only a wee mouse,' she said disgustedly.

'And its name is Mickey,' I said with a snigger. She giggled and went to poke her brush under the machines, calling,

'Here, Mickey Mouse! Come and see yer pals. They're all waiting for ye tae run up their skirts!'

By the time Wullie came the mouse had disappeared down a hole and the girls turned once more into robots, all frantically trying to make up for lost time.

The girls were interested in how I spent my leisure hours and one or two looked rather surprised when I regaled them with a few of my exploits.

'You make it sound so exciting, Chris,' commented those who were old-fashioned enough to think that disabled people as a whole must lead extremely dull lives. It was no use telling them my life not only *sounded* exciting. It *was* exciting.

I listened to their accounts of cinema visits and weekend

dances and thought how dull it all was. They simply didn't know how to get the most out of living or to appreciate the good times to the full. I had learned through the years of my disability that it was no use trying to impress upon able-bods the fact that, though my legs were not in perfect working order, everything else functioned beautifully, including my brain. This attitude was much worse in the older generation who often think that diminished faculties and institutions must surely go hand in hand. Fresh air lurks in the outside world, waiting to kill 'us' off if we don't muffle ourselves to the eyebrows in woollens.

We really oughtn't to have friends of the opposite sex. After all, if the question of marriage arose how could we 'possibly manage'. In a way I became a bit of a Jekyll and Hyde, wearing a different face for my various settings. I suppose we all do this to a certain degree. In my case the 'faces' were more deceiving, that was all. My social life at that time really was a breathless whirl. I went out with boys, and I was learning to swim. One night a week I went with a friend to the Turkish baths where I melted to a frazzle in the steam and the heat. Every weekend there was a party, and every Friday there was Ken at the club for Disabled Drivers, growing more and more relaxed in my company, joining in the parties, gradually abandoning the older crowd he had got caught up in and joining the younger set.

One night at the club he came up behind me and whispered into my ear, 'When are you going to marry me?'

Marriage was the last thing on my mind at that time and I just laughed at him and told him to stop joking. But as the weeks went on it became plain it was no joke to him. Letters from him began to arrive regularly, lovely fat letters, full of deep thoughts and feelings. On the flap of each envelope was a little drawing of Ken wearing an artist's smock and a beret. At the end of each letter there appeared a caricature of a little man peeping over the rim of a toilet pan, his hand on the chain ready to pull it. The slogan below read, 'If you don't marry me I'm gonna destroy myself.' With each letter the caricature was sinking lower into the pan with only the nose hanging over the rim.

I showed the cartoons to the girls at work. Gradually they were believing all that I told them.

'An artist?' they said in wonder while gladness and envy punched each other for first place in their eyes.

A month after the weekend of 'Hitler's Big Mate', the club held a barbecue. Ken was there and over the smoke and the flames we made eyes at each other and became so engrossed we burned our sausages to a cinder.

Gradually he edged closer to my chair. 'I've brought you a present,' he said shyly.

I was so overcome that I allowed half an hour to elapse before I opened the large oblong package. It was a set of oil paints and brushes in a lovely carry-case-cum-easel. I had mentioned that I was keen on dabbling around with oils never dreaming that he would take it so seriously. Later I learned that he had saved for weeks to get me the gift but all I could say at the time was, 'Oil paints!' in the way a gibbering fool might say, 'Nuts!'

Soon we were going out regularly. I found him considerate, courteous and kind. He was also a slave to convention which didn't suit me in the least. It was the sort of thing that stifled individuality and I had no intention of letting anyone smother me into oblivion.

One day in Sauchiehall Street, a rather posh street in the city of Glasgow, I took a banana from a paper bag at my side and began to peel it. My chair came to an abrupt halt as Ken stopped pushing. 'You can't do that *here*!' he hissed in deep shock.

'Do what?' I asked, stupidly.

'*That!* Eat a banana in the middle of the street.'

'I'm doing it,' I said calmly and went on eating my banana.

That was when I discovered his red hair really did signify a temper. Without another word he stalked away and left me in the middle of the pavement eating my banana.

Passers-by smiled politely and eyed each other but I sat where I was, eating my banana with slow deliberation while Ken lurked in a doorway till I was finished.

I discovered other things about him that were slightly disconcerting. He was embarrassed by window displays of ladies' lingerie. One day I stopped to gape in at an attractive show of frilly pants and bras. For a full minute I talked non-stop about all the things I would like to buy before I discovered that my listener was a delighted male stranger. Ken had disappeared into the crowd!

Despite him I went on eating bananas and sucking lollipops in the heart of sophisticated thoroughfares. To think Telly Savalas took a trick sucking lollipops and grinning his big grin! I was doing these things long before he ever got round to it!

But we were good for each other, Ken and me. He became less serious and laughed more often. I lost some of my impulsiveness and began to be more considerate and tolerant of the feelings of others.

My family were growing curious about Ken, wondering what special quality he had that was holding my attention for so long.

'Bring him up for tea,' said Kirsty.

'We'll size him up and tell you what we think,' smiled Callum.

I squirmed at this but duly presented Ken to Kirsty, Callum and Margaret. Kirsty was anxious to please, Callum, respectful and silently watchful, and Margaret was her usual pleasant easy-going self. Ken was shy yet assertive about his feelings for me. We were all very polite. What a contrast was that first meeting to the fun-filled nights of future family gatherings.

Ken left and his praises were sung.

'He's all right,' stated Callum in his soft Hebridean voice.

'All right! He's smashing!' cried Kirsty. 'Handsome too. I could fine go for a wee moustache like his.'

'Why don't you grow one?' grinned Callum sarcastically.

'Kirsty married and Chris with a steady,' murmured Margaret. 'I'll have to get my skates on.'

With winter coming on, Bertha was like an ice box but when you're young the blood runs thick and warm. When you're in love it boils over and so it was with Ken and me. But comfort is nice if you can get it and innocently I offered to baby-sit for Kirsty.

'Ulterior motives,' she smiled but took me up on the offer. So Ken was initiated into the intricacies of baby-minding, but it wasn't too difficult for little Sarah was a contented baby and crooned in delight from her cot at the sight of us kissing on the couch.

The time came for me to meet Ken's parents. We didn't want to make it too formal a meeting so managed to get Bobby, Marie and Wee Sadie, as we had come to call her, invited as well.

It was a dark, foggy night when we arrived at Ken's street. Gravestones loomed and I gulped, wondering if I had wandered into a cemetery but it was only the yard of a monumental sculptor. Bobby came up beside me, opened his window and roared, 'Have we arrived at Count Dracula's castle?'

A waver of torchlight shone in the gloom and Ken peered in at me. 'Nearly there, just follow me.'

The house was a former manse, grey and forbidding-looking in the fog, with a flight of steps leading up to the door.

Bobby as usual made a great noisy fuss as he half-fell, half-walked upstairs but for once I was glad of his support. Ken gallantly staggered upstairs with me in his arms. Behind us toddled Marie and Wee Sadie. We were a variety of wheels, crutches and sticks but not one member of the Cameron family batted an eyelid. Mr Cameron was a small man with a serious face and twinkling blue eyes. He received us at the door and did not even flinch when Bobby's crutch almost screwed his foot into the floorboards.

The sitting room had floor-to-ceiling books, a large piano

and a lovely family atmosphere. Mrs Cameron had the same twinkle in her eyes as her husband. She was kind and gentle but one sensed the laughter lurking beneath the surface. Ken's young brother Scott was a dark giant of a boy, their sister Marjory a slim, pretty girl, deep eyes aglow with life. It was soon plain that to them we were people. Not disabled people to perhaps pity a little and make a fuss over, just people to talk to on the same par as anyone else.

Some able-bods feel ill-at-ease in the company of the disabled, never quite meeting your eyes, never quite addressing their remarks to you just in case you might not understand. Others quite simply ignore your presence altogether. You are not whole, therefore you are not wholly there, a kind of invisible entity. It takes a lot of hard work to get this sort to acknowledge that you exist, that is if you feel they are worth all the effort. Thank goodness they are in the minority group of able-bods.

The Camerons were an open-minded family and by the time we made our erratic way into the dining room we were all feeling quite at ease. It also turned out that they were a family of leg-pullers. Over tea, Marjory informed us that the dining room furniture had been hired for the evening. With a straight face Mr Cameron confided that the beautiful china teaset had been borrowed from a trusting friend.

They were also a family of animal lovers. When we went through to the kitchen two dogs ran to meet us and a great army of cats descended to fight for strokes and tickles. Because I had a permanent lap I was immediately exploited. Two felines draped themselves over my knee, another hung lovingly over my shoulder, deafening me with its purrs.

That night I was destined to discover what was going to be my greatest rival for Ken's attentions. He had a model railway. One of the upstairs bedrooms had been converted into a railway room. Up we went to see it. The skill and patience that had gone into that amazing lay-out of tunnels, mountains, lakes and stations could not be denied. I could not deny it, certainly not to a shining-eyed Ken so obviously anxious for my approval.

'It's . . . fantastic,' I said, my eyes glued to a busy little engine with a light and smoke that puffed from the chimney.

'Hey, Mac, you've forgotten your bunnet!' yelled Bobby in delight as the engine disappeared into a tunnel.

Mr Cameron met us at the foot of the stairs, grinning from ear to ear. 'I'm surprised my son let you escape. He's a stranger in this house you know. If he's not got his nose buried in an art book he's upstairs footering with his engines!'

We gathered to have a sing-song round the piano. Ken's parents were both musical with his mother a professional church organist and his father playing popular tunes on the piano. When Wee Sadie began yodelling the room shook with surprise. She was a great yodeller. No microphone was required by this tiny person with the big, melodious voice. It was an experience to hear her yodels bouncing from ceiling and walls and we all applauded with delight.

'Come again, all of you.' Mrs Cameron told us at the close of the evening.

Mr Cameron smiled his twinkling smile. 'The house won't be the same again till you come back with your yodel, Sadie, and Chris comes back with her giggles. She doesn't say much but she's a great giggler.'

'They love you, they love you!' Ken told me joyfully as he staggered downstairs with me in his arms.

'They think I'm daft,' I said mournfully. 'You heard your father.'

'He was only pulling your leg. You'll have to get used to that.'

The others phut-phutted away but Ken sat with me for a while in Bertha. We made arrangements to meet the following evening.

It was a night of thick fog. I arrived late at our rendezvous but Ken was nowhere in sight. Somehow I made my way to the nearest police station where a young constable carried me into the station. There I was fortified with tea and biscuits while the young constable parked Bertha in the yard then came back to phone for a taxi to take me home.

When I saw Ken a week later at the club he came running to explain he had waited ages for me in the fog and had eventually taken a taxi over to Nellie's thinking I might be there. Selfishly I was pleased to learn he had been frantic with worry over me but hadn't been able to get in touch because he had been in bed with 'flu.

'I ended up drinking tea at the police station and getting a taxi home,' I laughed. 'You won't find me driving around in the fog if I can help it.' I really shouldn't have laughed because fate has a knack of throwing frivolity back in your face.

It was a November of filthy weather. One night I came out of work into a world of pea soup. Quite literally I couldn't see my hand in front of my face let alone the tip of Bertha's snub snout through the tiny circle I blew on the ice-covered windscreen. Bertha was not equipped with a heater. Ice patterns glistened on the paintwork of the metal interior. It was like sitting inside a refrigerator turned up to full blast. I felt like a human ice lolly but the cold was the least of my problems. To see my way home was first and foremost in my mind.

Wullie the boilerman hovered through the gloom. 'I'll guide ye oot the yard, hen,' he called and waved me on.

'Thanks, Wullie,' I yelled, then wondered what I was thanking him for because it seemed he had guided me not on to the road, but into a grey hell. Headlights came towards me and I realized I had strayed to the wrong side of the road. But I kept my cool, in my mind I mean. My body was so cool I couldn't feel certain vital parts of it! For a long time I sat at the roadside. I wasn't scared. I never really got scared in all the situations I had landed in since first taking to the road in rickety old Black Maria, my first invalid car. Whenever I landed in a sticky spot I thought of Mam. She was my guardian angel. From the day she died and went to her rest I knew inside myself that she watched over me.

'Are ye lost?' The voice was just outside but I couldn't see who owned it so I opened the door and peered out.

It was a young boy, grimy, tough and kind. 'Here, I know you,' he went on in surprise, 'Ye stay roon the corner frae me. There's nae buses runnin' the night so I've tae walk hame. C'mon, follow me, I'll haud my torch at my back. Just follow the light.'

Mam was with me.

For two solid nightmare hours I followed the gallant youngster. Through traffic jams he led me, past ghost figures that coughed and hunched along in the cruel sea of mist. Harassed traffic policemen loomed at crossroads, pale shadows of light filtered eerily from shop windows. And all the time that little light bobbed along in front of me. For me, at that time, it was the light of the world. My windows constantly iced over despite the wipers. I fumbled and somehow managed to light a cigarette and I held it against my windscreen to keep a little circle clear of ice in order that I could keep vigil on my Knight of the Torch.

Just when I thought my freezing limbs must surely snap from my body the boy was at my windows calling, 'We're hame! Open yer door and I'll help ye oot.'

And he did. Without bothering to fetch Callum he grabbed a hold of my chair and pulled me up the stairs and into the close as if he had been handling wheelchairs all his life. Before I could open my numb lips to thank him he was running downstairs, already being swallowed up in the fog.

'Where do you stay?' I called.

'Jist roon the corner!' The voice floated back at me, a ghostly echo without form.

No matter how hard I looked for him I never saw that boy again. He had appeared to help me in my time of need, sent by God, by angels, by any one of the higher powers that our unsophisticated minds could only just grasp at. I had faith and that was all that mattered.

All too often my circumstances placed me in some difficulty or other. Buggy breakdowns were a regular feature of my life and I could count on Bertha to sob to a standstill in the most awkward places — traffic lights and busy crossroads coming into the top ten. But always someone appeared to help. My guardians came in many disguises yet come they did, sometimes too well disguised for me to recognize them.

Soon after the fog incident the whims of the elements placed me once more in a fix. I had spent the evening with Ken and now we were parked in our favourite spot on a hill overlooking the railway station. Between kisses Ken liked to watch the trains coming and going but his arms were round me. We were cocooned in our own little world. The whirling snowflakes outside belonged to another planet. We were warm and safe inside Bertha.

But Ken's common sense began to get the better of him. It was late. The snow was beginning to lie so he became quite masterful and ordered me to go home. Sulkily I went. Anxiety did not come till I came to the foot of the long, steep hill that wound into the housing scheme where I lived. When other roads were just mildly slippery, Wormy Brae was a treacherous skating rink. Now it was a thick icy ribbon that snaked upwards to white eternity.

Bertha only had one rear driving wheel. Halfway up the brae it began to spin, juddering Bertha along sideways. But somehow I slithered my way to the top with my heart racing faster than my valiant little engine. At the top of the hill the snow was thicker. I was just starting to congratulate myself for conquering the Wormy Brae when Bertha ground to a halt in a pile of rutted snow.

I looked at my watch. 12.45 a.m. and not a soul in sight. With slow deliberation I reached out and switched off my engine. The uncanny silence of the snow-covered country-side wrapped round my ears like a muff. I opened the little flap in my Perspex window and peeked out. A street of houses lay in front of me and not a light in one of them. The residents of High Wormy Brae were asleep. I was on the fringe of the housing scheme, a quiet rural-like stretch on top of the world. Behind me, far in the distance, the outlines of the Campsie Braes were half smothered in yellow-grey snowclouds. In the deep, dark bowl beneath, the lights of the city winked, cold and remote.

Lighting a cigarette I told myself help would come. There were always taxis coming up and down this road. If I sat tight and waited something would turn up.

Half an hour and another cigarette later I began to have doubts. Nothing stirred in the cold, white world. Then a brilliant idea crept into my mind. Why not dig the snow away from the driving wheel? Anything was better than nothing. Looking around for a suitable shovelling item I found a few rusting spanners which, even to my optimistic eye, would be of little use in the marathon task ahead of me.

When you are cold and tired, inspiration very rarely comes in blinding flashes. For a long, blank eternity I stared at the tiny, square wooden box which served as a storage space for essential bits and pieces and also made a useful if uncomfortable seat for hardy escorts. I grabbed the removable lid and stared at it. Just recently Ken's bottom had warmed it. At the thought of him I began to feel self-pity. He would be tucked up in his nice warm bed unaware of the plight of his little darling.

Swallowing hard I looked at the box lid with affection and told it, 'You are a shovel and you are going to dig me out.'

I opened the door and started to heave my chair outside. The cold blast that rushed through the door was somewhat repelling but without any more feelings of spirit-quelling self-pity I heaved my frozen cheeks on to the chair.

Armed with the makeshift shovel I began my task but it wasn't easy. The brakes of my chair weren't too efficient and I kept sliding forward, bumping my head so often on Bertha's flank I began to see stars. Reluctantly I arrived at the conclusion that I would get on better if I got down on my knees. The ground was hostile to limbs already numb with cold but my box lid was making a good impression and I was able to scoop quite a quantity of snow away from the driving wheel. But in a careless moment I lost my balance and slithered away from both Bertha and my chair.

'Oh hell!' I said angrily as I lay upon the icy ground, wiping my running nose with my sleeve. 'The Queen doesn't know what it's like!'

Why I picked the poor Queen to vent my feelings on I shall never know. I was quite fond of the Queen in a remote kind of way. Perhaps my mind had latched on to the one person in the land least likely to ever know the kind of experiences I was experiencing now.

'*She's* got servants,' I told a large lump of snow irrelevantly before I heaved myself up on my hands and knees and crawled up the slippery slope to my chair.

It was a sodden apology for a human being who eventually sat in Bertha, praying a silent prayer before I let in the clutch. Joy! She was moving! I had done it! Christine Marion Fraser was of the stuff who didn't need flunkies! I slithered into a hard-packed rut, Bertha let out a long, low sigh . . . and wouldn't budge another inch.

Quickly I reached for my cigarettes. My frozen thumb flicked at my lighter but it refused to light. Like Bruce's spider I tried and tried again, flicking at the lighter till my thumb was raw and no vestige of a flint remained to give off even a spark.

The part of my brain that had recently concentrated solely on my plight now pivoted round the problems of getting my cigarette lit. For ten frantic minutes I rummaged through every corner of the buggy. Eventually, joyfully, I found half of a match. I stared at it, loving the little pink head, beseeching it to light. I had no box upon which to strike it but, undeterred, I struck it against a rough bit of bodywork under the dash. The little pink head disintegrated, crumbling away like tablet, leaving pink streaks on Bertha's blue paint.

My pent-up frustrations came out in a rush. I hurled

abuse at the snow, at Bertha for having so little pulling power, and at myself for being such a fool as to get myself into such a ridiculous situation in the first place.

But swearing was not going to get me anywhere. Rubbing at my damp knees I came to the awful conclusion that I would have to get out and push myself home. Under normal conditions the half-mile journey would have been tiring but possible. In present conditions I could not assess my chances. It was now two o'clock. There was no sign of a living soul in that unfriendly white world.

Slowly and painfully I hoisted myself over the hostile terrain. Wheels skidding and sticking I cursed every curse known to me and when I stopped to get breath I looked back at Bertha sitting on the brow of the hill. All at once she seemed like a small haven, a familiar thing in a desolate land. Looking round at the empty streets, the gaunt buildings, I felt frighteningly alone. Till then my feelings were those of a person bereft of the normal comforts of everyday life, now fear began to creep over me. Quite recently, not far from this very spot, there had been a murder. I wasn't very sure of the facts but the word *murder* whirled round in my head with all its terrible implications.

A wood lay ahead of me, snow-covered branches reached out long arms, pointing me out as the next . . . victim?

'Stop it,' I told myself fiercely. 'Just keep moving.'

It was then I heard voices, male voices, still a good way off but coming ever nearer in my direction. The men were not talking loudly but in the silence their voices carried clearly and I could tell they were a real pair of keelies (which is a colourful Glasgow word for 'hard men').

My heart beat a tattoo in my throat. 'Help me, God,' I prayed silently.

The men got closer, my heart beat faster. One of the men cried, 'My God, Shug! Look! A wee lassie in a chair! She must have got stuck!'

They raced over, showering me with concerned questions. Breathlessly I explained.

37

'Haud tight, hen,' said Shug, a little smout of a man with two missing front teeth. 'They don't call us Samson and Charlie Atlas for nothing. We'll take ye back tae yer wee caur and push ye hame.'

I said it would do if they just gave me a shove home in my chair but they wouldn't hear of it.

'No fear, hen,' said Charlie Atlas stoutly. 'The weans would have yer wee caur dismantled come mornin. We might as well dae the job right. Put yer feet up and haud on.'

Bertha's engine started quite readily and the men each put a hand on a window jamb, a shoulder to the rear and off we skited. They heaved, slithered, fell and cursed. Every so often they stopped to get breath and to blow their noses in the snow. My house lay uphill, ever higher. Bertha's engine whined, the men pushed with all their might. For an eternity in time my world was a snow-caked box filled with pants, puffs, groans, oaths. The Land God Gave To Cain seemed a far better deal than The Land God Gave To Christine. But in my land he had placed two knights, the salt of the Glasgow earth.

Somehow, sometime we arrived at my close. The men were bent double, rasping, wheezing, fighting for air. In a moment of panic I thought they were going to die but a few minutes later they were fully recovered, laughing, jubilant. They looked at the steps up to the close.

'How dae ye usually get up these?' asked Shug.

'If the family are in bed I just bum it.'

'Intae yer chair,' ordered Charles Atlas, 'We'll cerry ye up.'

At the top of the stairs I tried to thank them but they brushed my words aside cheerily.

'Think nothing of it,' shouted Shug as he slithered away, 'Ye'll maybe dae the same for us sometime!'

The house was quiet and warm. Little Sarah slept peacefully in her pram, a cinder crackled in the grate.

For a long time I sat and thanked God for my Knights of

the Snow and it seemed in the stillness that Mam's hand touched mine the way she had touched it in the far-off Govan days when the warmth of her presence stilled my childhood fears.

3. Another Milestone

The rest of the winter passed in a jumble of work, parties, club outings and family affairs. 1962 had been a good year for me. In its duration it seemed I had crammed in everything denied to me in my earlier teenage years. Most important of all, it was the year I found Ken and discovered what real love between a man and woman was all about. It seemed he had had his eye on me from the very first night I had quaked into the club with Marie in a flurry of nerves and shyness.

Now I not only knew Ken, I was getting to know his family too, and to love them like my own. They were very patient with me while they waited for my shell of shyness to crack. Bit by bit I crept out and blossomed and it was perhaps just as well that they only gradually got to know the real me, complete with madcap schemes, impulsive moods, and Mam's sense of humour. But Mum Cameron was of the north east too. Her own mother had belonged to the north so the family had strong ties with Speyside. Mum Cameron's sense of humour was like Mam's, warm and couthy, but like Mam she had breeding and knew instinctively who could take it and who couldn't.

Dad Cameron was full of an old-fashioned chivalry that was bewitching. If Ken kept me out too late at night then Dad Cameron would drive the family crazy by recounting all the things that might happen to me on my lone journey homewards. It was difficult for Ken in that I saw him home instead of the other way about. It was the peculiar circumstances of the affair that reversed the roles. He had no car. I had Bertha Buggy. It would have been ridiculous for him to see me home then take a taxi back if he missed the last bus. He was still at the art school and not financially equipped to indulge in expensive forms of transport.

At first it had taken much persuasion to get him to travel with me in Bertha but by the time 1963 had winged its merry way in he was quite at home on the little box-cum-stool at my side. Rather uncomfortably at home because he had to squash in beside my wheelchair and it was as well he was slimly built.

We made the most of that first lovely summer together and went camping all over Scotland. Surrounded by camp gear we were like a couple of badly squashed sardines inside Bertha. It was not ususual for her to refuse to carry us up long steep hills and quite often Ken had to unload all the stuff at the bottom and carry it up to where I was waiting at the top of the hill. We made the most of every minute of every day. We were at the zenith of our pre-marriage days, enjoying our freedom, knowing and loving each other more every day.

By September of 1963 he had graduated from art school with a diploma and was now with a firm of technical designers, working on contracts to the Admiralty, NATO, IBM and Scottish Aviation, which was all away above my head but sounded pretty good, and Ken was happy which was all that really mattered.

It was at this time he decided it was high time we were engaged. This was just at the beginning of September when I was staying at his house for a fortnight. Kirsty and Callum were away on holiday and Ken's parents had left the day previous to spend two weeks at Croft na Geal with Great Aunt Agnes. Marjory was working in Arran so, with the exception of Scott, we had the house to ourselves. Of course there was also the army of dogs and cats to feed and tend which was in itself a full-time task. But without actually saying so Ken and I pretended we were married and keeping house.

For two whole weeks we lived out of tins. I had the

marvellous excuse of not being able to get into Mum Cameron's kitchen which was up a short flight of steps from the main kitchen-sitting area. While I developed a strong wrist from continual combat with a tin opener the two boys gallantly concocted makeshift meals which we ate on trays in front of the television. Ken was a great one for 'bloody pudding'. In cookery books this can be found to be 'bread pudding' but in the Cameron family the first term was favoured ever since the time Ken had suffered a whole week of soup and a main course with never the taste of any sort of pudding to wet his whiskers. By the end of the week he could contain himself no longer and had finally simmered over, frothed, bubbled. Whatever you care to call it, Ken had done it. There and then at the dinner table he had thrown a red-haired tantrum, claiming that there were so many 'damned cats' supping all the milk there was never any left for the humans. 'I want a bloody pudding!' he had raged, emphasizing each word by banging his soup spoon on the table top. 'A bloody, bloody pudding! I want especially a bloody *bread* pudding! I'm sick of cats getting all the milk! I'm sick of cat's hairs in my tea and cat's hairs on my clothes! They should all be kicked out on their necks!'

For a few minutes the family had been dumbfounded. Ken was a very placid chap, you see. He seldom complained, harped, shouted, or any of the unpleasant sort of things that people like myself indulged in, but when he saw red . . . brother! It was scarlet, crimson, blood red that he saw! I had witnessed one such temper myself when I had arrived late one night at his house for tea without any firm excuse for being so. The bloody pudding incident saw Mum Cameron tripping up the kitchen steps to cry over her hot stove while Dad Cameron lectured Ken severely and Scott and Marjory screamed with such uncontrolled laughter that very soon Mum Cameron was crying tears of mirth and Dad Cameron's eyes twinkled. All but Ken had laughed . . . but he had won the day, or rather the bloody pudding, because the next night one lay steaming at his place, a bloody bread pudding, thick with jam and raisins and a fluffy meringue topping.

When Mum and Dad Cameron had been away for one full week at Croft na Geal Ken declared that he had had enough of tinned food. Scott and myself were instructed not to enter the kitchen premises and Ken disappeared into them for a good part of Sunday afternoon. Dinner time came. The table was beautifully set. A milk jug instead of a bottle, jam in a dish, butter on a tea plate instead of a greasy paper. No soup spoons but knives, forks — and pudding spoons. The first course came, extremely palatable mince and tatties. Scott wolfed his down. He always did this, like a puppy trying to get more than its brothers and sisters. I was a very slow eater, compared to Scott that is. My jaws worked very, very hard but the food on my plate went down very, very slowly. Scott on the other hand hardly seemed to move his jaws yet his food just disappeared. If ever a food-moving machine is invented then Scott was the prototype.

I ploughed my way through the last potato. Scott was politely sitting with folded arms looking positively starving, Ken was oozing with impatience. I had hardly swallowed my last bite before my plate was whipped away by Ken who went into the upper kitchen and shut the door. The oven rattled, plates banged, burnt fingers incurred a few curses. Then the door was ceremoniously thrown open and down the steps came Ken bearing a steaming bowl in the manner of a chef carrying a haggis at a Burns' supper, slowly, proudly. The bowl was set on the table and of course it was a bread pudding, rich, reeking, like the mealy beastie but without the gushing entrails. Ken's breader was really quite something to look at. Thick black crusts poked out from the surface like the towering skyscrapers of big cities like New York, raisins lay in hilly mounds on a sea of oozing marmalade mixed with blackcurrant jam. Scott took one look and let out a great guffaw of mirth. He had a very loud and infectious laugh. It infected me and we both rolled in our seats.

Ken was always good at keeping a straight face. It was straight now, so straight his chin almost hit his knees. 'I know it doesn't look like Mum's,' he said with dignity, 'I don't know how to make that frothy stuff but I can assure you it will taste delicious.'

He spooned out great dollops. Scott seized his plate and began wolfing. I was not one for stodgy puds but dutifully I began on Ken's bloody breader . . . and it was absolutely scrumptious. We fought over the remains in the dish. The cats were ringed round the legs of the table waiting for scraps but they were out of luck that night.

'Now you know,' said Ken when the meal was finished, 'looks don't always count.'

Later that evening, when Scott was out and I was ensconced on the couch with Ken, he put his arm round me and said, 'I want you to come into town with me next week so that I can buy you a ring.'

'I don't like rings,' I said without comprehension.

'Not even an engagement ring?'

'We don't have the money for things like that,' I said lazily.

'I've got it,' his voice was quiet, his blue eyes very blue. 'I've been saving up for it ever since I started work.'

'But, there are more important things,' I protested even while my heart raced with joy at the idea of a fancy ring on my finger.

'A ring is important. I want to do everything right for you. I want to give you everything. It might take the rest of my life but I'll do it. You deserve much more than you've ever had. No one has spoiled you or pampered you and that's maybe why you're such a great kid . . . but it's time somebody pampered you a wee bit and that honour is going to be mine . . . because I love you, my lamb.'

My lamb! Mam's pet word for us children. Before I ever told Ken this he had used it as an endearment, and it seemed right and beautiful coming from him, like a continuation of Mam's love. He was like Mam in many

44

ways, gentle and considerate. Right from the start I had loved him for his kindness, now I loved him for everything that he was, even his red-haired tempers. He was a truly good, and human, human being. He had never fussed about my being disabled, never wondered about how we would manage this and that *when*, never *if*, we were married. He drew plans of houses on paper, wonderful concoctions with everything just perfect for a wheelchair, his clever, sensitive fingers making a pencil do magical things, while his enthusiasm bubbled over in words tripping one upon the other.

'Ken, I don't need all those fancy houses,' I told him one day, 'I'd live in a tent with you if I had to.'

'All right then,' he had laughed and immediately began to draw pictures of fabulous tents with every kind of convenience imaginable.

The following week we both took an hour or two off work and met in town. Ken trundled me into a well-known jeweller's shop where we both took a fit of nerves at the enormity of the step we were about to take. We also turned pale on seeing the price tags fixed to a tray of rings immediately in front of our vision. 'Let's get out of it,' I whispered.

The owner of the shop came forward, all smiles and folded hands, wanting to know if he could help. He did, of course, beautifully, tactfully, bringing out several ring trays with prices ranging from those in the three figure bracket to those hovering just over one figure. A solitary diamond caught my eye in a setting of platinum with little gold horseshoes embracing the precious stone. There was no price on it and my heart fell. It was probably too dear for the cost to be displayed.

'You like that one, don't you?' said Ken politely because the owner of the shop was standing with his hands on the counter beaming down upon my cringing spirit. He picked up the ring and looked at it lovingly. 'A lovely setting, horseshoes for luck . . . so appropriate for a young couple thinking of spending the rest of their lives together.'

The price tag was nestling in the little hollow left by the ring. The figure was nowhere near the single bracket . . . and nowhere near the upper. It came comfortably into the middle range and Ken's intense young face broke into a wide grin of relief. He looked at me and I nodded and of course the shop owner, obviously so familiar with such dumb exchanges between young couples, asked for my hand and slipped the ring over my finger. But it stuck at the knuckle. I was not the fragile-fingered type but this was only a minor drawback.

'Just a small adjustment . . . and you should have it next week,' said the shop owner.

'I would like it inscribed, with our initials and the date,' said Ken gently, then with a smile, 'so that I will never forget our anniversaries.'

'It's wedding anniversaries you're supposed to remember,' I pointed out wickedly.

'Och, that's just convention,' he returned with dignity. 'Engagement anniversaries should be remembered too.'

We went out into the street and looked at each other.

'I think I'll eat a banana in the middle of the street to celebrate,' I choked joyfully.

'Don't you dare!'

I hooted. 'A minute ago you were all for throwing off silly old conventions! Why don't you eat a banana too?'

Without a word he went into a fruit shop and came back with a bag of bananas, handing one to me and keeping one for himself before tucking the rest down the side of my chair. Slowly and seriously he peeled his banana. I followed suit with mine, and we set off down the street giggling like a couple of fools as we wired into our bananas with great enjoyment.

The girls at work were agog with excitement when they heard that I was officially engaged.

'Where's the ring?' they clamoured.

'At the jeweller's being inscribed,' I answered proudly.

For the rest of that week groups of girls huddled and whispered together. It was always the same when somebody got engaged. Secretive plans were laid to give the engaged person as many little surprises as possible. You knew the surprises were going to be for you but had to give the impression of being very nonchalant and unaware. It was a sort of little game which you played by instinct because games like that had no concrete rules to go on.

By Friday I was positively exhausted by my self-imposed restraint and was glad to get out of work. But there was no rest to be had that evening. Our elders were due home next day so we had a mammoth dish-washing session and dusted and polished till the house shone. We all sent up a silent prayer that the bin men had been that day to cart away our fantastic assortment of tins because we did not want Mum Cameron going into horrors about the lack of vitamins we must surely have suffered in her absence. She was an expert cook and hardly ever opened a tin if she could help it.

They arrived on Saturday afternoon to be met by sleek, purring cats and barking, bouncing dogs.

'Are you all well?' asked Mum Cameron through a mouthful of cat fur. 'Did you manage to cook and feed yourselves?'

'Great,' we chorused, giving a silent vote of thanks to the bin men who had dutifully carted away all the tins.

Dad Cameron was taking good note of the general condition of the house and upon observing its tidy aspect took his pipe from his mouth to say, 'Stone me, Mother, I think I'll fire you and take Chris on as my housekeeper. The place has never looked so clean.'

Mum Cameron smiled and sat down to drink the cup of tea brought to her by Scott. 'Ay, but I wonder what it looked like yesterday,' she proclaimed with a knowing nod. 'I don't doubt we would have got a nasty shock if we had come home a day earlier.'

Ken scurried for the teapot. 'Sit down, Dad,' he invited. 'Chris and I have a nice surprise for you.'

He told them about our engagement over tea and cakes.
'That was sudden,' smiled Dad Cameron.

'I've been thinking about it for a long time,' said Ken, 'but didn't have the money to do anything till now.'

Mum Cameron was delighted and true to character was already making plans for a party, before her coat was even off wondering what to bake and how many she would have to cater for.

'Steady on, Mum,' laughed Ken. 'We haven't even got the ring yet.'

I took possession of the ring the following week. It was passed round the work to be admired. All the girls tried it on and wished on it. All that week I was showered with engagement gifts of all descriptions. I was thrilled beyond words. I had made many friends during my year at the factory but never realized my popularity till then. Gifts came from the most unexpected quarters. Sheets, towels, pillowcases, some of these in sets with 'his' and 'hers' embroidered into them. Those two simple words brought things home to me. 'His' and 'Hers'. To be used on a marriage bed, mine and Ken's. That was what it was all about. Not just a ring and a party with everyone laughing. This was the future.

At the end of the week I staggered home, my head spinning with good wishes and Bertha loaded down with parcels.

Towards the end of September the doors of the Cameron household were thrown wide for the party. Kirsty and Callum were there, Margaret and Stuart, my dear half-sister Mary, and her husband, half of the Disabled Drivers' Club, with Marie, shining-faced, eager-eyed, and Wee Sadie, yodelling with all the might of her big warm heart. I had grown to love this small person with her wonderful spirit and her enormous courage. I can see her now, her sticks at her side, her face alight, her dark head thrown back to let her magnificent melodious voice soar free.

Ken's elder married brother, John, was serving drinks

behind the bar. He wasn't so well known to me as the rest of the Cameron family but I liked him just the same because he had a lot of Dad Cameron about him. Scott escaped his mother's eye in the large crowd and made merry with his first real taste of whisky behind the sofa. Marjory had managed to come home from Arran and looked lovely in a blue wool suit she had knitted herself.

I had bought myself a new dress for the occasion, pink, lacy and very feminine. I hadn't been able to resist it after seeing it in a shop window. It was the sort of dress I had always wanted but was so entirely frivolous that it wasn't a sensible buy because I would likely never wear it again. Marie had tried to dissuade me from it but she could have talked herself blue and I wouldn't have listened. I had a weakness for pretty clothes but in the past had never been able to indulge myself because I was always so short of money. I was still short of money but determined to have that dress even though guilt tore me in two when it finally belonged to me. I sat at the party, lathered in my pink froth, hardly daring to move in case I should put one flounce out of place. But the 'water of life' was warming my blood and eventually I threw both flounces and caution to the wind.

That night I flirted with my future father-in-law by sitting on his knee, cuddling him and telling him he was 'the best wee paw in the world'. And I really meant it. He was like a father to me, the sort of father I had never known in my childhood. I loved and respected the memory of my own soft-hearted tyrant of a father but he had been worlds away from me because of his great age, more than old enough to be my mother's father.

Dad Cameron was so different in every way with his pawky humour, his twinkling eyes, his teasing. He roared with laughter when I cuddled him and kissed the little bald patch at the crown of his head.

'Look, Mother,' he shouted, 'I've got a girlfriend! You'd better watch out!'

Happy times! Happy memories! I can recapture that

scene now, feel its gaiety and bitter-sweet sadness. For Dad Cameron was ill, with a tumour in his lung and the years I was to have him for a father were to be short . . . but sweet and happy just the same.

He got up to play the piano and we all burst into song and all the while the doorbell kept ringing to announce the arrival of more people to swell the ranks. One of the latecomers was Mr Cubinski, the buggy repairer. He had been invited but being the fisherman he was we had expected him to be away for the weekend. He was greeted with open arms by all the disabled in the room who owed so much to his diligence in keeping us mobile. He rushed over to me and kissed me heartily. I blushed while the whole room cheered. A parcel was pushed into my hand which I was all for opening later but he wouldn't hear of it.

'Now, Christina, open it now,' he insisted. 'I went to a lot of trouble for this one.'

A pink gossamer nightdress fell out of the wrappings. 'Something nice for your wedding night,' smirked Mr Cubinski with satisfaction. 'The shop assistant told me it was just the thing for a young girl on her first night but, do you know what?' He grinned delightedly. 'I have a sneaking suspicion she thought I was buying it for my mistress.'

Everyone cheered again while Ken's blushes vied with mine. He was very handsome that night with his red-gold hair shining and his trousers neatly pressed. Normally he was rather sloppy about his appearance, definitely Bohemian in his attitude to clothes but for special occasions he conformed and tonight was one of the most special occasions of his life.

Kirsty had made lots of lovely little dainties for the party. Dad Cameron bit into one of her cakes with relish. 'These are delicious, Kirsty,' he approved with a twinkle. 'I think I'll have to swop Chris for you, you'd be a great asset as a daughter-in-law.'

'Too bad I'm already married,' grinned Kirsty.

'Wait a minute,' I clamoured indignantly, 'I can make terrific tablet! It melts in your mouth.'

'Oh well, in that case I'll keep you, you might come in useful after all.'

During the winter that followed Ken and I commandeered the big empty room upstairs and whiled away the long dark nights making rugs and painting bits of furniture. We had almost set the house on fire when first we lit a huge fire in the long-empty grate. The chimney roared and belched smoke and poor Mum Cameron went almost frantic wondering whether to call the fire brigade or evacuate the house. Neither course came to fruition thanks to Ken who came charging in with a bucket of water to throw over the fire. Black billows of smoke nearly asphyxiated us all, charred bits of paper flew merrily round the room, while the doused fire sent out acrid waves of rotten egg fumes. Dad Cameron gave us a good dressing down while his wife made inarticulate noises in the background that were meant to be apologies for not having had the chimney swept. She was a soft-hearted, kindly soul who hated hurting anyone's feelings, even indirectly. The sweep was called posthaste next day and we were able to sit before the comforting warmth of a blazing fire for the rest of the winter.

At Christmas the whole house was decorated with holly and mistletoe and a big silver tree that shimmered with fairy lights. Dad Cameron was the spirit of Christmas. He was like a small boy in his excitement. It was quite funny to watch him smuggling his presents out of sight because he was so furtive about it everyone knew what he was up to. On Christmas Eve large feathery snowflakes came drifting down silently to earth. By the time I came away from the Watchnight service with Ken a thick white blanket had draped itself over our world, giving everyday objects an aspect of beauty. Bertha slithered along to Ken's house and I knew I wouldn't make it home that night. I had warned Kirsty that if the weather worsened I would be spending the night at the Camerons' house. The old manse stood amidst the snow, the fairy lights winking in the window, warm, friendly, welcoming, so different from my first impression of it in the fog.

At the foot of the stairs in the hall Ken took my hands in his. They were warm and gentle. Like Mam's. 'Goodnight, my lamb,' he whispered softly.

'Merry Christmas, my dear Ken,' I murmured.

'Maybe next Christmas we'll be in our own wee house,' he said longingly.

'As long as we're together it will be all right,' I said and kissed him goodnight.

I lay on the big lumpy couch in the warm, silent sitting room with the embers of the fire giving the room a peaceful glow. Hundreds of cards were lined on bookcases, mantel-shelf, piano. I had never seen so many cards in my life. Under the tree lay heaps of beautiful parcels wrapped by Marjory. The whole room throbbed with love and happiness. I looked at the tree sparkling with tinsel and glass baubles and I was reminded of another tree many Christmases ago, a tiny green tree decorated with silver paper balls and squinty stars, sitting on the dresser of our dingy kitchen in Govan, and I remembered Mam's voice welcoming me home from hospital, anxiously hoping that the tiny tree pleased me, the warmth of her hands in mine conveying her love, her pleasure at having me home.

Now there were other hands, gentle, kind, full of reassurance, of a love that seemed somehow to have always been in my life, from the beginning. That was the kind of love that went on and on.

I looked at my wheelchair sitting like an obedient and faithful dog at my side. Wheels. It seemed they had always been part of my life too. I wondered where they would lead me next. What the next bend in the road would hold for me.

I held up my hand to look at my ring and the firelight glinted into the heart of the little diamond, making it shine so brightly it dazzled me. A precious stone, a stone that symbolized love, but most of all . . .

'Another milestone, Mam,' I whispered and fell asleep, contented.

4. Pastures New

New Year was barely over before Ken and I began the exciting business of looking for a house. After more than a year of courtship we felt we could wait no longer to get married. It would be untruthful of me if I said I had any qualms or doubts about marriage. I was a wild, carefree, impulsive creature and, as I have already said, I lived only for each day. I was not the sort of girl to lie in bed at night and think, 'Hell, I'm disabled. What's going to happen to me? Will I get married?'

I had not entertained the idea of marriage till Ken's arrival into my life. Before he had arrived on the scene I'd had three proposals of marriage but I was too busy enjoying myself to consider any of them seriously. Men liked me – I suppose I had that elusive thing commonly referred to as sex appeal. I enjoyed flirting enormously, I found it a wonderfully stimulating way of passing my time at a party and I had the knack of being able to escape from the person I had spent the whole night teasing and tormenting.

Ken admitted that the only worry he had was of finding a suitable house. The idea of being married to a disabled girl did not unduly distress him. In fact he revealed to me on more than one shamefaced occasion that he often forgot that I was disabled and perhaps did not come to my assistance as often as he should. This suited me down to the ground. I could not have married a man who felt obliged to run about after me like an obedient dog. At the time of meeting Ken, financially I was an extremely hard-up girl. I was so busy catching up with life that any talents that might have been born in me were pushed well to the background. So what did an able-bodied young man see in a young disabled girl? He admits to this day that it was my untamed free spirit that appealed to him.

'How do you feel when you're pushing my chair in public?' I asked him once.

'Proud,' came the answer.

'You're not just saying that? After all you're a very shy sort of chap.'

'When I'm with you, you give me courage.'

So that was that, no more needed to be said between us. Later on, of course I found out that it was *other* people who had misgivings.

'Do you think your son is doing the right thing?' Mum Cameron was asked by neighbours. 'She's a lovely girl but how will she manage?'

'The way she's always managed,' Mum Cameron replied with asperity.

'Oh, of course, Mrs Cameron, she's so independent but — well — she looks so perfect from outside . . . but what about — inside? You know?'

These of course were the fool kind of things that many people wondered. Because your legs were disabled it followed that your internal organs were too — especially the reproductive organs! As far as I knew, without actually peeping inside myself, my organs were all in perfect working order and were the least of my problems. On the whole, though, everybody was very pleased about our pending marriage. The Camerons had many friends, kind, wonderful, sensible people who gave not one thought to my organs or my disability. My own family were delighted, though Kirsty, perhaps feeling it her duty, took both Ken and me aside and gave us a talk on the practicalities of the married state which she told us was difficult enough even with a house, money and possessions.

We had none of these things but didn't care. Neither of us was materialistic and it didn't worry us greatly that we would have neither money nor lavish furnishings to start us off.

Our search for a suitable house took us far and wide. Always we came up with the same obstacle. Stairs! Those that were on a level were too disreputable for even our Bohemian tastes and the first thrill of house-hunting wore off with depressing rapidity.

Our spirits were at a low ebb when Ken heard of a couple who were living in a rented cottage outside Glasgow. They were in the process of buying a house which meant that the cottage would be empty in a few months. We arranged to go and see it and went through a nail-biting spell till the great day came, both of us feeling that hordes of young couples might possibly be waiting to pounce on 'our house'.

The day came and into Bertha we squeezed to follow a map obligingly drawn out for us by 'the cottage couple'. Our way wound through country lanes and past white-washed farmhouses. Crows flapped angrily into the sky at the intruding 'phut, phut' of Bertha's engine into the sleeping countryside. Up hill and down dale we scooted, charmed by the tracery of winter trees against the sky. Glasgow straggled far in the distance, its smoking chimneys, church towers, and the spire of the university piercing the clouds. The city lay in a basin, flanked by the Campsie braes with the snowy hills of Perthshire crowded into the gap between Drumgoyne and the Dumbarton slopes. Above them Ben Lomond loomed, an almond of frosted white. Away in the west the gleaming white peaks of Argyll crowded together in gregarious splendour.

'Oh to live here!' I cried in ecstasy, mentally comparing the scenery around me with the drab monotony of the housing scheme.

We almost flew over a humpy bridge then turned to make our way up a rutted farm road. The ruins of an old mill poked through the bushes on our left and away to the right we glimpsed the distant hills once more and with a nervous snigger I saw that Ken's fingers were crossed. It was obvious that he too would like it if we started off our married life in the country.

I rattled noisily into the yard sending squawking hens flying in every direction. I shut off my engine to look at the cottage which was attached to the main farmhouse building. A terrific clucking issued from a long, low building opposite the cottage and Ken said briefly, 'Battery hens, hundreds of them.'

Nervously we approached the cottage door. 'Only *two* steps,' breathed Ken and already he began to make quick excited plans about a ramp. But I wasn't listening. I was staring at a thin, straggly, miserable-looking twig that adhered precariously to the flaking whitewash round the doorway.

'Look,' I said in delight. 'Roses round the door!'

A few seconds after this exaggerated observation the door was thrown open and we were ushered up a narrow cavern of a hallway and into the living room. Furnished as it was with the cottage couple's tasteful possessions it was charming. A big fire burned warmly in a corner fireplace and a central window provided a somewhat restricted view of the fields and hills. The obstacle that blotted out the landscape was a huge hayshed stacked high with bales of winter feed.

Coffee was served out of an elegant coffee pot such as had only come to my attention from the wrong side of expensive china shop windows. I was so full of unnatural etiquette I could hardly speak and wished only the disappearance of the couple that Ken and I might view at leisure this little paradise of a place. We were shown the bedroom which opened off from the living room, then up a tiny hallway to a quaintly antiquated bathroom, across from it a dining room, then to the kitchen where a back door opened on to a grassy yard with the fields beyond. Into the scene came Mrs Murdoch, the landlady, a tall, well-built, kindly-looking soul with soft grey hair waving about her pleasant face and a 'country air' about her.

After introductions we proceeded to give her a sketchy account of our long wanderings in search of a suitable house, ending our tale of woe with warm praise for the cottage and how it would suit our particular case. We also painted our characters in an unnaturally rosy light and listening to the glibness of Ken's tongue I fully expected him to sprout a halo there and then. I pushed all thought of wild parties out of my mind and shook my head in solemn agreement with Ken's every word. Mrs Murdoch looked at us long and hard and with, I thought, a good deal of suspicion. But then, joy! She told us that the cottage would be vacant at the beginning of March and the rent was payable two months in advance.

We went away in a trance of happiness to count our meagre savings and decided we could just manage the rent with enough left over for a quiet wedding.

Our wedding plans forged ahead with all the arrangements preceding such an event.

'We'll hold the reception in our house,' Kirsty told us and I could have hugged her for our limited finances would not have allowed the hire of even the smallest hotel. Halls and caterers were also out of the question. I had no parents to indulge my smallest whim so we resigned ourselves to a rather quiet wedding. Nevertheless, I had decided I was going to be a white bride and Marie came into town with me to a gown-hiring firm. The fitting rooms lay up narrow flights of stairs so while Marie giggled and assistants looked at me askance I performed a fine 'bumming' display, pulling my folded chair up after me with spasmodic help from my merry friend.

I tried on several dresses deciding eventually on a close-fitting lace-covered satin. It was much too big for me so the kindly assistant stuck pins around various parts of my anatomy, mumbling through mouthfuls of them that I had made a fine choice and would most certainly be a beautiful bride. Whether she still maintained the opinion as I thumped noisily downstairs I shall never know. I last glimpsed her peeping from behind a row of dresses, a few pins still sticking to her tightly closed lips.

By early March when the cottage was vacated Ken and I could hardly contain our longing to go and look over it properly. The cottage couple had barely moved out before we swooped to crow over and comment on every little thing. I went charging through empty rooms, my wheels making squelching noises on the bare linoleum. We laughed and our laughter echoed; we poked and pried into cupboards; peered with delight at insignificant details, and shouted, 'It's ours! Ours! Ours!'

Then we made tea on the Primus we had brought. There was no cooker, it had been removed by the cottage couple but the tea tasted lovely brewed on our camp stove. We took the steaming mugfuls through to the dining room to perch ourselves on the broad ledge and gaze out at rolling brown fields and a romantic little glade carpeted with leaves through which wild daffodils were poking. Mrs Murdoch's vegetable plots lay some yards away while under the dining room window was a patch of rough ground that had been promised to us. In my mind's eye I could visualize a profusion of flowers and so much of an optimist was I that I ignored completely the fact that beds of nettles and ground elder had established themselves so completely it would take more than the efforts of an amateur disabled gardener to remove them.

We could hardly bear to tear ourselves away from 'The Cottage' which was the unimaginative but apt title of the little house. Already we had planned where to put our few sticks of furniture that we had either made, converted or wheedled. These possessions were pitifully few and inadequate but to us they were wonderful. Looking back I wish that I could get the same pleasure now from simple things. Yet I have never completely lost the childlike pleasure they give and I think it is a good thing not to start off with too many possessions. Otherwise, it is easy to take things for granted and never experience the euphoria we felt in the gradual gatherings of life's necessities.

Kirsty donated a passable-looking fireside chair. She also agreed to let me have our little budgie complete with cage and stand. Da had taught him to speak and he yelled things like, 'Where's Pop? Put that juke box aff!' and 'I've lost my een!' He was also an accomplished mimic, making realistic cat noises, wolf whistles, and a sound like a saw rasping through wood.

Ken had made a cabinet with sliding glass doors in which we planned to keep the lovely glasses we had received as engagement presents. We coaxed an old cupboard from Mum Cameron and painted it white with a view to using it as a kitchen cupboard to store the dishes we hadn't yet come by. I had spent the winter making a Readicut half-moon rug embellished with tan and orange autumn leaves which we could well imagine parked in front of a roaring fire. It was to be our only form of floor covering for many a long day.

To complete our collection was a little raffia stool made by Ken, a tiny rocking footstool, Marjory's discarded double bed, and an old dressing table and wardrobe painted white. Mum Cameron presented us with a complete bedding set as a wedding present and, with these worldly goods removed to the cottage in a van borrowed by Callum from a workmate, we felt dizzy with smug satisfaction.

A cooker was to prove a problem. Almost every one we looked at was too high for me to reach in comfort from my chair, but after much searching we came upon a shop in which there reposed a neat little double Belling. We put down a deposit and sailed from the shop in a state of delight. When it arrived at the cottage we assembled it on a coffee table next to Mum Cameron's cupboard, which now contained an assortment of 'jumble sale' dishes together with a galaxy of delft cups in every hue imaginable.

What we lacked in home furnishings was made up for in wedding gifts. I will never quite get over the excitement of that time with every new day bringing parcels from far and wide. Great Aunt Agnes sent an exquisite table-cloth of hand-painted silk together with a crumpled five pound note neatly folded. A typical Great Aunt Agnes gesture. I had visited this old lady of eighty in her croft near Loch Garten and immediately her rickety wooden gate closed behind me I had felt myself transported into the past. She was a

Victorian figure with her long white aprons, bird-like bright eyes and snowy locks of hair. She ran the croft single-handed and was up at the crack of dawn and last to go to bed. Muffled cosily in my bed the first morning I had almost died of shock when she rapped on the door at dawn to announce that breakfast was ready. Creeping blearily from my warm layers I had gone to the window to see her scuttling with agility over the fields in search of her cow.

A crate of Pyrex ovenware sent me into raptures even though I knew that most of them were far too big to go into the tiny oven of my cooker. I visualized them grandly decorating my kitchen in the way one sees such things displayed in glossy home magazines. The girls at work gave me sheets, glasses (we got dozens of them but still no decent cups!) pillowcases, towels, ornaments and cutlery. The two cleaning ladies clubbed together and presented me with blankets.

The whole of the Disabled Drivers' club assembled to watch us receiving a double electric blanket. Speeches were made, ribald laughter echoed when someone told Ken that the gift didn't say much for his abilities as a bed warmer.

In the midst of the excitement we rushed around in Bertha, posting banns, visiting suit-hirers and florists shops, receiving quiet advice from the minister of the church where we were to be married. We impressed upon him that we wanted a quiet wedding without even a church organist. What we omitted to tell him was that we were too financially embarrassed to afford the services of an organist!

The day of the wedding drew nearer and my workmates made furtive plans. Another girl was getting married the week before me and I looked with horror at her machine which was gaily decorated with garlands of bows and bits of waste material. A crude wooden archway had been assembled over her head, bearing a cardboard cut-out of a squinty-looking bride and groom surrounded by large 'L' plates. Every time someone passed the poor girl's machine her threads were cut and she spent the entire last day of her 'freedom' patiently rethreading her machine. At dinner time a bogie came trundling in and into this she was bundled to be dressed in a mock-up of a bride's outfit. Then she was wheeled outside where everyone joined hands and danced round her, before the men descended to kiss her. In the middle of the street she was enthroned on a large chamber pot, then subjected to more teasing and kissing before she was presented with the chamber pot in which she found a large bag of salt and a baby doll. Perhaps all this was a throwback to days of fertility rites but whatever it meant I didn't fancy any of it.

All week my mind swam with various plots to escape the fate. Miss Sims was quite kind to me during that week. She had always assumed a rather distant attitude towards me and I knew I was definitely not one of her favourites because she had them, 'older girls' whom she had known and worked with before she was hoisted to the upper rungs of the promotion ladder. Wee Jenny also condescended to mutter congratulatory words to me on my forthcoming marriage and to look at me with sour favour from behind her big specs. Wee Jenny was the supervisor of the overlocking section. Like Miss Sims she too had tottered up the ladder of success — and I really mean 'tottered' because her bandy little legs would most certainly have prevented her from doing much else. In a way she reminded me of Miss Black, my fearsome primary school headmistress with her swinging tawse and her cold, glittering eyes.

Like Miss Sims, Wee Jenny had her cronies, 'girls' in their fifties like herself. Miss Sims and Wee Jenny were both unmarried ladies and, from the latter at any rate, I had always sensed the unspoken thought, 'How did you manage it, and you in a wheelchair?' Wee Jenny had always looked delighted whenever she came to me with a bundle of 'returns', garments that had not passed the inspection test and which had to be unravelled and overlocked all over again. Returns had to be done in your own time otherwise you simply did not get much of a wage in your pay poke.

Your money was made by piecework and many's the dinner time I spent furiously going over my returns in between grabbing mouthfuls of sandwiches. These were the days I dragged myself wearily homewards without having had a break in the whole exhausting routine.

But on the week preceding my wedding not a single return came my way and Wee Jenny managed to summon up a belated interest in my engagement ring which had been on my finger for nearly six months. Friday approached and my hands grew clammy as I pushed garments into my machine. Careful though the girls were I could not help but notice the secretive collections for my presentation 'envelope', a packet of salt, a baby doll and a chamber pot.

'Don't be silly,' I told myself, 'they can't stick you on a chamber pot! Not in your condition!'

'What condition?' I asked myself wildly. 'Your wheel-chair won't get you out of this one! Not when you've convinced everyone that it's the least of your drawbacks.'

Should I pretend to be suddenly helpless? No! No! That would never do, not when I spent half my time boasting about my capabilities.

'Say you've got a boil on your backside,' I told myself with growing desperation. 'Tell them you can't sit on anything let alone a chanty!'

Wee Jenny began to look positively gloating and on Thursday brought a huge batch of returns to my table and dumped them without ceremony on top of the work I had piled neatly at my side. With malevolence I watched the retreat of her cowboy-style legs and felt like crying.

The girls were friendly, bright, chattering, yet I sensed a certain reserve in their attitudes. I was a shy one, never quite able to join with ease the ready repertoire of jokes and banter that flew around me. I had several steady friends but one of the mob I was not. I began to wonder if the girls' unease was incurred by the fact that they didn't know quite how to handle the coming situation. How to get me into that bogie, on to that chamber? Then horrors! I wondered if perhaps they were *not* going to treat me like everyone else. That for me would be even harder to bear than the indignities of being treated like any other bride-to-be.

That evening I went home with my belly in a tight knot and I was unable to eat my tea. Kirsty eyed me with concern and told me in big-sister tone that I needn't go into work the next day. She would phone Miss Sims with some excuse and I could spend my last day at home with Kirsty. We could have a rare old blether.

'It's going to be funny without you here, Chris. When I'm in bed at night I can't really get to sleep till you come in and I hear your wheels swishing through the house. I always say to Callum, "That's Chris, I hear her wheels" and then I go to sleep.'

Her voice was unexpectedly sad and I looked up to see the tears in her eyes. We had been together right from the start, first in Govan, now in this housing scheme. Margaret was away working in Newtonmore in the north in her fiancée's father's hotel, Alec had left home some time before, Ian had married a few years ago, so it was natural that I had become very close to Kirsty even though there was often a lot of conflict between us, something to do, I knew, with the frustrations she and Callum must have experienced sharing the home with a gadabout young girl who paid no court to time. I knew I wouldn't like to be starting off my married life with other members of the family in my home. But now the time of parting was near there was the inevitable sorrow of knowing that things would never be the same again, that we were all now on our separate roads through life. Her green eyes were very bright in those moments, her beautiful auburn hair shining in the light.

'It would be great — to spend tomorrow here with you,' I said gruffly.

And so I took the coward's way out. I could handle situations of mini-disasters with a fairly courageous heart, things like buggy breakdowns, being trapped in snowstorms, wheelchair obstacles, but anything that involved the human elements left me totally useless. Miss Sims proved very understanding. My 'envelope' she would arrange to be taken to an appointed place by one of the girls who hailed from my airt.

The last piece of news served to bring me out in a sweat of remorse but that night I went to the chosen place where a giggling crony met me with the largest chamber pot I had ever seen. She had carried it in her shopping bag and, whilst delving for her purse on the bus, had been forced to remove the chanty much to the amusement of passengers and conductress.

I apologized profusely but she waved her hand airily. 'Don't worry, the conductress was so taken aback she forgot to take my fare. Here, take the thing! I hope it brings you luck.'

She also handed me my envelope and in return I gave her chocolates to be shared amongst the girls and cigarettes for the men. The envelope contained ten pound notes which promptly went to the purchase of whisky and beer for the reception.

By the time Saturday morning came all my nerves seemed to have vanished. I was in no hurry to get out of bed and a frantic Kirsty had to resort to hurling abuse at me over the jumble of bedclothes. I had always been fond of a good lie-in but never imagined that I could ever feel so utterly drowsy on my wedding morning. The next few hours went by in a jumble of comings and goings. Margaret, who was to be my bridesmaid, arrived from the north in the early afternoon bearing more gifts. I remained stolidly calm during the procedure of donning my wedding outfit. My bridesmaid had taken herself off to the hairdresser so wasn't available to do such things as fasten hooks and zips and pin on my headdress. I had not bothered to book myself into a hairdresser, convincing myself that my naturally curly hair would only require scant attention. Into it I had wound a few rollers but they only served to make my hair even curlier and then I began to panic. But Mary had been there most of the day and now she took over the role that should have been Margaret's. She brushed my waving curls into good behaviour and now they shone and tumbled over my head though a few unruly tendrils escaped the veil. She gave me something old, something borrowed and finally a new lace hanky to tuck into my bra.

The family came to look me over and I knew from their faces that I passed the inspection test. Looking in the mirror I hardly recognized myself. Quite suddenly a will-o'-the-wisp seemed to appear at my side. An unruly tomboy with a dust-smeared jersey, bedraggled plaits and muddy shoes, a shadowy memory of myself at six years old. Now, here I was, a white bride with sparkling green eyes, burnished hair, clean white shoes . . . and wheels, something I hadn't had at six years old!

Little Sarah, a beautiful child with amber eyes and an oval face, touched my dress with chubby fingers. 'Lovely dress,' she said shyly and I kissed her fragrant hair, suddenly realizing how much I was going to miss my infant niece.

'Nearly time,' murmured Kirsty and the nerves bubbled into my throat.

'Take a good stiff half,' advised Callum and with shaking hands I took the proffered glass.

Margaret appeared, tall, elegant, very pretty in a turquoise dress. 'The cars have arrived,' she announced.

'My breath! My breath!' I wailed. 'The minister will smell the whisky!'

Too late. Callum swept me up in his strong arms and carried me down to the sleek car waiting at the close. Curtains twitched, windows opened, confetti rained down. Even the difficult families were in benevolent moods. 'Good luck, hen!' they called. 'Ye look smashin.' 'The bride o' the year!' 'Wullie, stop kickin' the caur ye wee bugger!'

'Look oot, there's money gettin' thrown!'

'Johnny, get in there first!'

'Stop pushin' you lot! Gie the wee yins a chance!'

The children swooped on the shower of pennies that Mary had thrown from the car window. The sleek car received a few hearty kicks and the driver swore. One snotty urchin peered through the windscreen and delivered a hideous raspberry, and white bride or no I immediately returned it. It was a cold March day, the sort of day on which I had made my arrival into the world, but the whisky in me kept me warm and it seemed we arrived at the church in no time.

The next few minutes went past in a whirl. Vaguely I heard the strains of the organ inside the church but thought it to be my imagination. But the minister was determined that our wedding was to have the usual trimmings and had arranged for the organist to be present after all. The sound of the Wedding March filled the church and I was wheeled in. The pews were packed to overflowing. My workmates had not taken umbrage. They were all there, right down to my chamber-pot bearer, beaming, waving, murmuring compliments about my appearance. Among them were members of the Disabled Drivers' club together with relatives and a good crowd of outsiders who had popped in to watch the wedding.

It had been decided that I would not follow the usual procedure of coming up the aisle. Instead I was brought in from a side door which took me almost immediately to the altar. Ken was there waiting for me, handsome in his black evening suit, not at all like the carelessly dressed artist I knew. Scott, his best man, stood tall and straight beside his brother, such a contrast with his dark hair near Ken's red-gold thatch. Beside them was Margaret, glancing at me in a moment of solemnity. In the front pews sat Marjory, Dad and Mum Cameron, and all at once I wished my own parents could be there that day, watching their second youngest, the tomboy of yesteryears, rustling into church in white satin, decorous, radiant, heart and mind bubbling over with emotions, with thoughts of the present, the future, the past. But then I knew they *were* there, Mam smiling, her silver halo of hair shining, looking exactly as she had looked the last time I had seen her alive — and Da, his thick head of iron-grey hair well brushed, his watch chain sparkling against his maroon waistcoat. How they would have taken to Ken, especially Mam with her ability to talk about every subject under the sun and her way of making people relax and laugh.

'Here goes, Mam,' I thought as I was hoisted up to the altar and placed beside Ken. His bright head was slightly bowed but he gave me a sideways intimate glance and his blue eyes reflected all that I felt myself: pride, excitement, joy.

The rustling in the church died down, the hallowed walls muffled the sounds of the outside world. Everything was hushed and peaceful. The ceremony began. The minister began by relating an incident that had happened recently. He had come up behind me on a hill, Bertha Buggy had panted and sobbed but had struggled blithely up the steep slope. The minister had been unable to overtake and that was the theme of his service.

'Christine's life has been an uphill struggle too,' he ended, 'but she has never allowed the steepness of the climb to slow her down nor has she given way to illness and allowed it to overtake her. Rather she has raced ahead of it to stop momentarily at the traffic lights where this young man, Kenneth Cameron, caught her up and would not let her go on again without him. Now the lights have changed to green and they can go on together, up the hills and down the dales of life's byways and I wish them both every happiness on their journey. They will come up with many problems and they will need luck, but from what I know of them they are the kind of young people who do not yearn for great fortunes, just the ordinary kind of luck that makes life happy . . . and it is my prayer for them that they will always keep such values in sight for they are beyond all riches.'

A great ripple of sniffing ran through the church,

handkerchiefs dabbed furtively and I felt myself reddening in a mixture of gratitude and embarrassment.

Soon after that Ken and I became man and wife. We found ourselves in the vestry where the Cameron family came to welcome me into their fold. John took a photograph as we signed the register and another when the minister presented us with a copy of the New English Bible. My mind was in such a daze I gave no thought to everyday affairs and only later did I learn that Ken had sought out the organist to pay him for his services and to give the minister a book token. In all the excitement I had forgotten such things but Ken never allowed jubilation to get the better of consideration. Paying the organist left us very short of money and our married life was started on ten pounds borrowed from Callum but this did not worry us unduly.

We were outside, being showered with confetti, posing for more photos, smiling with relief now that the formal side of the wedding was over and we could go away and enjoy ourselves.

We arrived back at the housing scheme and close on our heels came a string of bright blue buggies, puttering noisily into the terrace. Again windows were thrown wide and eyes stared as members of the club tottered and toddled up the steps and into the close. One after the other they came and the neighbours were agog.

The shrill uncouth voice of a small boy rent the air. 'Aw, look, Mammy, there's another wan!'

And yet another, 'C'mere, Mammy and see this!'

I really could not blame anyone for observations such as these though normally they were made in a less obvious manner. Having started life as an able-bodied child then, at the onset of my illness, being in hospital wards that contained by and large able-bodied folk, I had never been fully initiated into the world of the disabled till my introduction to the club. Unlike many of the members I hadn't spent much of my earlier life in specialized hospitals surrounded by a vast range of disabilities and so it was that I was mesmerized the first time I saw a tiny midget woman walk under a table. I was equally intrigued by various shapes and sizes and the frequently outlandish methods by which they got themselves about. But get about they did, and with such cheerful tenacity you began to feel that virtually nothing in the world was impossible. And very quickly I adapted, as people do, and often felt highly indignant when open stares were directed at my contemporaries though I suspect I was the only one who felt indignant because none of the others seemed to care.

My family had been used to just me, quite an ordinary-looking individual except for my chair, and they had been somewhat taken aback on meeting my friends. But the feeling didn't last. In fact, so much did Kirsty, Callum, Margaret and Stuart enjoy their company that they eagerly gave parties, greedy for more of people who knew how to get the most out of every minute of life. So they were made welcome with open arms and on that day of the wedding Kirsty came out to the close to usher my friends inside personally, giving a last haughty glance to the nosey neighbours before she shut the door.

Kirsty had made the wedding cake. Ken and I cut it together before toasts were made and telegrams read. Busy though the day had been some of the family had not forgotten to place their bets on the Grand National and Mum Cameron had won a small prize. Ken made a speech, telling the assembled company that lucky though his mother had been on backing a winner he felt himself to be luckier still with me as his winning little wife.

'Keep the whip handy and she won't turn into a nag,' quipped Callum, earning a glower from me and a laugh from everyone else.

The evening swung gaily along with Wee Sadie yodelling and the rest of the company in fine fettle. I watched little Sarah dancing and suddenly it seemed to me now that I couldn't possibly leave home to go and live in a strange house. I couldn't leave Kirsty and Callum and it was unbearable to think of parting with my little niece.

I poured out my doubts to my new mother-in-law but she merely chuckled. 'You've got him now, Chris, and I hope you'll have more success than me at making him change his vest and socks.'

Marjory grinned. 'Not only that it will be heaven in the morning without Mum having to yell upstairs to get him out of bed!'

Ken's morning exploits had already been recounted to me. One of his favourite tricks was to clump his shoes on the floor so that it sounded as if he was up and walking about the room. At first his mother had fallen for the ruse but became suspicious after a few mornings of diligent shoe-thumping and no Ken at the breakfast table. She crept to the foot of the stairs. Clump, clump, clump, went the shoes. Upstairs she glided to find Ken hanging out of bed with his eyes closed, a shoe in each hand marking time on the floorboards. Compared to me he was a Rip Van Winkle!

Contrary to custom my new husband and myself were among the last to leave the party. Ken was beginning to look at me with desperation and reluctantly I took the hint. Stuart and Margaret had left two hours before for the long drive to Newtonmore. They had told us that the Drumochter Pass was treacherous with patches of ice and snow and it was in Newtonmore that we had planned to spend a few days' honeymoon after a couple of days' settling in at the cottage. A rather tearful Kirsty ran into the bedroom because she couldn't bear to bid me goodbye. Ken and I slipped away and were both rather silent during the journey to our new home, suddenly shy of each other now that the time of our being alone together as man and wife had at last arrived.

More snow came down during the night, silently draping the sleeping countryside in a soft thick blanket.

5. Halcyon Days

We woke to a white land. I lay still in the big warm bed and gathered to my stirring senses the strange sounds that filled my new world. Hens clucked, an occasional bovine bellow came from the barn, chains clanked from the byre which was separated from our quarters by the wall of the hall. The cottage had at one time been a dairy with the byre adjoining it. With joy in my heart I looked at the bedroom walls adorned with speedwell-sprinkled paper. A great rush of contentment swept over me. I had always wanted to live on a farm, now here I was, in this dear little cottage, a very new bride, far removed from city smells and sounds, safe and secure with my new husband snoring beside me.

He stirred, grunted, then his unruly golden head hove out from under the blankets. 'Good morning, lamb,' he greeted me with newly-married decorum. 'I'm getting up to make breakfast so you just lie there till I get organized.'

I needed no second bidding and smothered a giggle as a muffled curse followed quick on the heels of his feet touching the freezing lino. The cold hastened his advent into his clothes and he ran through to switch on the electric fire we had acquired through cigarette coupons. In minutes he was back to report that the snow was at least two feet deep and it was unlikely we would make it to Newtonmore on schedule.

'Oh well,' I said comfortably. 'It will be nice to potter about the cottage. I might paint the fireplace if I get the time.' I lay back to contemplate the quaint fireplace and was visualizing it in white covered with flower transfers when Ken came back, proudly bearing a laden tray.

'For you, my dear little wife,' he said tenderly, fluffing the pillows at my back before setting the tray on my knees. I gulped and stared at a burst egg yolk that was running in greasy rivulets over the white. Two fat sausages had split to reveal sickly pale innards, and the bacon burned to a crisp, lay in a pool of congealing grease.

'How lovely,' I managed to say and Ken smirked with satisfaction then took himself off to his own breakfast.

Like lightning I hoisted myself to the bed end to pull up the lower sash of the window. The cold air rushed through my nightdress as I grabbed the plate and threw the contents into the snow. Closing the window I heaved myself back under the bedclothes to fortify myself with an excellent cup of tea and buttered bread. A triumphant crowing and squabbling came from outside and I knew that the hens had gathered to gobble up my breakfast.

'Everything all right?' asked Ken, coming in to survey my empty plate with silent approval.

'Lovely,' I said with genuine gratitude for his well-meaning efforts. 'I'd love another cup of tea.'

'For you, my darling, anything.'

Later in our married life his cooking improved immensely but my disposal of that first breakfast was a closely guarded secret till I wrote this book but he has forgiven me.

By Tuesday the snow had cleared considerably. Till then, Mrs Murdoch had tactfully left us to our own devices but when she saw Ken putting luggage into Bertha she came in to present us with a wedding gift and to wish us well in our married life. 'I hope you'll be all right travelling in this weather,' she said doubtfully and I could see she hadn't got used to the idea of a disabled person withstanding the elements although I must say that not once had she shown surprise at sight of my wheelchair. She accepted it from the start without fuss or ceremony and that was one of the many things I liked about her.

'It's really very cold,' she continued. 'We found some of the free-range hens dead yesterday and can only think it was the cold that killed them.'

'Oh,' I murmured stupidly, my hand flying to my mouth and my thoughts to the hens that had eaten my breakfast. I knew nothing of the ways of poultry and the sort of things they ought to eat, but I dismissed the notion that they had died by my hand though I couldn't help but hide a smile at the idea.

The drive up north was enjoyable, owing to the fact that we had filled our hot water bottles, placed them at our feet then wrapped blankets over the lot. Bertha was a regular little ice box in cold weather. She was such a small craft that a window always had to be open to combat condensation so we were experts at insulating ourselves against icy draughts.

At Drumochter walls of snow loomed on either side of the road but after a few impromptu waltzes on the long uphill stretch we reached Newtonmore safely there to be greeted by Margaret and Stuart at Briar Cottage where a warm fire and a hot meal awaited us. Our honeymoon was spent walking through Christmas card countryside by day and playing cards or Monopoly in the evening when Margaret nearly always won amidst shrieks of triumphant laughter.

Our bedroom had two single beds so Ken and I spent our first nights squashed together in one of them.

'Never mind,' he consoled me, 'we'll have a proper honeymoon in the summer — maybe camp in Skye or somewhere exciting like that.'

'Ach, I've enjoyed it all,' I said contentedly. 'It's been the best honeymoon I've ever had.'

Ken laughed. 'Do you have them often then?'

'I will from now on,' I replied smartly. 'Our anniversaries and my birthdays fall within days of each other so every year we'll make it a honeymoon.'

The honeymoon over we were thrown into a hectic life of work followed by a rush home to light the fire and cook a meal. On my first day at work I crept on silent wheels to my machine, wearing that nonchalant expression that people wear just after a honeymoon. All morning I received some teasing remarks but couldn't understand it when some of the men came up, sniffed the air and said they smelt burning. I sniffed with them till finally in some anxiety I got into my wheelchair to search through the bales of material behind me to see if by chance something was smouldering amongst them. Oh, naive girl that I was! My actions earned a few well-smothered sniggers yet still I did not construe anything but the utmost innocence from the men's comments and in fact it wasn't till a good few years later that I found out what they implied.

Each night Ken and I were only too glad to flop by the fireside to amuse ourselves with model kits, read, or listen to the radio. We never even entertained the idea of television. So much else was needed before we could afford such a luxury and as Ken told everyone,

'The day we get a TV our honeymoon will be over.'

It was quite a problem getting coal up to the farm. The local coal merchants would not consider bringing anything less than half a ton which was beyond our pocket so we had to resort to small bags which we loaded into Bertha two at a time, four nights out of seven. We were three miles outside the suburbs so it was a rather trying journey coming home loaded down with coal, not to mention groceries that had to be bought almost every night despite a shopping expedition each Saturday.

Several problems unfolded the longer we were at the cottage but we took them all in our stride. Life was a whole lot of fun, blessed as we were with youth and a love of the green fields. Towards the end of March the little glade beside the house burst into a riot of wild yellow daffodils; young bullocks butted each other playfully; we witnessed the births of twin lambs in the 'maternity ward' of a farm we passed every day. 'Our' farm went in mainly for beef cattle and hens, both battery and free range. I was in the habit of throwing bread to the birds, amazed at the rapidity with which it disappeared till I discovered it being gobbled up by the hens. They began to look upon me as some sort of benefactress and I couldn't open the back door without a battalion of hens running helter skelter from the fields. One old hen had a short leg which caused her to run with a lopsided gait. We nicknamed her 'Hopalong Cassidy', favouring her with the occasional potato.

With the cottage we had inherited two cats named Penny and Twopence. Penny had belonged to the cottage couple and had known the farm from kittenhood. She was a beautiful half-Persian tortoiseshell with big green eyes and affectionate ways. She became so attached to us that she came on walks to the bottom of the farm road but would go no further and stood watching us as we left her, tail waving in anger at our desertion of her. She loved a ride on my knee and even if I was outside she would settle down with purring contentment, sucking and padding at my jumper like a little baby.

One thing that grieved us about Penny was her habit of climbing trees to rob nests of baby birds which she carried proudly to us, certain that we would be pleased to receive the gift of a scrawny fledgling. At first she had been greatly angered by the fact that she couldn't have Jockey and would sit on top of his cage with her claws curling longingly round the spars while the budgie wolf-whistled and mewed at her. He adored the big fluffy cat and exhibited all his little tricks to her while she surreptitiously tried to kill him. But he did everything in his power to draw her attention, to the extent of picking her pink nose with his beak when she pressed her face against the bars. He had become an expert at calling her and for many a day his calls brought her running to see if her dinner was out only to discover the whole thing was a hoax. When the weather became warmer, out went Jockey in his cage. He went into ecstasies listening to the wild birds and pecking at tasty bits of grass that poked into his cage. Beside him rolled Penny in the sun, gripping the spars of the cage with hooked claws which Jockey immediately began to manicure with his hooked beak. At first the cat was highly indignant at this but as time went on she appeared to enjoy it and lay beside him purring, her eyes closed as the busy little beak nibbled between her toes.

Summer approached and the peaceful nights in the country grew shorter. We were getting used to our life on a farm and the mice in the rafters no longer kept us awake with their scampering and squealing. These sounds became part and parcel of our lives. Owls hooted, chains rattled, hens clucked, dogs barked, larks spilled golden music into summer skies, and we loved it all.

Each night we raced home from work to prepare a hurried meal then we were off into a scented world. Down the farm road we went, beside the stream, competing with each other to see who could hit the most times a big log that stuck out from the bank. My chair made an ideal receptacle and round me Ken piled stones so that we would have a continual supply of ammunition. Mr and Mrs Murdoch must often have wondered why each time a rut was filled with stones they just simply disappeared.

'Bouncy ball' was another of our favourite games which we played on the quiet road till we came to 'the fairy knoll' our name for an enchanting little clearing beside the bluebell woods where Ken and I dreamed of building a house. He drew it down on paper.

'A revolving house that follows the sun,' he said exictedly, 'with a lot of glass to let in the light. Everything on the level and a lift going up to my art studio so that you can come up to visit me . . . with a tray of coffee and biscuits!'

Halcyon days! Full of simple pleasures that cost nothing yet gave us so much joy. Talking in bed at night we often wondered how we had been able to bear living in the city for so long. On clear nights we could see that same city far in the distance with lights strung out like jewels against the velvet sky. Our city friends came to visit us often and it soon became a familiar thing to hear the 'phut phut' of a two-stroke engine crashing into the stillness.

Marie came one day when I was up to my elbows in soap suds at the kitchen sink. I did not even think of a washing machine in those days, or a spin dryer for that matter. If the weather was good the clothes went outside, if it was bad they went up on the pulley to drip into basins and buckets strung strategically beneath. I had adapted myself to housework from my wheelchair, developing a method for carrying pots, plates, kettles, without the need to guide my wheels by hand. I used my feet in a sort of 'walking' movement, pushing with one to turn a corner, pulling with two if I wanted to go forward. This left my hands free to carry such things as are necessary in day-to-day chores. Ken said that mine was the only walking wheelchair he had ever seen while I became so used to the new habit that I could get along quite easily without using my hands at all. Quite often people thought that my chair wa propelled by electricity and in one instance 'a little engine hidden under the seat'.

Marie's eyes were sparkling that day and she kept waving her left hand about under my nose. Engrossed in the task of extracting as much dirt as possible from Ken's socks I took scant notice of my friend's hands.

'For heaven's sake,' she said in exasperation. 'Don't you notice anything different about me?'

Leaving my soap suds for a moment I eyed her searchingly from head to foot. 'You've got a new pair of shoes,' I acknowledged with slight envy because my one and only pair were now showing distinct wear in the region of the toes, the penalty for having a 'walking' wheelchair.

Wee Marie gave vent to a loud sigh. 'My hand, look at my hand, silly!'

'Pink nail polish!' I said triumphantly while I strove to bury my own broken nails in the folds of a towel.

'Do you need specs? My ring! Look at my ring!'

'You're engaged!' I cried joyfully. 'To Don?'

'Of course, who else?' she cried, implying that there could be no one else in her world but Don, a well-built boy with both legs amputated below the knee. They had made each other's acquaintance at the club. Where else? A tireless cupid seemed to be at work there, firing little arrows tipped with love potion and tying knots and what have you all over the place.

'We must have a party,' I decided. 'A combined housewarming and celebration for your engagement. We'll have it when Ken and I get back from Skye but we'll have to ask Mr Murdoch's permission.'

Mr Murdoch was outside in the byre. He was a tall thin man with high cheekbones and smiling blue eyes, invariably dressed in dungarees, an old cloth cap and Wellington boots. Ken and I already thought the world of him, loving the way he always made a point of passing the time of day with us no matter how busy he was. His long loping stride was a familiar and welcome sight. Often we came upon him in his big estate car carrying a calf in the back seat. The first time we had witnessed this we laughed in delight while the calf lovingly licked Mr Murdoch's ear with its green-coated tongue.

The smoke from our cigarettes mingled with the rich scents of the dung midden. We put forth the question about a party and he willingly gave his permission.

'It's partially to celebrate Marie's engagement,' I explained.

Mr Murdoch looked down at Wee Marie from his great height but showed not the least surprise that such a small person had become engaged with a view to marriage.

'Big or wee, we're all alike,' he told us later with a simple philosophy that was endearing.

Our second honeymoon was memorable in many ways. The trip to Skye was a marathon drive even though we stopped at Newtonmore for the night to break the journey. It was a warm morning when we took our leave of Briar Cottage and we opened the windows wide to let in the breezes. I felt comfortably happy spinning along the open road with my excellent navigator beside me. I had little sense of direction and could have been driving to Timbuctoo for all I knew but Ken was there to keep me right. Up hills and down dales we bobbed, in and out of bends through a breathtaking panorama of scenery. By the time we saw the Five Sisters of Kintail I felt as if I had been on the road forever. Bertha was overheated and on a particularly steep hill we puttered to a halt halfway up.

'Oh no,' groaned Ken but got out and put his shoulder to the door jamb. In minutes several motorists had come to our aid, and we plodded on to Loch Duich with diminishing ardour. At Loch Alsh the excitement of seeing Skye at close quarters lifted my flagging spirits. I forgot my blistered hands, full bladder and empty stomach and fairly pelted up the road to Kyle of Lochalsh. We groaned afresh on seeing the rows of cars all waiting to board the tiny ferry but got ourselves into the queue. A collection of children gathered to look with languid interest at Bertha.

'It's a bubble car,' declared one.

'No it's not — it's a motor bike,' contradicted a knowing, toffee-smeared girl.

'I wonder how it goes,' said another. 'I think it has to be pedalled.'

'Don't be daft,' scorned the first child, sucking noisily at a large gob-stopper. 'It goes itself! You don't have to drive it, it's a great new invention!'

We sat sweltering in our 'great new invention' for almost an hour till our turn came. In mild panic I wondered how such a small craft could possibly bear any weight without sinking to the bottom of the sea but serenely we sailed over the sea to Skye without mishap. On dry land once more Bertha roared into life and we kept hopeful eyes open for a good camping spot. We did not like organized sites, preferring to be on our own whenever possible. Acres of moorland, pitted with peat hags and peat bogs, abounded, but no little oasis of green was to be had anywhere. We toured the length and breadth of Skye and were now desperately considering pitching the tent any old where. When we reached Bernisdale we realized we had come round in a circle and we were so exhausted by then that we nearly considered spending the night in Bertha. Outside Dunvegan we suddenly spotted a lush patch of grass which was right on the edge of a cliff.

'There's just enough room to put the tent up,' declared Ken after a swift reconnoitre.

'Aw hell,' I protested dismally but one look at Ken's tired face made up my mind. It was a good little clearing, scattered with boulders and whin bushes but these didn't encroach on the little patch of green. As I helped Ken knock in tent pegs I looked in fascination at the furling white banners churning below. I had no head for heights yet I stared down the craggy cliff face to the sea spuming and crashing against the rocks, spraying frenziedly into the air as if clawing to reach us.

We had waited so long for a meal we had now lost our appetites and Ken threw his fried egg down the cliff face where it was pounced on by a flock of seagulls who had been wheeling about since our arrival. A fresh clean wind blew in from the sea, rustling the tent and rattling the dried seed pods on the whins. It was really very beautiful looking out over the vast reaches of the Little Minch to the tip of Lewis in the purpled dusk.

But when darkness came down I took a fresh attack of the shakes knowing that bedtime was imminent and just a couple of feet of solid ground separated us from a precipice. I tormented Ken with unanswerable questions.

'What if the ground crumbles away and we crash to our deaths?'

He grunted.

'What if we roll out of our beds in the night and go right over the edge?'

'Don't be daft,' he said in tired tones.

'What if we dream we're falling over the cliff and waken up to find we really have gone over?'

At that he couldn't help smiling. 'If that happens we'll never wake up again so don't worry,' he said and crawling into the tent flopped into bed.

'Some honeymoon,' I mourned but there was no answer.

Ken had pitched the tent side on to the drop so that the doorway at least was facing solid ground. I got down on my knees and crawled inside, folding my chair and pulling it in after me, arranging it just inside the flaps. Ken normally performed such tasks but exhaustion had gained the upper hand of valour this time. I had spent too long pondering over our possible fate. By the time I wriggled into bed he was already snoring. The sea boomed dully far below and I was grateful that Ken had put his bed on the side nearest the drop. Nevertheless it worried me that he might roll out during the night or if he didn't I might perhaps perform the amazing feat of rolling, bag and all, over him and out of the tent to the waiting sea. The idea was so ridiculous that I smiled to myself in the darkness and almost immediately fell asleep.

It was still dark when I awakened with a start, not knowing why I had wakened but blearily glad that I was still safe in my bed. It had been raining. Staccato drips bounced drearily off the fly sheet to the ground. Ken was breathing steadily in his corner and I felt unreasonably angry at him. Yawning disgustedly I thought how quiet everything was, only the sea sighed restlessly. Then I heard strange noises outside the tent. Something or someone was blundering about, shaking the canvas, pulling at guy ropes. My heart hammered into my throat and without further ado I yelled, 'Ken!'

Before my cry was answered the tent began to shake and tremble. There followed jumbled impressions of wobbling poles, sagging roof, an alarmed Ken sitting bolt upright in bed. Quite gracefully the tent folded about us and I got a mouthful of wet canvas just as I was getting ready to give full throttle to another call for help.

'What's happening?' cried Ken in a muffled frenzy, fighting to lever a pole from his sleeping bag. Scared though I was I felt sorrier for him than I did for myself. At least I'd had some warning while he had been rudely awakened from a satisfying sleep.

'Chris! Are you there?' he yelled, his voice clearer now that he had managed to extricate his face from the soggy clinging canvas.

'I'm here,' I gasped, 'But the tent isn't — at least, it's down!'

'Don't I know it — but how?'

'There's someone outside! Tripping on the guy ropes!'

'I can't hear anything. Hell, I'm soaked! Are you all right, lamb?'

'Shh,' I warned imperatively.

'Keep quiet,' hissed Ken as if I hadn't spoken.

I trembled under my soggy covering. 'What if it's a murderer?' I croaked. 'This is an awful quiet place. No one would ever find us if anything happened.'

'Shh,' he returned sharply.

I lay back and waited for doom to overtake us. Something cold dropped on my face and I almost screamed before I realized it was only one of the big black beetles that had crawled in from the grass. A beetle was preferable to the unknown thing that stalked the night beside us.

'I'm going out to see,' hissed Ken in the 'silent hero' voice that he kept for tricky situations. But before he could move there came another sound, one so ordinary and familiar that we both gave joyous croaks of relief. It was a gentle 'moo' followed by a long drawn-out bellow.

'It's only a cow!' I cried, even as Ken was burrowing his way outside. I untangled myself from my weighted sleeping bag, gritting my teeth at the touch of the cold groundsheet against my feet.

Attired only in pyjamas and anorak Ken valiantly hoisted our dejected tent erect while the cow stood placidly by, peacefully chewing cud while it watched proceedings out of the corner of its eye.

Seven o'clock saw us breakfasted and haggardly pale, our bloodshot eyes searching the grey landscape with little interest. But by eight o'clock the sun began to break through ragged gold clouds. Lewis lay like an opal on the sapphire sea, the gulls dipped and splashed sending diamond drops sparkling into the light and on a barnacle-encrusted boulder a heron stood poised on one leg looking like a delicate piece of sculpture.

That day we drove to Glenbrittle and came to the Cuillin Hills, blue and beautiful in their sombre grandeur. Ken pushed me over peat and heather till we could see Rhum and Eigg and all the other enchanting islands that had till that moment just been names on the map to me. It was as if someone had taken a handful of emeralds and scattered them at random over the sea where they had grown more beautiful with the passing of time. We sat on top of the windy cliffs for ages letting the strong breezes balloon our clothing. We laughed and shouted and Ken picked me up and waltzed with me in his arms.

We stayed for several days on Skye and the place where I had been loath to set down roots now held an enchantment for me.

'We'll have a proper honeymoon some day,' Ken told me earnestly as sadly we struck camp, but I shook my head.

'No, this has been a proper honeymoon, our kind of thing. It wouldn't be the same to go to a hotel and be all posh and formal and try to do things right. Things have happened to us here in a natural order and it would be wrong to ever try to go back.'

He looked at me in some surprise, his madcap impulsive little wife suddenly dripping words of wisdom. 'You're really serious, aren't you?'

'Of course I am . . . anyway,' I looked at the upturned toes of the shoes I kept specially for camping. I suppose I looked like Billy Connolly's idea of an extra for *Kismet*. When I had gone camping with Wee Marie I had not foreseen the catastrophe that a 'crawling camp' could bring to shoes and I had been forced to wear the one pair all the time, even to places like hotels. In retrospect I suppose people must have thought my feet were shaped like rockers, a sort of part of my disability, and my Kismet shoes had been made specially for my rocking feet! 'Can you imagine me in a hotel with my rocking feet and my squeaking wheels. I'd bring the bloody house down!'

Ken roared with laughter and we set off for home in the highest of spirits.

The following Saturday our house was all ready for the housewarming. We had now gained another item of furniture in the shape of a horsehair sofa offered to us tentatively by Mrs Murdoch. We jumped at the offer and placed it carefully in the living room. We dusted and polished then sat back to admire our domain. A big fire roared in the grate, mirrored in the glasses that Ken had placed in readiness on top of the cabinet he had made. On a table near the door stood two candleholders presented to us by Dad Cameron. Gleefully we had rushed out to buy coloured candles and now we lit them, awed by the romantic glow they gave to the room. Above the table was a picture of a little girl kneeling in prayer. What didn't strike us at the time was the fact that the table now looked like an altar. Our eyes were too masked by a joyous simplicity that saw only beauty in every little thing that came our way.

The party started quietly but by nine o'clock there were twenty people in the room. We had issued invitations wildly, never expecting half of them to be accepted, but the doorbell kept ringing till it seemed that the entire club was crowded into the cottage.

No one seemed to mind the lack of chairs. Many had brought their own in the form of wheelchairs while the rest just squatted on the floor. Small gifts were laid on the table till quite a pile sat between the candles. Guitars, banjos and mouth organs were in full swing, Wee Sadie's voice almost split the rafters. During a break in the singing one of the boys wheeled himself to the table and cried, 'Where is the holy watter! We must have the holy watter!'

He said the words in a passable Irish brogue and the room

85

went into an uproar. For the next half hour everyone jostled for a position in front of the 'altar' in order to make some funny comment. Wee Sadie's eyebrows were creeping slowly towards her hairline till suddenly she bellowed, 'It's blasphemous! They're swearing and it's blasphemous!'

'But, Sadie,' I spluttered, 'it's not really an altar — it just looks like one.'

'Well, just the same, they've no damned right to make a fool of it.' Suddenly her eyes twinkled, 'I might as well make a wish while I'm here.' And she got up to toddle to the altar where she made her 'wish'. At three in the morning the last guest left and we were left to look at our 'altar'.

'Why didn't we see it?' I wondered.

'Maybe because we saw only the candles in Dad's candlesticks,' said Ken rather sadly.

'Well, I think it's lovely and we will keep it as a sort of altar, a wee corner we can pass and know that God's always there.'

We were silent for a moment.

'Bring the holy watter, Patrick,' said Ken and giggling we retired contentedly to bed.

6. God's Corner

Our first year at the cottage was like one long holiday. Sun shone, soft rain fell, the hay grew high and golden and the harvester whirred all day. Ken offered to help and went off happily to the scented fields, his hair vying with the rich tawny grasses. The air was heavy with the sweet warm smell of newly cut hay. When it lay in neat bundles over the fields we sat aloft them and cuddled together. Windswept and brown we gazed out over the rolling country to the hills of Argyll.

'Some day we're going to live there,' said Ken once, but I just smiled because at that time I was perfectly content where I was.

In time the bales were stacked in the barn for winter feeding but the young bullocks got the scent of it and were forever breaking out of the pastures to go rampaging joyfully through the shed. Sometimes there were two or three at a time, nibbling away at the bundles and pulling great bunches to the ground. We could see them from our living room window, butting each other in argument over a few strands.

We were pretty used to cattle by that time though our first encounters had given them complete mastery over us. The first time was during a walk when we decided to take a short cut over the fields. The bullocks were grazing peacefully some distance away so we felt safe as we made our way over the rutted ground. We were greatly surprised therefore to turn round and find them following us from a wary distance.

'They're only curious,' said Ken who had had some

experience of bovine ways during school holidays spent at Great Aunt Agnes's croft.

'They look a bit mad to me,' I gulped. 'Look at the whites of their eyes.'

Ken quickened his pace behind me but the faster we went the faster went the bullocks and before long we were all thundering over the field, the wheels of my chair rattling on stones while my skeleton did the dance of the bones.

'There's *millions* of them!' I exaggerated in panic.

'If they get too near, belt them with your handbag!' gasped Ken.

I got ready the proposed weapon, twirling the handle round my fingers so that I could give a good swipe if need be. Then abruptly and most unexpectedly we were stopped in our mad flight by a hidden boulder and I was pitched out of my chair. In a split suspended moment the sky and fields spun crazily before I landed with a thud on my belly. Close on my heels came Ken, hurtling over the back of the chair to land on top of me with a force that squeezed my lungs of wind and almost relieved my bladder of its contents. We lay in a jumbled heap, unable to do anything for a moment let alone extricate ourselves. With a struggle we helped each other to sit up and looked vengefully to where the bullocks had skidded to a halt and were now grazing tranquilly, seemingly unaware of our existence.

The rich warm smell of dung pervaded our nostrils for we had landed on ground liberally sprinkled with cowpats, both ancient and new.

'Keep down low,' Ken urged me as he helped me to slither into my chair. 'Someone might see us!'

'*See* us! They'll smell us first!'

We made our chastened way home, both of us reeking horribly but having to suffer the smell while we waited for the immersion heater to warm the water.

'Never mind,' called Ken when I at last lay soaking in perfumed water. 'They say dung is good for the complexion so you should count yourself lucky!'

I was alone when next I came face to face with a young bull. I had gone through the gate to my little garden to spend some time freeing my plants from the crushing embraces of ground elder. My pansy family seemed to smile at me with velvet eyes, my tom thumbs flowered colourfully among the nettles. Gently I prised a green caterpillar from the leaves to let it go marching in hump-backed zest over my hand. A movement in Mrs Murdoch's cabbage patch caught my eye and I held my breath at the sight of a baby rabbit having a good feed.

Ken and I loved such little creatures, always hopeful during our rambles of seeing them. We adored the purposeful shuffling hedgehog with his little pin legs and busy snout. Moles were more elusive but once we had come upon a tiny baby sound asleep in a bed of moss. He didn't waken as we peered at him and we were able to study in detail the twitch of a whisker, the rise and fall of his soft furry belly. Ferrets, field mice, even a fox, had charmed our eyes at some time though we weren't so keen on the latter when we heard that one had crept under one of the hen houses and eaten the legs off the hens as they roosted.

I was watching the rabbit with great fascination when a soft little groan sounded near at hand and I looked up to see the frisky young bull. He was a wild one, continually bossing his companions about and forever escaping from the fields. He fixed me with a calculating stare and I swallowed hard when I saw that I had left the garden gate swinging. Through it he began to make his way to stop just a few feet from where I was sitting. I felt particularly vulnerable from my lowly position and was glad that I had left my hoe to hand. Grabbing it I hoisted it at the ready like a knight with a lance except that I had no lively mount to carry me away from danger, only a rather creaky wheelchair which was badly in need of repair.

The pride and joy of my garden was a huge sunflower which had attained a height of five feet. At the top was a big juicy bud just ready to burst into flower. Wickedly the bullock began nibbling at the leaves while one bloodshot eye kept me firmly in view. Ken was in the living room with a book and would never hear me if I shouted for help, so instead I muttered a feeble 'go away, get, you brute'.

The beast went on browsing among the leaves of my sunflower, his neck stretched higher and his soft lips caressed the fat bud at the top. Ecstatically he slobbered over it and the action lent me some courage. Half-heartedly I wielded my hoe, he jumped back momentarily then came bouncing back with more bravado than ever, the gleam in his eye now more pronounced. Playfully he butted the few feet of air that separated us and I was just about to have a nervous breakdown on the spot when a coy little 'meow' came from behind. I turned to see Penny bearing down on us, tail erect, a look of determination on her pussy face. The huge bullock and the tiny cat faced each other. Penny's pink nostrils were aflare with anger, her bushy tail waved menacingly. The bullock lowered his head and kicked his legs in the air in a show of defiance. Penny ran at him and with a bellow of fear he stomped round her and into the vegetable patch. Penny had saved the day. At least she had saved my day — the garden's days looked decidedly numbered as the enraged bullock 'bronco-bucked' through the potatoes. With a purring Penny on my knee I made a hasty exit through the gate just as Mrs Murdoch's son came on the scene and sent his dog in after the bullock. Wilfully it ran, head down, back legs kicking high, all round the garden, before it submitted and allowed the dog to chase it back through the field gate.

It took one more incident before we gained the upper hand over the cattle. We had just gone to bed one night, snuggling thankfully between the sheets with contented sighs. It was a cold night for summer and the warm bed was more than usually welcome. I was at the pre-sleep stage when all the muscles relax and the abyss of dreamland floats tantalizingly behind the eyelids. Strange sounds penetrated the haze bringing me back to consciousness with a jerk.

From the gravel yard outside came curious crunching noises, furtive and uncanny.

'Ken, what's that?' I whispered, while the life forces leapt crazily within me sending a rush of blood through my ears that sounded like a stormy sea.

Ken's voice came back in a tense hiss. 'Shh! I'm listening!'

The sounds came closer till eventually they were right outside the bedroom window.

'It's an intruder,' I said with authority, 'listening at the window.'

'Don't be silly, lamb,' said Ken, hotly and bravely in my ear. 'It's probably Mr Murdoch out for a breath of air.'

'At this time of night? They go to bed at ten — it must be past twelve now. No, it's a thug. We'd better phone the police.'

I popped my head out of the blankets to seek out our red phone gleaming dimly and comfortingly on the chest of drawers. The crunching began again, louder than before, till now it seemed there was a whole army of thugs marching about in the yard. Visions of the window being broken and gangs snatching us from our bed made me tremble.

'There's a whole crowd of villains out there,' I told Ken with shaky conviction. 'The Murdochs won't hear a thing, their bedroom's at the back of their house.'

We lay sweating under the blankets while the sounds grew in volume and it seemed certain that the gang had gathered outside the window for a mass attack.

Ken crept slowly out of bed. 'I'm going through for the poker. You stay where you are.'

He padded into the living room, coming back armed with our heavy steel poker.

'Be careful,' I warned. 'They might have a shotgun at the ready.' I was an avid reader of crime stories and felt I knew just what to expect from a gang of thugs. With bated breath I watched while Ken twitched back the curtain a fraction.

His sudden laughter startled me almost as much as the outside noises.

With a flourish he threw back the curtains and shouted, 'Look!'

There against the window panes was a huge pair of nostrils blowing twin puffs of steam against the glass.

'It's these damned bullocks,' choked Ken. 'The whole herd of them! They've broken out of the field to go on a midnight rampage! I'll have to get out there and try to get them back into the field.'

As soon as he was out of the room I shuffled to the end of the bed to look outside. It was a moonlit night with the sky awash with glittering stars. The countryside stretched, moon-bathed and peaceful, but for once my attention was too taken up with other matters. Ken was dancing about in the yard, waving his arms and wielding a big stick against dung-encrusted rumps. Kicking hooves sent up showers of gravel, the bullocks mooed, butted and generally played for time but in the end Ken won and they began to make their unhurried way down the road to the field. I got into my chair and went through to the cold kitchen to make cocoa for Ken's return.

'Mrs Murdoch is in for a shock when she sees her front garden tomorrow,' he came back to report twenty minutes later. 'They've eaten most of the flowers and trampled the rest to the ground. The place is a sea of dung so watch where you put your wheels in the morning.'

'My rose, what about my rose?' I faltered, referring to the sickly twig at the front door into which I had poured love and liberal helpings of dung. My labours had been rewarded with shiny new leaves and a single fragile rosebud. Now . . .

'It's gone, lamb, everything round our door has been trampled.'

'Hell! I'll never have roses round the door,' I mourned, in that moment relinquishing the picture that I carried of a lush bower, thick with scented pink roses, framing a little cottage door.

After that night our future encounters with straying cattle held no more fears for us for, while I hadn't actually participated in the events of that night, I had seen that it was quite effective just to wave your arms about and make authoritative noises. During our four years at the farm we often had to get the beasts back into a field, I at one end to cut off the retreat of any that broke from the main stream, Ken at the other, his arms thrashing while he yelled out firm commands.

Winter gradually crept in bringing hazards that we had half-expected and others that we hadn't bargained for. Bertha was not the most ideal machine to cope with snowstorms and ice. Often we were snowed up, unable to get near the main road and then Ken had to walk three miles to the station to get a blue train to work. If he was lucky he got a lift, if he wasn't he was forced to trudge through thick snow to arrive at work cold and damp to make his excuses for being late. Miss Sims always sounded suspicious when I phoned to tell her the reasons for my absence. My work lay in the heart of town where snow never stayed long enough to hold up the flow of traffic and to those used to city amenities my excuses must have sounded pretty feeble. These were the days when Ken had to walk through tracts of virgin snow to collect food and fuel; when I often got stranded in snowdrifts and when once in a blizzard Ken had to come out searching for me. But they were also the days of snowfights and snowmen, cherry-red noses and ravenous appetites; evenings of blazing fires and cosy contentment, with Ken making models for his railway and me settling down with jotters and pencils to write and write, never able to get the words down fast enough, a glow of excitement in me as my mind untangled plots and Ken had to speak twice to me before I knew he had spoken at all. Already I had drawers full of grubby jotters, cupboards crammed with reams of poetry. The stories were mainly schoolgirl adventure stuff, very amateurish, but the poems were good. I had always written poetry, secretively, furtively, never letting anyone see it till Ken came into my life. From the moment he read them he encouraged me to keep on writing and he encourages me to this day. Those nights of our first winter together, of our contentment, of my renewed interest in writing, were the start of my apprenticeship. At the age of thirteen I had sent a tatty, handwritten manuscript off to a publisher and had waited with almost unbearable suspense for the result. Back came the jotters full of my best child's handwriting with a kindly little letter of refusal. After that I wrote only for my own pleasure and told myself I didn't care a fig if any of it ever got published.

A fortnight before Christmas I had a bad miscarriage and owing to the incompetence of two doctors didn't land in hospital till four days had elapsed. During that time I almost bled to death yet still dragged myself to work where even Miss Sims looked alarmed at sight of my white face. On the third day, during a visit to Kirsty, she made me go down to a second doctor who listened languidly to my description of my symptoms, then told me to come back the following week if I was no better. To be fair to the doctors I didn't even know I was pregnant owing to the fact that I was so indifferent to my bodily functions. I hadn't even bothered to look at calendars, and so forth. It turned out that I had been four and a half months 'gone', as Mam would have said, so it was little wonder I had suffered such agonies all during that first frightening night.

But I was back home for Christmas and when we went for Christmas dinner to Ken's old house Mum Cameron told me that the WOOPOS had been at it again. These letters stand for Welfare of Other Persons' Organs Society, a name thought up by me of course, and we were all able to laugh at Mum's descriptions of simpering ladies with their enigmatic smiles and veiled questions.

The winter also saw the onset of muscular sclerosis in Marjory. I put it as bluntly as that because I still can't get over the shock of seeing a vibrant, able-bodied girl, just out of her twenties, going downhill as quickly as she did. It began gradually with violent headaches and dizzy spells. The first time I saw her staggering into the living room carrying a tray in her shaking hands I honestly thought she was pretending to be drunk. But she had had hospital tests and the results came back as MS, a wasting of the nerve tissues of the body. The process could be gradual, sometimes taking years to really disable someone. On the other hand a young person could be affected quite quickly and Marjory was very young.

Grief also came to Mrs Murdoch at that time. Her husband went into hospital for an operation to remove his ulcer, a week later he was dead from meningitis. The farm was a changed place without his ready smile and his long, loping figure working in the fields. The spoken word of commiseration is of little use in times like these. You try to reach out to the bereaved one with awkward groping well-worn clichés but 'doing' is really better by far. I think we helped Mrs Murdoch by doing the little things for her that her husband would have done. At least I like to think we helped. Ken was very good in situations like these. He never said very much but he showed his sympathies by doing. I on the other hand, tended to let misery paralyse my actions but perhaps that was only because I could never do as much as I would have liked.

Sometimes I suppose I got really frustrated by my disability because so much I would like to do to help other people was beyond me. I had learned how to cope with my own problems, had overcome them over the years by all sorts of methods, but to sit and watch something being done for somebody you love and not being able to help is, I think, the worst mortal agony to bear. Your mind is so active, it sees all that needs to be done, but your legs won't, or more accurately, can't, work in conjunction with your thoughts.

One day I stopped at 'God's corner' in the living room. I thought about Marjory growing thinner and weaker, I thought about Dad Cameron with his smiling twinkling eyes and grey, tired face, a death sentence hanging over him though he didn't know it. Tumours had spread from his lung to other parts of his body and already he had spent a year of the two that the doctors had given him to live. I thought about Mr Murdoch, working in the fields one week, dead the next, and I said in an angry voice, 'Are you there, God? Are you helping any of us?'

A reproachful silence seemed to shroud God's corner and I could find no comfort, none of the sort of comfort I had experienced in the simple world of childhood when I had accepted Mam's kind of faith without question. I remembered Iona, the beautiful girl who had died beside me in a hospital ward, her acceptance of God carrying her fearlessly to that other world she was certain awaited her, a world without pain. But Iona had been just a child. I think it is easier for children and old people to accept what the Bible teaches. It is the in-betweens who perhaps find it harder, with all sorts of scientific theories about The Creation cluttering searching minds. It has made things difficult for young people, more so now than even then, and I think it must be a better thing to keep the bigger issues as simple as possible. Far better to believe what you really want to believe.

Life is too short to go on wondering about such big issues and perhaps never arriving at any sort of conclusion. I had been through a good part of my search at that time, Bible classes, Sunday schools, churches, studies on the scientific aspects, and I was at the stage where I was too confused to make much sense of any of it. My own Mam had always had a wonderful childlike fa th that saw her through a hard life and finally into that other unknown existence with the hand of God firmly leading her along. Even tough old Da had whispered his prayers at night, ghostly whispers in the silence of the kitchen when he had held long conversations with God. Mum Cameron had a faith that never faltered, not even now when her husband was dying and her only daughter was teetering on the edge of a serious illness.

I looked at the picture above the 'altar', of the little girl kneeling in prayer. It was a picture of innocence but that was all, the light shining on her face made it look too clean, the folded hands to her lips were too posed, her warm-looking, virgin-white nightdress would have perhaps looked more natural with the collar twisted just a little bit. If she had been dressed for bed the way I was as a child, in baggy bloomers and an old vest, then I might have identified more with her. Her knees were planted firmly on a cosy rug which perhaps made her look so smugly comfortable. At my childhood bedside there had been only cold hard lino and I had said my prayers muffled under the warm blankets.

> Oh, to be a child again
> To say your prayers and then 'Amen'.
> To know a whisper in God's ear
> Will be all right for He will hear.

I made the little verse up on the spur of the moment and said it aloud but the words had an empty echo and gave me no comfort. For me at that moment I could only ask, 'Are you there, God?' and wait for the answer that time alone might bring.

As winter melted into the spring of 1965 our spirits became more uplifted and everything began to take on a brighter aspect. Surely people we loved could not be dying when the hedgerows were bursting into life and little baby pheasants, newly hatched and looking like tiny eggs on legs, went waddling down the farm road after their mother. Hawthorn blossoms hung heavily on branches in bowers of pink and white, carpets of bluebells lay thick in the woods and pale green ferns unfolded tightly curled tendrils to the sun. Delicate grasses swayed by the roadside interspersed by dazzling wild flowers, seagulls screamed after the tractors, small animals bustled in the undergrowth. Picking great bunches of hawthorn and bluebells I filled the cottage with them.

In God's corner I placed a huge vase full of fragrant pink

hawthorn and it seemed somehow to bring the 'altar' to life. It might have been for me that God belonged more to the great outdoors and in bringing a portion of it into the room I had brought something of the Creator in too. Mrs Murdoch looked at my flower arrangements and after commenting on how charming they looked added gruffly that they would just create a mess. It seemed that country people did not go foraging in fields for wild flowers but I knew I would never share such an outlook even though I lived in the country for the rest of my days.

By this time we had aquired a Cyril Lord carpet and a three-piece suite with the couch folding down to make a comfortable double bed. Kirsty and Callum came with little Sarah for a week with the latter sleeping on an air bed in the dining room while her parents shared the couch. Kirsty almost died the first night when she heard the mice rattling plaster inside the skirting and the cattle clanking their chains in the byre next door. Unlike me, Kirsty had never been one to take creepy crawlies lightly but after a few days of beetles wandering under the crack in the kitchen door her yells of protest diminished in volume . . . until the night she found a 'crocodile' in the bathroom. We were all sitting talking in the living room except for Kirsty who had gone to have a bath. The peace was shattered by ear-splitting screams. 'A crocodile! There's a bloody great crocodile on the wall!'

We all rushed through to see the 'crocodile' which turned out to be an enormous slug that had somehow got in under the kitchen door, marched through the kitchen and round the corner to the bathroom. It was a beautifully patterned slug, rather like a crocodile in its fancy golden pin stripes but there the resemblance ended. It was adhering to the wall above Kirsty's head and though she had hastily covered herself with a towel at our intrusion I don't think she would really have cared if we had seen her starkers at that moment. But for several minutes none of us were capable of helping ourselves, let alone Kirsty. We howled with glee, even little

Sarah who couldn't decide which was the more interesting sight, her mother lying hysterical in the bath, or the big shiny slug stuck to the green wall. Eventually Callum recovered sufficiently to pluck the creature from the wall only to set us all screaming when he put it on his face where it adhered quite happily.

Country-bred Callum took a fiendish delight in such tricks. I will never forget the night he and Ken went out for a drink leaving Kirsty and I blethering our heads off. Back came the men folk and there was Callum with several black slimy slugs decorating his face. He knew that slugs and other such legless horrors did not come into my favoured category in the insect world and fairly smirked with joy as both Kirsty and I almost swooned in disgust before he set us fleeing all round the house with himself and his slug-covered face in hot pursuit.

Because the new furniture was on the never-never our purse strings were stretched to the limit yet almost every weekend we went off camping to our favourite spot at Loch Eck in Argyll. Marjory came to stay with us for a few days and I sneaked a few days off work to be with her and to take her to Lock Eck for the day. She had always been a slim girl, very slightly built, but now there was nothing of her and she was having to get around on sticks. From the minute I first saw Marjory I thought she had that look about her of someone not destined for a long life but at the time I brushed away the idea because she was so filled with a zest for living, a vitality that would not let her rest. Yet despite this there was a feeling that somehow she didn't belong to the world, that somehow she had landed into it by accident, a ghost that inhabited a human body.

Before Marjory there had been another little girl, one who had breathed life for only a week before she died. When Marjory came along a year or two later Mum Cameron said she was so like the first little daughter that it was like having her reborn. Like me, Marjory was a girl who loved animals and didn't mind things like beetles and mice. As a small girl she had kept a white mouse in a cage from which it regularly escaped, terrifying the whole family by appearing where it was least wanted and sending visitors into hysterics by leaping up on the table when everyone was partaking of dainty cups of tea. Now Marjory was very ill but made light of it. In fact she made nothing at all of it, no questions, no self-pity, just an odd kind of acceptance that was strangely disquieting.

While she was staying with us Twopence gave birth to yet another litter of kittens. We were fed up with Twopence who had demented us on many occasions with her nocturnal howlings that attracted all the farm moggies for miles around. The results were strings of kittens and after a year and a half we felt we could take it no more. The first batch had arrived in the hayshed not long after our marriage but when Mum Cameron saw them there she had implored us to take mother and offspring into the house and shower them with tender loving care. For the sake of peace we deposited the whole feline family into a large box and set it in a corner of the dining room. Because we were both out working we left the window open so that Twopence could get in and out as she pleased. She was a restless creature with none of Penny's home-loving ways. Twopence was delighted with the arrangement and lay in her box preening her kittens while Penny glowered and went off in a huff for two days. The happy situation didn't last long. As the kittens became older the mother went in search of mice and birds with which to nourish her growing family. The dining room soon took on the appearance of a battlefield with corpses everywhere. Gruesome remains in the shape of birds' legs and mouse heads made our stomachs turn. Out went Twopence and the grown kittens and as Ken set about clearing away the mangled corpses he said bitterly, 'I will never listen to Mum again.'

Now we decided it was time Twopence had her marching orders though we waited till Marjory went home before taking action. The latest batch of kittens were fearsomely wild. They had never known anything but the great outdoors but would follow Twopence into the kitchen when she came to be fed. One of the kittens was a meltingly beautiful creature, fluffy and white with big blue eyes and fangs that would have put Dracula to shame. When casually I mentioned this kitten to a crowd of my workmates one of them immediately cried, 'A white kitten! We've been looking for one for ages! Could you bring it in, Chris? I'll take it home on the bus.'

'It — it's a bit — wild,' I told her in a reckless understatement because I was feeling guilty about the fact that Ken and I had decided to take Twopence and her family to a distant farm and there let them adopt a new set of human mugs. We had carefully observed the fact that this particular farm had so many cats already they would never notice a few extra.

'Och, I'll tame it,' said The Optimist eagerly. 'Bring it in tomorrow.' That night Ken and I lured Twopence into the house with food and behind her trailed three bushy-tailed kittens, alluringly charming in their wide-eyed beauty and so wild that they spat at the reflections of themselves in a tin tray. We had a big box ready and into it bundled Twopence and two of her kittens. But they were having none of it and there followed a furious battle of wits. As soon as we stuffed one kitten in another got out. Howls, hisses and snarls filled the kitchen. Both Ken and I were torn and bloody where the kittens' razor-sharp claws had slashed through our skin. Panic set in, both animal and human. Mother and kittens were streaking all over the kitchen, knocking down pots and breaking precious plates and cups. Ken raced through to the bedroom to search for his winter gloves. By the time he came back, looking like a boxer, the kittens had quite literally climbed the walls which were smooth with no footholds. But climb the walls the kittens did till they were all rowed decoratively under the ceiling with their ears pinned back and most unkittenlike growls issuing from their bared jaws.

'Bloody hell! I'll have to get the ladders!' said Ken and rushed away once more. Penny came back with him but stalked away to the fire in disgust at such undignified behaviour from her very own great, great and double great grandchildren. Ken ascended the ladder but each time he lunged at a kitten the whole lot edged away from him as one, and all over the kitchen went the ladders after the kittens. But determination triumphed till one after the other the darling bundles were seized unceremoniously by the scruff of the neck and handed down to my double-gloved hands to be stuffed into the box which we hastily tied with stout rope. Leaving the white kitten still hooked ferociously to the ceiling, we set off through the darkening countryside till we came to our destination. There Ken opened one end of the box in a barn at the side of the road and we watched with glee as Twopence emerged followed by the kittens. With a nonchalant air she gave them a good wash before setting off determinedly in the direction of the main farmhouse buildings.

During our absence the white kitten had detatched itself from the wall and had obviously exhausted itself streaking around the room because by the time we got back it submitted enough to allow us to place it in a box where no doubt the attraction of food settled it down for the night.

With some trepidation I wheeled myself into work the next morning.

'The kitten! Where's the kitten?' yelled The Optimist excitedly.

'In a box in the buggy.'

'Och, the poor wee thing. I'll bring the box in and put it near my machine then I can poke some food through to it at dinner time!'

All that day, enthusiasm bubbled out of The Optimist. Everyone was clamouring, demanding to see the beautiful white kitten, until at four o'clock The Optimist could contain herself no longer.

'We'll just have a wee peep,' she decided and opened up

one flap of the box. For a moment nothing happened. Everyone held their breaths, myself included till I was almost asphyxiated.

Suddenly a silver-white streak blurred out of the box like a bullet, scratched the nearest set of limbs, shot through Jenny's conveniently shaped legs, before it disappeared with a flick of its tail down the length of the factory.

'My kitten! My kitten!' wailed The Optimist and went bounding full pelt after it.

'My legs! My legs!' moaned the scratched one.

The Optimist's voice echoed through the factory. 'Somebody catch my kitten! Don't let it get out of the door!'

Obligingly everyone downed tools and set about trapping the kitten but from the yells and curses that followed it was evident this was not proving to be easy. The kitten had now made its way into the knitting machine section where a goodly number of males abounded.

The catching of the kitten was a challenge to their egos. Soon it seemed the entire factory had ground to a standstill. The robots forgot about work in a diversion that was both hilarious and tinged with fear of the flying claws. Even Miss Sims forgot for a moment about the example she ought to be setting and went prancing after the elusive white streak with everyone else. But a well-aimed blow at her legs brought her back to her senses and with her stockings in tatters she cried, 'Send for Wullie! Get Wullie in here!'

Wullie came, complete with thick leather gloves, but with a twist of irony the kitten belted past him and out to the boilerhouse from whence Wullie had just come. To this building The Optimist and Wullie took themselves hastily and as it was now four thirty, the time I departed work, I slid discreetly into my chair and made my surreptitious way outside. There was Wullie, holding the kitten at arm's length by the scruff of its pretty white neck and behind him trailed The Optimist, all smiles, looking as if her troubles were over instead of just beginning.

But there must have been a touch of Barbara Woodhouse

in The Optimist for I was to receive glowing reports about the kitten turning into a lovely home-loving cat, although the first night had been difficult with him clinging to the ceiling and refusing to come down even for food.

I could hardly wait to meet Ken and tell him about the day's events and though he smiled he said firmly, 'We won't have any more animals, Jockey and Penny are enough to cope with.'

We stuck fast to that resolution till the day Margaret and Stuart appeared on our doorstep. They were now married and living in Briar Cottage though they came to see us quite often.

'Come out to the car,' said Stuart with a grin. 'We have something to show you . . . but stand well back in case you get attacked.'

He opened the car door with a flourish. We peered in and saw an exquisite pup shivering shyly in a corner. It was my first introduction to a Samoyed and I will never forget my awe of that pure white fluffy bundle with biscuit-tinged ears, a jet black button of a nose and a fringe of white lashes coyly hooding brown eyes still smudged with baby blue. I picked up the soft little bundle and buried my face into her downy head. She sat snug in my arms, her mobile pink tongue coming out to give my nose a good wash. In the house she lost her shyness and after drinking some milk frisked about and barked her puppy bark which came out with such gusto it sent her rolling backwards once or twice.

'Some day,' I said decidedly, 'I'm going to have a pup like her.'

'Just you bide your time,' said Stuart. 'When Judy grows up we'll let her have pups and you can have your choice.'

Judy snuffled under the table in God's corner, scratched an ear and fell over. She lay on her back, legs stretched immodestly, her pink pot belly bare to the winds. In seconds she was sound asleep, her tongue lolling, her steady breathing fluttering a little corner of the cloth that covered the table in God's corner.

7. Joys and Sorrows

It was our habit at Christmas to pile Bertha with gifts and go down to Ken's old house to hand the family their presents. The Christmas Eve of 1965 was no exception and Ken went back and forth to the buggy with the gaily wrapped bundles. At eleven o'clock we set off down the farm road, jogging in and out of the usual ruts. It was a clear frosty night with millions of stars winking in the heavens with the North Star hanging like a silver lantern above the trees. The freezing cold seeped through Bertha's many chinks and I shivered, thinking of the warm fire we had recently abandoned. But it was Christmas Eve and I wasn't going to let the cold take away my surging spirits. Above the roar of the engine I began to holler 'Jingle Bells'.

'C'mon,' I urged Ken who was unusually quiet in his cramped little corner, 'Join in.'

But he just grunted and cheerily I went on with my song, negotiating bends with familiar ease, chanting down hills and waltzing slightly as my driving wheel hit icy patches. Quite suddenly Ken crumpled up and gave a cry of pain.

'I'm in agony,' he gasped. 'Stop the buggy!'

Cold fear gripped me and I slid to a halt at the roadside. With great difficulty he got out of Bertha. It was a feat he normally performed with agile ease though his was a restricted seat, wedged in at my side with my folded wheelchair leaving hardly enough room for a sardine, let alone a human being. He staggered outside to lean his forehead against the cold roof of the buggy.

Instinctively I knew he wanted only to be quiet in those minutes. He was a silent sufferer, never telling me if he felt ill till he really *was* ill and then creeping off to his bed to be alone in much the same way as a dog slinks off to a corner to nurse some misery. But it wasn't flu or any of the relatively minor ailments that was causing him to stand outside in the bitterly cold night. Taking a small bottle from his pocket he spilled some white tablets into his hand then crammed them into his mouth. Panic gripped me and I demanded to know what the tablets were for.

'Indigestion,' he gasped, 'I've been taking them for months — but — a minute ago I felt something bursting inside me.'

He was unable to swallow the pills. They fell out of his mouth which was wide open as if he couldn't get enough air inside himself. In similar situations I normally remained cool and prided myself that I was quite a good help in emergencies. But that was with other people, not with my wonderful husband who had been such a tower of strength to me since our marriage, who had given me a prop such as I had never known before, who had showered me with love the Christmas before when I was weak and ill after my miscarriage. Now . . .

My heart pounded with fright and the quick-witted brain that had figured ways out of so many difficult situations in my life just wouldn't function.

But Ken took the problem out of my hands. 'We'll have to go back to the cottage, Chris. I'm sorry this had to happen on Christmas Eve, my lamb.'

He was in agony yet he called me 'my lamb' and apologized for being ill. How he got back into the buggy I don't remember but in a dream I was turning Bertha and traversing the dark country roads back to the cottage with Ken at my side, slumped forward, his head resting on the handles of my chair. With every sense urging me to hurry along I forced myself to go slowly, my reactivated mind now racing with terrible dread. I knew Ken wasn't suffering from appendicitis because he had had his appendix removed as a child and amateur doctor that I was I couldn't think of anything else to cause such pain. The journey back to the cottage was interminable with Ken urging me to drive ever slower till we were barely crawling along. At last we reached the farm and I looked desperately to see if the lights shone in the farmhouse but there were none, only blank dark windows gaping gloomily into the freezing star-spangled skies.

Ken walked like a bent old man to the cottage door and there was no way I could help him. By the time I got into my chair and hauled myself over the gravel-strewn drive he was in the bathroom retching sorely. He emerged, gaunt and grey and I announced my intention of calling a doctor. Stubbornly he insisted he would be all right, it was something he had eaten at tea time, but my senses were coming to the fore and sternly I ordered him to bed. 'If you don't want me to call the doctor I'll phone your folks instead. They'll be wondering why we haven't shown up and they'll be able to advise me about you.'

Inwardly I felt utterly helpless. It wasn't often I despised my disability but at times like these I hated it. How easy it would have been to run to the farmhouse and knock up the household. It would take me ages to get there in my chair over the gravel chips and there was a high doorstep to be negotiated before the bell could be reached. I helped Ken on to the bed, taking off his shoes and loosening his tie. He was rolling about in agony now and I felt terribly alone and afraid. The only sounds in the cottage were the ticking of the clock, the crackling of dying embers in the grate and Ken's awful moaning.

With shaking hands I picked up the phone, dialled the wrong number and had to start all over again. Mum Cameron's familiar voice crackled over the line, reassuringly covering the distance that separated us. Quickly she grasped the situation. 'I'll phone the doctor, Chris, don't listen to Ken. He was aye a thrawn rascal. I'll get the doctor to pick us up so that we can show him the way — he would never find it otherwise and time's precious. Don't worry, everything will be all right, we'll be there as quickly as we can.'

I clung to her comforting words in the hour that followed. The hands of the clock moved slowly while I made Ken as comfortable as possible. His eyes were dazed with pain yet he never complained, just groaned softly and implored me not to speak to him because he only wanted to be left alone. For a time I sat in the living room, shivering although the fire now glowed warmly. The shimmering boughs of our little tree glistened in the firelight, cards called gay greetings from the mantelpiece, but I felt that Christmas was everywhere except our little cottage, that the house was still and waiting in fear like me.

The crunch of tyres on the gravel startled me although I had longed for no other sound in the last hour. All at once Mum and Dad were there with the family doctor who went straight into the bedroom. Dad's face was drawn and pale. His coat hung on his thin shoulders and I knew he shouldn't have come out in the night air. I often wondered if he realized how ill he was but he gave no indication of his innermost thoughts and still dragged himself out to his manager's job in a Sauchiehall Street store. He bent and put his arm round my shoulders, comforting me without words.

The doctor came out of the bedroom. 'Ruptured ulcer,' he reported quickly. 'I'll have to phone for an ambulance. Where's the phone?'

'In the bedroom,' I told him while my innards turned to jelly. Mr Murdoch had suffered from ulcers in his stomach and now he was dead. I felt sick with fear but I had learned to hide my feelings since the days of my childhood illness and even now I presented a calm facade to the world.

The doctor, who was a real family friend, came out of the bedroom to put a firm arm round Dad's shoulder. 'C'mon, Brigadier,' he said, using the affectionate nickname that always brought a smile from Dad. 'Let's get you home. The two girls here will see your son into hospital.'

When they had gone, Mum went to make a cup of tea and

I went into the bedroom to pack pyjamas and toilet articles. Ken had turned a frightening yellow colour and all at once I could find nothing to say to him. All the intimacies we had shared, the times of loving, of laughter, were tightly locked in my heart. I knew if I was to speak it would only be small talk and Ken was in no state to listen to that. We had both been pitched abruptly out of our nice world of normality into one of the unknown and were utterly helpless in our respective states. That is when touch is better than words and I touched him gently on the brow, his hand clutched mine briefly and I smiled though it was the last thing I felt like doing.

During the time of suspense, waiting for the ambulance, Mum, in her practical way, asked me what I would do after I had seen Ken into hospital. I felt I couldn't come back to the empty cottage and the manse was out of the question because of all the stairs. But Margaret and Stuart were now back living in Glasgow so I phoned their house and they were only too anxious to help, saying they would wait up till I arrived and there would be a bed ready for me. Mechanically I put the guard over the fire, took plugs from power points. The ambulance arrived and Ken was carried out on a stretcher. With Penny on my knee I turned my back on the warm little room and went outside. Mum was going with Ken but I had decided it would be wiser for me to make the journey in Bertha as I was going to need my little buggy afterwards. Penny stood mewing dismally, angry at being ousted from the fireside, her fur ruffling in a cold wind and her big eyes glinting in the ambulance headlights.

I followed the tail lights of the ambulance down the farm road, watching till the red glow of them merged together in a watery mist because at last I was crying.

'Please, God, let him be all right!' I called despairingly to that Greater Being, automatically turning to Him in my time of need.

I suppose many of us use God as a convenience, only

calling on Him when we are in trouble. During my journey I made all sorts of rash promises to God. I would be a better person, a better wife, a better Christian, a better anything, not just for now but for all time, if God in His turn would make things better for me now by helping Ken.

The gaily wrapped parcels rustled on the shelf behind me. The lump in my throat got bigger when I remembered the gifts I had for Ken under the tree in the cottage. He wouldn't be opening them this Christmas morning that was certain. We had prepared so keenly for the festive season. Weeks beforehand I pestered Ken with questions as to what he was getting me but his answers were always non-committal. On previous occasions he had hidden things on topmost shelves but he soon abandoned the idea that lofty places were beyond my reach when he caught me with a brush trying to poke a parcel down from a high shelf in the bedroom cupboard. Of course I would never have looked inside the parcels. It was all just a game and we had both howled with glee at my antics. He was never content to give me one gift, always there were 'bumpers' as well. Thinking of all this turned the ache in my heart into a physical pain and I felt sick by the time I drove through the gates of the infirmary.

Ken was rushed to the x-ray department and I waited with Mum for what seemed an eternity till eventually he was wheeled out and we followed the trolley up to the ward. The spirit of Christmas was there in the brightly decorated wards. Shimmering trees stood tall and green in the corners of the sleeping hospital. I use the word 'sleeping' metaphorically because a hospital never really sleeps. In the dark watches of the night when the thread of life is at its frailest, the task of tending the sick is perhaps more intense than daytime, with the shadowy figures of nurses detaching themselves from deeper shadows to keep an ever-watchful eye on those whose lives they hold in their hands.

Ken was taken immediately into a ward and a desolate loneliness washed over me. I knew my dear husband was in capable hands yet I felt cheated, as if I was a part of him no longer. Strangers could be with him yet I who loved him was excluded. In that state of mind I heard faintly the voices of carol singers drifting peacefully through the silent corridors. Nurses practising so that they could bring the tidings of Jesus' birth to those who were far from home.

'Silent night, Holy night . . .'

It could have been angels singing in the hushed stillness of the nightwatch, and all at once I felt the presence of Jesus as surely as if He had touched my hand.

'Gentle Jesus, meek and mild . . .'

His presence embraced the sleeping figures in the beds, comforting the sick, soothing the unrest of the recovering, taking away the fears of the dying.

'Silent night, Holy night . . .' the words of my favourite carol echoed peacefully inside my head.

A nurse appeared and led us into the dim quiet ward. Ken lay in a bed by the door. At first glance he was just a tangle of tubes and sticking plaster but then I saw it was only one tube going up his nose, distorting the shape of it, the sticking plaster on the tube pulling the skin on his face. Into a huge syringe a nurse was drawing vile yellow fluid from Ken's stomach.

He gave me a lop-sided smile and when he spoke his voice was so normal I just stared at him. 'I'm sorry I gave you such a fright, Chris. I feel a lot better now that this stuff is being pumped out of me. How will you manage tonight?'

'F-fine,' I stammered, 'I'm going up to Margaret's. Are you sure you're all right? You're still a bit yellow.'

'I'm fine – just you worry about yourself, lamb.'

A nurse came up. 'You'll have to go now,' she whispered. 'Your husband will be going to theatre shortly.'

My fears came back anew. 'What will they do to him?' I asked as soon as I was out of Ken's hearing.

'Clean out his stomach and put a few stitches into that ruptured ulcer. Don't worry, it's quite a commonplace operation. If you phone at seven you'll get the night nurse

111

before she comes off duty and she'll let you know how he is.'

'God rest ye merry gentlemen let nothing you dismay.'

The words drifted, mere whispers from another building but I heard. I was neither a gentleman or in any way merry but somehow I wasn't as dismayed as I had been earlier and I managed to bundle Mum's fur-coated figure into Bertha and take her home before making my way through the quiet streets to Margaret's house.

The next day I went back to the cottage to collect Ken's presents to take to the hospital, feed Penny, and generally tidy up. Penny gave me a rapturous welcome from her favourite perch on the barn roof. Here she spied out the land and pounced on mice coming or going through the skylight. In her hurry to get to me she skated down the roof, threw herself straight into my lap, and I gave her a lift into the cottage. I opened a tin of dog meat for a special Christmas treat. She preferred it to cat meat but we rationed her intake because it had a dire effect on her bowels, usually in the middle of the night.

While she ate her dinner I wandered through the quiet rooms, realizing how different it all was without Ken. It was no longer a home, just an empty lonely house, slightly tired and neglected-looking with its empty grate piled up with grey ash and the dark green carpet liberally coated with Penny's hairs. A dismal chirp made me squirm in horror. I had forgotten all about Jockey and his little blue head was huddled miserably into his shoulders. Guiltily I filled his dishes with fresh seed and water and put the electric fire near him because the room was cold. A delighted Penny came to sit by the fire to give herself a good wash while I went through to the bedroom. It was chaotic with sheets and blankets all jumbled together and I busied myself making the bed, crawling round it on all fours as there was not enough room on either side for me to get round in my chair. Before my marriage I would have thought nothing of this but now Ken did such tasks and I realized how much I had come to depend on him to alleviate hardships in my life.

Mrs Murdoch knocked on the door and came in full of concern, having heard the news on the phone from Mum.

'Let me help you wi' that,' she offered but I had espied a pair of Ken's socks under the bed. Ah! Little habits that can be so irksome in day-to-day life but which become endearing little traits when the offender is no longer around to vent your wrath upon.

'No! I can manage!' I protested in red-faced vehemence. 'But, I wonder if you could take Jockey into your house till Ken comes home. I'm staying with my sister.'

'Ay, I'll take him ben the hoose,' she said readily. 'Just gie me his things and don't worry aboot Penny, I'll feed her as well.'

At the hospital I traversed a labyrinth of corridors before reaching Ken's ward. Automatically I went to the bed where he had been the night before but the eyes of a total stranger looked dully into mine. My belly churned and for a few seconds I knew eternity before a nurse came up and pointed down the ward where a dear familiar face had lit up at my entry. Later I learned it was good that Ken had been shifted as the beds near the door were reserved for emergency cases. Ken's face was gaunt and pale making his eyes look very blue. The tube was still in his stomach, draining away the remainder of the poisonous fluid from the burst ulcer, and a drip was suspended above him. Tubes and drips are always rather frightening at first sight but I had had my share of them in my younger days and knew that they served a good purpose. His fine artist's hands lay on the counterpane but he reached the free one to me and said, 'Merry Christmas, lamb. It's a silly thing to say to you after me causing such a fuss. It's great to see you, I've been lying here worrying about how you must be managing.'

'You're talking to an expert on independence,' I laughed shakily, 'How are you before I open your parcels for you?'

'Och, I'm better now though I feel as if I've been kicked for weeks. I got a present from Santa,' he smiled, 'One of

the doctors dressed up — and do you know what he gave me
. . . a new pair of socks.'

'Hell! I hope you'll keep them good and not throw them
under the bed when they're dirty!'

'Did you open my parcels to you, yet?'

'No, but I will now that I know you're going to be all
right. It seems a year since last night already but it's let me
see one thing — I couldn't do without you, dirty socks and
all!'

For a fortnight I divided my time between the homes of
my two sisters, spending the nights at Kirsty's because she
had less steps than Margaret's, the days with Margaret
because her home was nearer the hospital which I visited
twice a day. I realized then the value of sisters. We often
niggled and fought but basically we were very close and in
times of trouble the strong bonds that held us brought us
even closer. Stuart and Callum were good to me too.
Brothers-in-law can often be infuriating and just as often
great fun with good strong shoulders for crying on. We
three sisters were lucky in that we had married men
who suited our temperaments ideally. They all came
from different backgrounds, Callum a 'teuchter' from the
Hebrides, reserved, deep, but toughened by a spell in the
Merchant Navy; Stuart from a 'moneyed' background with
a boyhood spent at boarding school and parents who owned
one of the biggest hotels in Speyside, yet he was more at
home having a drink in the pub with the boys, unsnobbish,
down to earth. And Ken, an artist who had spent some
years at art college, who was sensitive and deeply intelligent
and could mix with people from all walks of life. All three
had married Govan girls and all three delighted in hearing
stories of our tenement days, roaring with laughter at our
descriptions of childhood pranks. Mam would have liked
them all, Da would have gotten on well with Callum, a bit of
a 'he man' like himself.

The day before Ken was due home I went to the cottage
to get it ready. For the first time I spent the night alone in

our little house and went to bed expecting to feel nervous but was so exhausted with all the running about that I slept like a log. I awoke to see a beam of sunlight dancing on the ceiling. I felt it to be a good omen and for the first time in two weeks my heart was singing as I got dressed. A taxi had been arranged to bring Ken from the hospital so I had plenty of time to get everything ready. The house I had cleaned the night before, clearing away the sad little tree that had shed all its needles, cleaning cat's hairs from the carpet on my hands and knees, with a hand brush because we didn't have the luxury of a vacuum cleaner. All that remained was to light the fire but my first attempts failed dismally with the paper flaring up briefly then dying away leaving charred sticks. Thrice I pulled out paper, sticks and cinders, reset the lot, then applied a match but all my efforts failed. Frustration mounted in boiling bubbles of temper. I was good at lighting fires having plenty of tuition from Da in the Govan days but light that fire would not! I had wanted everything to be perfect with the cottage beautifully warm but instead I was like Polly Flinders sitting amongst the cinders only I wasn't warming my pretty little toes . . . or my bunion and hammerheads for that matter! I was sitting amidst the wreckage of my fire with aching knees, longing to drag myself back into my chair but stubbornly refusing to give in. Imagine Ken coming home to a filthy coal-stained wife and a freezing house!

Mrs Murdoch spoke from the hall. 'Can I dae anything to help?'

Not wanting her to see that I had failed in my duties I scuttled into my chair and sat back trying to look nonchalant. 'Not really,' I croaked, praying she would come in and offer to light the fire.

She stopped in the doorway. 'I've brought some pancakes for Ken's tea . . .' Her eyes strayed to the empty grate, 'Oh, ye havny got the fire lit yet!'

Tears of rage had made a dusty passage down my face and

I quickly scrubbed a hand across it and said carelessly, 'It's all right, I was just about to light it.'

'The hoose is that cauld,' she commented suppressing a shiver, 'Here, let me dae it, you're too thrawn a lassie for your ain good.'

Within minutes a warm blaze was roaring up the chimney and the room immediately took on a welcoming look. Leaving my landlady to put the kettle on I rushed to clean both myself and the grate and by the time wheels scrunched on the gravel outside everything was in order. Ken was so thin his clothes just hung on him but his smile was radiant when he came through the door.

'My, it's that good tae see ye hame, Ken,' beamed Mrs Murdoch.

My heart was too full for words. It was wonderful to see him back in the surroundings we both loved. He was off work for six weeks, growing stronger each day till the nightmare of Christmas was a thing of the past. I tended him to the best of my abilities during his time of convalescence and it was then that we both decided it would be better if I didn't go back to the factory again. I had found it hard going, working and keeping a home, and a great sense of relief washed over me. For all the money I made at the factory it just wasn't worth all the effort. We had paid off the carpet and the suite and though we had far to go before we would ever be able to afford the things that many people take for granted, we were content enough with what we had.

As it happened I stopped working at a most opportune time. Judy was going to have pups at the end of May and Margaret was taking her up north for the event where there was a big summerhouse in Stuart's mother's garden. When Ken and I heard all this we packed camp gear into Bertha in readiness for the journey. Margaret had made the suggestion that we could camp in the garden behind the bungalow so that I would be near to assist in the delivery of the pups if need be. Somehow my sister had got the idea that I was a wizard with dogs and she was expecting me to act as chief midwife but the vet had told Margaret that it was unlikely there would be complications.

It was fun to set up our tent in the huge garden. The rockeries were ablaze with colour, clouds of golden alyssum and purple aubretia drifted over the stones, in the little wood behind us were clumps of primroses and a mass of bluebells. Margaret had made a cosy den for Judy in the summerhouse but she showed a marked preference for the bungalow kitchen where she foraged restlessly in the broom cupboard. It was past midnight when we finally got her settled into the summerhouse. Ken made a wooden barrier so that she wouldn't wander away from the bed of layered newspapers and we settled down to wait. By two in the morning we were all feeling tired, Ken's face was white and I ordered him to go to bed because he wasn't able to stay up too long since his operation.

'Do you think we should stay up all night?' Margaret asked me. 'We could make a couple of camp beds in here.'

I looked at a large black beetle that had wandered indoors then at Judy blinking sleepily in the dim light we had hung on a hook above her bed. She didn't look ready to give birth just yet so I told my sister we would go to bed for a few hours.

'Mind and give me a shout if you're up before me!' I warned as we made our way into a cold clear night.

It was 7 a.m. when Margaret's voice penetrated the mists of sleep.

'Wake up, Chris! Judy's had four pups!'

'Eh?' I yelped, extricating my legs from the sleeping bag and losing one of my woolly socks in the process. I felt guilty as I shivered into my clothes, feeling I had failed in my duties as midwife. But Judy, lying contentedly with four tiny bedraggled white pups sucking at her belly, looked smugly satisfied at her prowess in giving birth unaided. We drooled with silly human sentiment over the babies and Judy tholed our presence admirably though as

117

yet she wouldn't allow us to handle the damp bundles.

Margaret's fair skin was flushed with excitement as we huddled over the electric fire. 'I thought she would have had more than four,' she commented, 'Samoyeds usually have big litters.'

'She's having more contractions!' I breathed. 'A pup is going to be born any minute!' My voice held a professional note for I had been kicking myself for having been absent during the first births.

A dishevelled Ken joined us to look in wonder at the newborn. Three more came, one upon the other, a short pause, then another two, and as poor Judy churned them out we began to wonder if they would ever stop coming.

'It's like watching a sausage machine,' I said in awe, as one pup after the other squirmed into the world.

Judy was lying back exhausted, letting the latest arrivals crawl their own way to her belly instead of pushing them in as she had done with the others. But one more was yet to come bringing the total up to ten. It was the tiniest pup of all and none of us knew it had arrived till we saw a feeble flick under Judy's tail. She didn't acknowledge it and it lay in its little skin bag, breathing fish-like, its skin beneath the sparse covering of white fur turning an alarming blue colour. I put out my hand to it and immediately Judy's head jerked up. She grabbed the little blue baby to her, nicked off the bag and began licking with her warm tongue. The pup lay on its back, tiny paws in the air, the only indication of life showing in a feeble heaving of its skinny rib cage. Judy licked harder, the pup turned from blue to pink, then began the instinctive search for sustenance. Blindly it searched for a vacant teat but was bullied out of the way by a big bruiser who was so satiated the milk was running from the corners of its greedy little mouth. Quickly I removed him and shoved the tiny late arrival into position. Its body was warm and fragile in my hands and in that brief moment I knew it was going to be my pup. She was to be one of the most beloved of the four-legged companions I have had in my life.

'That one is mine,' I told Margaret. 'It's a bitch, I got a

good look at it when Judy was cleaning it. It will always be smaller than the rest so don't sell it to anybody else — it's mine.'

'I'll remember,' promised Margaret before going over the dew-wet lawn to fetch Judy a bowl of warm milk laced with two switched eggs.

Margaret had to remain in the north for eight more weeks till the pups were old enough to be sold. Stuart travelled back and forth every weekend and was able to give us reports on the pups' progress. He brought photos of them, now grown into fluffy balls of beauty, looking for all the world like miniature polar bears. We heard of Judy's methods of educating her young, teaching them the kind of things she felt might be of use to them but certainly to no one else. Once she dug a tunnel under a fence, going down two feet before coming up on the other side. Margaret was completely unaware of this till she looked from the window and saw Judy silhouetted on the skyline, her ten babies bringing up the rear in a perfectly straight line with my little one straggling valiantly at the end.

In the run the pups fought and squabbled, the bullies among them tearing the meeker ones into submission. One day they all escaped and got into the bungalow via the back door. The expensive carpets provided them with a new and exciting game. Underneath them they tunnelled from one end of the house to the other before they were discovered and shown the door. On another occasion one of the bigger pups jumped up to grab the clothes line and down the whole lot came to be set upon by the rest. Yipping and snarling they had a wonderful tug-o-war, tearing most of Margaret's smalls to ribbons before she came out and sent the pups about their business with a few hefty whacks from a rolled up newspaper.

Not till the very last minute did we ask Mrs Murdoch's consent to keep a dog in the cottage. We had delayed the confrontation, dreading that she might refuse after Judy, on a weekend visit to the cottage last autumn, had killed a lot of hens, piling them up at our back door, very pleased with herself and sending Kirsty into hysterics because it was she who had innocently let Judy out.

Fingers crossed we approached Mrs Murdoch. 'Ach well,' she said after hearing us out. 'A wee puppy will get used to the hens but you must aye keep it on a lead when you're aboot the farm.'

'You're a real pal,' I told her joyfully.

'Daft more like,' she returned dryly.

On the following Sunday we went to Stuart's house to be presented with a cardboard box in which reposed the pup. No sound came from the box, not so much as a whimper on the drive home. Into the cottage we went to set the box down on the carpet. My breath caught when I beheld the ball of white fluff that looked up at us from shy brown eyes. She had the same biscuit-tinged ears as her mother, her nose was ebony black matching the rims of her eyes and the pads on her feet though these had been like pink rose buds at birth. Long white lashes fluttered, hiding her eyes because she was hanging her head in an agony of trepidation. I picked her up and she trembled but she grew still as I buried my face into the soft fur on her head which was like a swan's down powder puff. She smelled of warmth and when she opened her mouth to yawn there was the faint fragrance of onions that all pups have on their breath.

'Shona . . . Shona of Cairngorm,' I told Ken in ecstasy. 'She was born in the Highlands so what better name?'

Ken laughed. 'Shona of Cairngorm has just christened the carpet. I'd better get a cloth.'

We made a cosy bed out of an old drawer, lining it with a blanket under which we placed a hot water bottle. After feeding her on Farleys made with warm milk we placed her in the drawer in the kitchen and retired to our own bed. All night long she cried. My heart melted but common sense told me that if I started the habit of bringing her into the bedroom it was a certainty it would continue. But Ken was just as soft-hearted as I was.

'I'll go and get her,' he said and went to the kitchen to bring Shona, drawer and all, into the bedroom. Her head peeped above the rim, she looked at us consideringly, then turned round and promptly went to sleep and all three of us slept soundly for the rest of the night.

It was my habit to get up with Ken in the mornings and run him to work. Next morning we went off as usual only this time we had an extra passenger in Shona. She was a born traveller, lying on the ledge behind my seat, her nose in her paws, every so often having a surreptitious gnaw at her new lead which was attached to a collar so big for her we'd had to pierce extra holes in it.

On the Wednesday evening we took Shona to the old manse. From the hall I could hear Dad typing away busily in the living room. He was a past master of the masons and did a lot of writing about it. I think at that time he was compiling some sort of book. The clacking of his little portable typewriter was a familiar sound in the house. It clacks away still, but different fingers operate the keys — my fingers, for I became heir to it. With his little Imperial Good Companion I have written millions of words. I hope he looks down and is pleased with what I have created.

Because he was busy we went straight into the kitchen and Marjory held out her arms to take Shona to her. I saw the glint of tears on her eyelashes and turned away. She was now in a wheelchair, virtually helpless — in less than two years just a shadow of herself. Ill and tired though he was, Dad had redecorated Ken's old railway room ready for her to come home to after a spell in hospital. All the things she loved were poured into the room: the proud heraldic symbols of Scotland hung from every wall, a bookcase was filled with the works of Scottish writers, walls were tastefully papered and tartan rugs laid on the floor. But Marjory only glimpsed it when Scott carried her upstairs for a peep because by that time she had been forced to abandon her sticks for a chair. The bright new room decorated with love, sweat and tears lay empty.

'I'll just have to bum it like Chris,' laughed Marjory gaily but she was too frail for such strenuous behaviour.

The dogs and the cats were excitedly examining Shona and Dad came through, peeved because we hadn't gone straight to him. My heart jolted at the sight of him. He had outlived the medics' predictions by some months but death was on his face that night. At fifty-six he was suddenly an old man, his voice barely a whisper in his throat.

'We didn't want to disturb you,' I said forcing strength into my voice.

'You know I love it when you come,' he chided. He spied the pup and for a moment the old twinkle was back in his eyes. 'Stone me! What next! It looks like a cross between a polar bear and a wolf!'

'Meet Shona of Cairngorm,' said Ken lightly but his eyes were a mirror for my own bleak thoughts.

At midnight on Friday we were sitting by the fire in the cottage. As usual I was writing, and beside me dozed Shona, her head resting on my foot, the trusting warmth of it making me unwilling to move though I knew I must soon make tracks for bed. Ken was absorbed in making a model aeroplane, his brow furrowed in concentration.

The sound of the phone made us all jump. Shona went running under a chair while Ken and I looked at each other wordlessly. In that split second we knew that Dad had died. Ken went through to answer the phone. When he came back I knew it was all over.

He was very pale. 'Dad died ten minutes ago . . . and I wasn't there with him . . . nobody was . . . he died alone in his bed — very peacefully.'

He dropped on his knees beside me and I crushed him to my heart, stroking his hair, trying to comfort without words because I could think of none that would make any sense. I knew so well what it felt like to lose a loved one, to love so well and then to lose. I had been through it, first with Mam, and had felt at the time I couldn't go on without her. Fourteen months later tough old Da was gone too, dying in his own bed like Ken's father, the house full of family but no one beside him in his room in those final moments . . . just like Dad Cameron.

In a daze we drove to the manse to be with the stricken family. Ken went to the bedroom where his father lay and I sat silent, feeling useless, trapped by my own sensitivity, my own knowing of what it felt like to be broken-hearted.

'You should have phoned us earlier,' I told Mum quietly but she shook her head wearily.

'None of us knew, Chris. He seemed to be resting easier when I went in a couple of hours ago then I went through with his tea and he had gone, just slipped quietly away. It's funny, isn't it? You live with someone for almost a lifetime and at the end you don't even get the chance to say — goodbye.'

A few days later Dad was cremated. The house was overflowing with those who had loved and respected him. When they left with the funeral cars I stayed behind to be with Marjory and help her in any way I could. It sounds strange that, me in my wheelchair helping Marjory in hers, but she was so weak the smallest tasks were beyond her. She hadn't shed a single tear but I knew that was the worst kind of grief.

Everyone was dressed in black that day, the stamp of the mourner, making dark rooms darker but wearing the clothes because it was the conventional thing to do. I felt sure that Dad would have hated seeing everyone so dismal-looking but he would have been pleased at how many folk came to bid a last farewell. Pleased but a little shy for he had been a reserved man, one who had loved his family, who had lived for them, and who had left them with bruised hearts that would take a long time to heal. Ironically he had paid off the last instalment of the house mortgage a few weeks previous. If he had lived he would have had less financial burdens — but at least he had left none for the family to bear.

His ashes were taken to Loch Garten and there sprinkled

123

on the clean wind-rippled waters he had loved. I like to think that the spirit of 'the best wee Paw in the world' roved free and happy among purpled mountains and the silent sentinels of tall green pines that guarded the secret of his favourite loch.

8. Smokey Joe

It was as well for us that Shona came into our lives when she did. She helped us over the difficult black days after Dad's death. Her love of life was utterly infectious and oh! the joy of walking down the farm road with that tiny waddling white bundle; of hiding in long grasses out of her sight and making silly noises till she hurled herself at us, growling her puppy growl, her sharp baby teeth pulling delightedly at our ears and noses. Of course having a puppy meant having a lot of problems also. Every morning after seeing Ken to his work, I made my way back to the farm. Those glorious mornings, with heat lying over the fields and the larks soaring musically in the peaceful blue skies. At the bottom of the farm track I stopped to collect the milk, tying Shona's lead to the tiller bar of the buggy while I got my chair out, her body trembling with pleasure as she sniffed the country smells, till I came back laden with milk bottles which I set carefully on the back ledge before folding my chair up and pulling it into Bertha. Once up at the farm I had to go through the whole procedure again, only as well as milk bottles to contend with I also had a lively young dog on the end of a lead and the gravel chips to the cottage door hampering my progress.

On the first such morning we had a confrontation with Penny which I had been dreading. She was on the barn roof and when she saw me getting out of Bertha she came leaping down, anticipating her breakfast of cornflakes. I settled myself into my chair, arranging the milk bottles at my side before lifting Shona out. Keeping an anxious eye on Penny I began to make my way round the corner of the barn to the cottage. The cat stalked towards me, the pleasure on her face turning to horror at her first sight of Shona. Her back arched, her long fur rippled and stood on end, her tail bushed out to twice its normal size, green eyes threw sparks of hatred at the pup who sensed that all this fury was directed at her and began to whine.

'Nice Penny,' I simpered horribly, slowly edging my way over the difficult gravel. The milk was clanking at my side, sliding forward with each turn of my wheels. With one hand on Shona's lead, the other clinging to the milk bottles, I had to pull myself forward with my feet, an inch at a time. Penny saw her opportunity. She flew at Shona, her flying paws drawing blood on the black little button of a nose. In an excess of cowardice Shona made an almighty spring and scrambled somehow on to my chair to snuggle into the small of my back, shivering and whining in terror. Penny was withdrawing for another attack. She turned and came mincing towards us sideways, fluffed up like a wildcat, ears back, fangs bared. I knew that if a fight developed I was the one who would undoubtedly come off worst between Penny's murderous claws and Shona's razor teeth.

Panting for breath I somehow managed to get myself, the milk and Shona into the cottage intact. I gave Shona breakfast, waiting till she was finished before I rushed her outside again to 'perform'. This she did gladly . . . the minute I had taken her back over the threshold! Having mopped up I then went to put Penny's cornflakes at the back door but my calls to her went unanswered and I guessed she would be sulking in the hay shed, having a quiet think about this outrageous intrusion into her idyllic life.

After that we played a sort of 'juggling' game with the animals. If Penny was in the living room we made sure Shona was shut safely in the kitchen and vice versa. In this way we hoped that the two would get to know each other's scents before another encounter. But work it did not, certainly not in the first week of Shona's arrival. On

Tuesday I took Shona for a walk by the edge of the newly cut hay field. She was bounding along, delighting in everything she saw, from bits of hay blowing in the wind to bees hovering round the clover. Neither of us saw Penny creep up behind. Without warning she hurled herself straight on to Shona's back, hooked claws clinging to the soft flesh beneath the fur. There followed a few minutes of bedlam with Shona yelping in terrorized pain and Penny snarling, spitting and howling. I made a lunge at the cat and grabbed her by the scruff of the neck and she dangled, her claws full of Shona's fur. Seizing the opportunity the pup hurled herself at me and crept once more in at my back to huddle in bloodstained misery. During the first weeks of her life her brothers and sisters had given her a rough time of it but a cat was obviously worse than anything she had yet enountered.

By the end of the first week we wondered how we had gotten by without a dog in our lives. Walks took on a new meaning with Shona ambling, sniffing, burrowing, pouncing along beside us. The beasts were fascinated by her. Whenever they saw her coming they would stop scratching hairy necks against convenient posts and come over one by one to the fence to puff, bellow and roll bloodshot eyes. Poking their heads under hedges they drowned the pup in chlorophyll fumes. The first time she sat quite still and stared, the second time she barked with a hint of bravado in her small voice. In those early days she would quite often fall sound asleep during a walk and we just popped her into the back of my chair. She grew quite used to this, cuddled up against my spine like a hot water bottle, and when the day came that she was too big to travel like this I don't know which of us was the sadder, Shona or myself.

The hens, too, looked with beady-eyed curiosity at her and she sat down in front of the boldest hen to take stock of yet another kind of creature. The hen strutted on splayed feet and waggled its comb. Cautiously it clucked and one of

Shona's ears flopped in amazement. Never once in all her time at the farm did Shona molest a hen. Instead, when she was older, she patted their combs with a gentle paw and they grew so used to her they would actually roost on top of her softly heaving flanks as she lay sleeping.

Only once did she chastise a hen and this happened at Great Aunt Agnes's croft which was situated near Loch Garten in Speyside. We went there three weeks after Dad died. Shona was very well-behaved in Bertha, sitting contentedly on her cramped ledge for mile after mile. Great Aunt Agnes never seemed to change. Her snowy hair was as tidy as ever except for a wilful strand that she kept tucking away; her cheeks were the same apple pink; her blue eyes still bright and inquisitive. When she saw the buggy approaching she patted her hair quickly into place and smoothed her long white aprons.

'My, my, but it's grand to see you,' she greeted us. 'Come away ben, I've got the kettle on.'

It was lovely to be in her kitchen again, sniffing the familiar odour of boiled eggs, soup, delicious fresh home baking. A huge range reposed in black-leaded splendour along one wall with a little pelmet strung below the old-fashioned mantelpiece. A great oak dresser stood in one corner with dozens of brass-ringed drawers. On a little shelf near the cooker was an extremely modern transistor radio, its clean sharp lines looking out of place in the old-world kitchen where time seemed to have stood still. But the old lady liked to keep up with all the latest happenings in the world and since her old wireless had been 'on its last legs' she had obviously decided to risk investing in a piece of 'modern trash'. To her all things that had been made in the last twenty years were just rubbish.

A tiny scullery led off from the kitchen where a galaxy of shelves groaned under an assortment of delft crockery and preserving jars. The sink stood under a small window and I smiled when I saw the countless packets of soap powders that flanked the draining board. It looked as if the old lady couldn't make up her mind which was the best brand to use and throwing her usual thrift to the winds had decided to invest in one of each kind.

While waiting for the tea to 'mash' she began reminiscing about Dad and I began to worry about Shona cooped up in Bertha. Great Aunt Agnes didn't know we had brought the pup along. Shona had made no sound when we left her, hadn't betrayed her presence by so much as a whimper. The old lady wasn't partial to dogs. She adored Clover, her cow, and two rather decrepit cats which she kept for the mice, but dogs did not rate highly in her affections unless they were working beasts who 'earned their keep'.

'Did you know we had a pup, Aunt Agnes?' I said conversationally.

She tapped her fingers on the table and her eyes looked to the window, perhaps hopeful of seeing Clover wander past her line of vision.

'Ay,' she murmured absently, 'Mary mentioned it in her letter when she wrote me aboot your holiday here. Of course, your mother was aye a softie wi' dogs, Kenneth,' she finished accusingly.

'She's a lovely pup,' said Ken. 'Too young to be left in kennels and we didn't like to ask Mum to look after her after what she's been through.'

'Ay, they're a lot of work right enough,' said the old lady in tranquil agreement. 'I've nothing against them myself but I'm aye scared they'll go for my hens. There's a great brute comes aboot here, a black thing wi' red eyes. I must admit he hasny touched the chickens — so far.'

'Shona's great with hens,' I gushed. 'We have them at the farm and she never looks near them — well, she looks but that's all. We couldn't leave her . . . so we've brought her.'

'Eh, what was that?' murmured the old lady, suddenly hard of hearing.

'We've brought the pup . . . she's out in the buggy,' Ken supported me.

'A pup here! A pup here!' she said, her pink old face

inscrutable. 'And you've left her out in that wee bubble car? That's no way to treat a young doggie!'

Ken made a quick dive to the door and was back in a few moments with Shona in his arms. I wondered how anyone could be indifferent to such a glorious bundle of snowy fur. Her thick paws hung over Ken's arms and she peeped shyly at Aunt Agnes from lowered white lashes.

'Hmph, you'll have a job keepin' that one clean,' commented the old lady gruffly. 'What do you call her?'

'Shona,' I volunteered eagerly.

'Shona — Shona,' the old lady repeated the name softly, 'That's the Gaelic for Jessie — your grandmother was called Jessie, Kenneth. I'll call your doggie Jessie.'

If anyone else had called my dog Jessie I would have protested, but not with Great Aunt Agnes.

At that moment a scraggy tortoiseshell cat appeared along the narrow passage from the back door. It stopped in its tracks as the smell of dog reached its nose and its bony back went into an arch. Shona, wary and respectful of all cats, stayed me quite still in Ken's arms.

'Come on, puss,' called the old lady. 'Puss, puss.'

But puss fled back along the passage and rather resentfully the old lady went to get the stewed tea from the hob.

Later, when we were sitting cosily by the range, the old lady began talking about the state of the world, while Shona surreptitiously chewed at her slippers. Frantically I tried to draw her attention away from the slippers but the old lady stayed me with a sharp command.

'Leave her! She's no' doin' any harm! These are my auld baffies. I got a fine new pair two years ago but I only keep them for visitors.'

I hid a smile, wondering what category Ken and I came into. As usual she read my thoughts and treated me to a coy smile from under snowy brows.

'I don't mind the same when it's family. I like fine just to be myself.' She giggled girlishly and I felt honoured to be classed as 'family' by the old Highland lady who could be sparing with her favours.

A pleasant hour passed, Shona chewed happily; the old lady talked and dozed intermittently; the clock ticked lazily from the depths of the hall; pine cones crackled in the fire. Every time the old lady jerked awake it was all that Ken and I could do to keep back the giggles. The mouth which had been hanging wider and wider closed with a snap and she blinked in surprise at finding herself in the kitchen.

'My eyes must have closed for a minute,' she excused herself each time.

Never would she admit that her naps were due to old age. In all the time I knew her I never once heard her blame her age for the various aches and pains that beset her from time to time. Invariably they were the fault of the weather, pollution, or 'these nuclear bombs they keep banging into the atmosphere'.

Great Aunt Agnes rose stiffly. 'I'll away and fetch in some kindlin' for the mornin'.'

'Can't I do it, Auntie?' asked Ken who had offered all day to do odd jobs only to meet with polite refusal. But we were now past the formal 'settling in' period.

'Ach well, if you're sure it's no bother. There's a pail behind the door and the wood and coal are in the wee oothoosie. I'm runnin' a bit short o' cones — when they're dry they're grand for gettin' the fire going.'

'We'll collect some tomorrow,' I said, joyfully visualizing a prowl through the woods.

'Ay, well, if you're sure you can manage,' she returned, eyeing my chair with some doubt. She had almost accepted the fact that I was of the stuff not to let things stand in my way but the first time she had witnessed me 'bumming' upstairs she was filled with horror.

'Lassie! Lassie! You'll get a skelf in your backside,' she had said with utmost sincerity. 'I wouldny like to be the one to take it oot and ye canny well ask a man to do such things!'

Ken came back from the 'oothoosie', dumping the pails

131

behind the back door before coming inside to the kitchen to say, 'Time we made tracks for bed.'

I was hugging Shona and said in muffled tones, 'All right, I'm coming. Goodnight, Aunt Agnes.'

'Here, what aboot the doggy?' asked the old lady sharply. 'She'll need to sleep ootside! Doggies are happier when they're out of doors.'

I could sense Ken's disappointment was as sharp as my own but he lifted Shona's warm little body from my lap and bore her away. Her paws hung over his shoulders and the look she left behind would have melted an iceberg but icebergs and Great Aunt Agnes were not made of the same stuff and I knew it was useless to pursue the matter.

'Aunt Agnes is a changeable besom,' I said angrily when Ken and I were settled in the big soft bed. 'One minute she's all for Shona, the next she's glowering at her.'

'Her bark's worse than her bite,' soothed Ken. 'She never did like dogs in the house. Just one of her old-fashioned ideas. She'll come round eventually, she always does. Don't worry, Shona will be warm enough. I put a bit of a blanket on the buggy floor.'

A light tap wakened us at seven the next morning. 'Are you awake?' came the sharp question. 'I've set breakfast to warm. The porridge is on the stove and will be ready in five minutes. I'm just away to feed the hens then I'll be in so see and be up!'

Warm and sleepy I listened to her clumping downstairs. Ken was snoring obliviously but a hefty nudge from me made him get up out of bed to pad over to the window.

'It's raining,' he announced dismally. 'Aunt Agnes is out there muffled in a million raincoats. She looks like a big nose out for a walk in the rain.'

This description of the old lady cheered me up immensely. My imagination began to work and in my mind's eye I saw a weird and wonderful vision of a huge nose with little matchstick legs dancing and prancing about in the rain splashing happily in all the puddles.

'Chookie! Chookie! Chookie!' The sounds came strongly from below and I choked.

'A nose that talks! That's really something!'

We were at the table when she came rustling in from the rain.

'Ach, whit a day!' she declared vehemently, removing her rain hat and showering us with raindrops. 'These daft hens will hardly budge from their hooses in weather like this — no' even to be fed. I've to cry on them for ages. Now then, sit you both in and I'll get the porridge oot.'

The porridge was thick, creamy and delicious. Soft-boiled, double-yolked eggs followed with crispy rolls and butter. I kept thinking about Shona and hurried over my breakfast that I might attend her the quicker.

Uncannily Aunt Agnes read my mind once more. 'Where's the doggy this morning? She'll be hungry, will she no?'

'We haven't had time to fetch her yet,' said Ken.

The old lady looked at us accusingly. Her changes of heart were annoying for you never knew when they were going to happen.

'Well, you should have made time!' she snapped. 'You canny have a young doggy like that then forget to feed the poor wee brute. I'll put oot a bowl of porridge and you can take it to her.'

We went out of the back door and into the fenced-off yard. In days gone by there had been no fence and the hens had paraded at will through the back door, but when a broodie was found one day cosily ensconced on the quilted bed in the guest room it was decided it was time to erect a fence with a stout gate in the middle which led into a field of grass kept short by the ever-pecking poultry.

We went through the gate, shutting it behind us carefully. Shona heard us approaching and her small face appeared at Bertha's window. She leapt at us, a joyful whirl of ecstatic licks and barks. Ken examined the interior of the buggy for damage.

'She hasn't chewed a thing,' he announced in amazement then he laughed. 'She's piddled plumb in the middle of the spare wheel, she must have thought it was a bedpan!'

The rain was easing off and the air was warm and damp. We went off to the woods, Shona running in circles in front. The interior of the wood was dry with the mossy earth covered in pine needles. Ken set me on a level piece of ground before he went off to a little glade below. When we separated like this Shona was faced with an agonizing decision. She didn't know which one of us to stay with. Naturally she wanted to have fun running about after Ken but she hated leaving me on my own. At barely three months old she was already showing an endearing loyalty. She dithered between us, looking at Ken's disappearing back then at me. In the end she came to a compromise, going after Ken but coming back at regular intervals to check that I was all right.

I gathered cones, enjoying the sweet smells of earth and pine trees, thinking about Loch Garten not minutes away from Croft na Geal, in my flights of fancy imagining that Dad Cameron's spirit was roaming free through the woods and glens.

The rain had gone completely by the time we made our way back to the house. Mouthwatering smells wafted from the kitchen and Great Aunt Agnes called, 'Send Jessie in. There's a platey of mince for her in the scullery!'

After serving an enormous meal the old lady took herself off to a neighbouring croft and we lay back bloated. The hens clucked lazily under the window; a plane droned somewhere high above; behind the net curtains a bee buzzed spasmodically. The peaceful sounds made me feel sleepy though I noticed that Ken was keeping a wary eye on the bee. He had a phobia about bees and wasps and I had had many a laugh at his antics when trying to escape them. Once a wasp had flown into the buggy and without ado he had ordered me to stop the machine in order that he might make good his escape. I skidded to a halt at the verge and out Ken hopped . . . with the wasp close on his tail. He had pelted up the road with the wasp in full chase leaving me helpless with mirth inside Bertha.

'Where's Shona?' I asked, suddenly missing the pup.

'Somewhere here, I hope,' answered Ken, still with his gaze on the bee.

'Did you leave the back door open when you went to the buggy for cigs?' I questioned.

'Yes, it's that warm in the kitchen. She'll be all right playing about in the yard.'

Five minutes later agitated sounds came from outside, a mixture of chicken screams and puppy yaps. With one accord we made a dive for the door though Ken was well ahead of me as I skidded on the polished lino of the hallway. Reaching the gate I was in time to see a petrified hen running helter skelter away from Shona who had just deprived it of most of its tail feathers. She looked very comical with a row of feathers sticking from her mouth. One large brown feather had got stuck in the fur at her ears and she was trying to dislodge it with a paw.

'Oh Lord!' gasped Ken. 'I must have left the gate open. Aunt Agnes will have a fit when she sees her baldy hen!'

'It could have been worse!' I choked. 'She was out here for ages on her own. Probably she started chasing the hen and couldn't resist a mouthful of feathers.'

Ken gave the pup a hearty wallop and she hung her head in shame but seconds later she looked up at us with an ingratiating smile on her face. Samoyeds are known as the 'smiling' breed. Some just look as if they are smiling when they sit with lolling tongues, others, like Shona, really smile with their teeth. Just lately she had begun to show her teeth whenever she welcomed us. When she was really excited she stripped her jaws to expose her growing fangs. To some it was a sign of fierceness and they backed away from her but we knew it was an expression of her fun-loving personality. When she grew older her smiles grew bigger and if ever she was in trouble she would beam at us with rows of gleaming teeth for she discovered early on in life it was a sure way to get round us.

Samoyeds also 'talk' and Shona was already showing signs of becoming an excellent conversationalist. She would begin by pursing her black lips into a tight ball to 'woo, woo' gently or she could bring the sound from deep down in her throat so that it came out in a roar of sheer ecstasy. Also, from the time we got her at eight weeks old, she would dump her paw into any available hand without being asked. It is a trick that comes naturally to Samoyeds. I have known four of these beautiful creatures in my life and not one of them had to be taught to give a paw.

Shona held hers out to Ken now, a big, fat, floppy, puppy paw, quivering in an abject appeal for forgiveness. She held it for several seconds in mid air and Ken could not refuse to take it though he said gruffly, 'I'll kill you the next time you touch a hen, you wee bugger.'

Hamish the roadman was coming over the field with a paper tucked under his arm. 'Will you hand this in to Aggie?' he asked us. 'I know fine she's away blethering up at Croft Beag but she'll girn if she doesny get her paper . . .'

The hen with the bare bottom streaked past his vision to disappear round the corner of the byre, 'My me,' he said in some bemusement, 'That's an awful bare-arsed chicken!'

'It had a slight accident,' admitted Ken and proceeded to enlighten the old roadman whose ruddy face broke into a crinkled smile.

'Bloody hell,' he chuckled, 'the poor brute will be getting pneumonia up its parson's nose. Don't worry, I'll no' let on to Aggie for you would never hear the end of it. She thinks more o' these damt hens than she does of people!'

Later that day Great Aunt Agnes came into the kitchen, shaking her white head in puzzlement. 'Queer, gey queer!' she muttered. 'One o' my hens has all the feathers missin' from its backside. None o' the others seem to be smitted but you can never tell wi' poultry. I'll need to keep a close watch on them for the next few days.'

We did not enlighten her about the 'accident' though both of us turned red and went out of the room on some pretext.

The old lady was like Da in many ways. She never showed her emotions to the world. That night I heard her in the kitchen talking, using the sort of silken tones normally reserved for Clover. 'Ach, Jessie,' she murmured softly. 'You're a bonny doggy that you are. Leave that auld slipper alone and come and sit on my knee. There now, you're like a wee pie wi' all that fine fur roon' aboot ye. My, my, your lugs are like dandelion puffs, it's a wonder you can hear at all with a' that hair aboot them but I know fine you're listening to every word I'm saying . . .'

I slunk away on wheels that Ken had oiled earlier, not making one squeak in my exit from the hall for I knew the old lady would be angry and embarrassed if she thought one word of her conversation with Shona had been overheard.

Two nights later Shona was allowed up to the bedroom! 'I told you Auntie would come round,' said Ken smugly. For the remainder of the holiday Shona spent her nights curled up contentedly in the huge chamber pot in our room and when we said our goodbyes to the old lady there were tears in her eyes when she stooped to fondle the pup's soft ears. She put up an impatient hand as if to tuck away the wayward strand of hair but in the process her hand brushed against her eyes to wipe the tears away. Absently she patted Shona who was leaning against her knee, 'Well, well, Jessie, I'll get peace now withoot you under my feet.' Shona grinned at her engagingly. 'My would you look at it!' exclaimed the old lady. 'Barin' its teeth and it just a wee doggy! I hope she'll no' turn oot to be a fierce beastie!'

'She's smiling at you, Aunt Agnes,' I explained. 'She only does it to people she likes.'

'Oh ay, and maybe Cheshire cats bark,' came the smart reply. She bent down to Shona. 'Are you smilin' at me, Jessie?' For answer the pup gave an ear-splitting grin. 'Here, you're right,' came the astounded words, 'the doggy does smile.' Shona lifted a chubby paw and dumped it into the old lady's hand. Aunt Agnes patted her with gruff affection. 'Ay, you're all right, Jessie, you'll maybe come to see me again betimes. Now, Kenneth I've a boxie of eggs here for your mother. Tell her to write and I'll be seeing her in September.'

She stood at the gate, her long aprons flying like scarves in the wind, her handkerchief fluttering above her head till we could see it no more.

When we got home Shona made another conquest. Penny was so pleased to see us she actually tolerated the pup too, and later in the week came down off her high horse long enough to nibble daintily from the side of Shona's plate. This was purely cupboard love because of her weakness for dog food but it was a start. Shona was very hospitable about such matters, allowing the cat to have quite a good start before she pushed her black nose in beside the little pink one. Although the pup had a very healthy respect for cats in general her high spirits sometimes got the better of her and she turned the tables by chasing Penny all round the house while Jockey screeched excitedly from his cage and wolf whistled happily.

By the time winter came creeping darkly in Marjory was completely bedridden with a nurse coming in every morning to bathe her and change the bed. She could do nothing for herself, the functions of her body were without control, her eyesight got so bad she could neither read nor knit the beautiful garments that had once rolled off the needles with ease. Yet never once did she say 'Why me?'

She just lay in bed looking like a little elf with her small white face framed by her dark hair. Her legs were twisted permanently, her body a riot of bedsores, all this in a girl who just two years before had walked and danced, climbed mountains, never still for a minute, even while sitting always busy doing something . . . cramming all the activity into a short span. I think it might have been more natural if she had cried a bit and asked 'Why me?'

I have always thought how traumatic it must be for an active adult, to find themselves pulled to a halt by some disability. My heart goes out to such people in their adjusting, their searching to try and put the bits and pieces of their lives into some sort of order. Some never do, the majority make the effort and eventually win. If you are born handicapped you know no other life so you adapt naturally as you grow up, if, like myself, you start off life as an active youngster overcome by a disabling illness, you perhaps go through a bad spell of mixed emotions and frustrations but you soon learn how to cope. Children are very tensile creatures — what was a bad dream last night is the next day something that slides quickly out of the mind because there is so much else crowding into it. But for an adult to find themselves having to start living life from a wheelchair . . . a fearsome transition! That is why I often think when people look at me in my wheelchair, 'Don't look with pity or such crude curiosity — tomorrow it might be you.' It is the last thing I would wish on anyone but life is such an oscillating state we none of us can afford to be too cocksure.

Marjory had no fight in her. It may have been that she was too weak to fight or simply that she didn't want to . . . But brave . . . oh God! How brave a girl was she. The unknown had always terrified me a great deal. Marjory knew she was facing the unknown but showed no fear. She faced the prospect of hospital after the New Year because she realized it was impossible for her mother to manage her much longer. Mum Cameron had already hurt her back turning Marjory in bed but it was her heart more than anything that was tearing apart with the pain of seeing her only daughter growing thinner and weaker with each passing day.

On Christmas Eve we left our warm little cottage and went to the old manse. Scott had carried the television set through to Marjory's room so we could all share the festive programmes together. When we arrived Ken hoisted Shona up on the bed beside Marjory who adored her. She was an adolescent pup now, eight months old, all legs, tail, and love. She loved to be with human beings but even more she loved to have physical contact with them. She was especially in ecstasy sleeping beside anyone who would let her, her head planted firmly on a pillow, legs stretched, belly to the winds, she would lie for hours unless ordered off the best bedspread.

Originally from Siberia, the Samoyed had lived close to man for centuries in the cold wastes of the Arctic. Their life with the Samoyed tribes meant long hours of work, herding the reindeer, patrolling the camp areas, always on the alert against attack by bears and wolves. At night they slept in the tents, huddled close to their masters for warmth and so it is that the modern descendant loves to share a human companionship.

Now Shona snuggled close, put her paws round Marjory's neck, gave her a watery kiss, and with a deep sigh drifted off into a contented sleep. Sultan, Marjory's spaniel, came on to the bed as well, then several cats and it was good to see Marjory laughing as gradually she became encased in a mountain of fur.

Despite her frailty her gifts to us were as beautifully wrapped as ever and it seemed a crime to open them.

'I've nothing better to do, Chris,' she said lightly. 'I'm just something the cat dragged in so I'd better earn my keep or Mum will fling me out on my ear!'

In the middle of January she was admitted to the geriatric ward of a hospital outside Glasgow. She was the youngest in the ward and was soon the pet of all the old ladies. Because smoking was about the only pleasure left to her now she soon earned the nickname of 'Smokey Joe' and she accepted the misnomer with good humour, saying that when she went it would be in a cloud of smoke instead of a blaze of glory. The nurses were lenient with her, so much so they allowed us to take Shona in for visits. Everyone laughed when the big white puppy belted up the ward to go straight to the kitchen for a biscuit or sometimes the ice cream that

Marjory craved but couldn't finish. It took us all our time to restrain Shona from jumping into the white hospital bed beside Marjory but as she grew worse the nurses often looked 'the other way' and it was worth it to see the joy on Marjory's thin face as her hands caressed the silvery bundle slobbering into her neck.

Whilst in hospital, Marjory's old Sultan had been put to sleep. None of us had the heart to tell her but she knew. From the day the spaniel closed his old eyes forever she never mentioned him again, knowing with an uncanny knack that she had lost him.

Despite our worries over Marjory our lives were otherwise full and happy. I was working again. Stuart had opened a driving school and he asked me to take over the running of the office. Shona came with me, of course, otherwise I would never have considered taking the job. With my wages I paid for Shona, not as much as Margaret had got for the other pups but it had been on my conscience for some time and once I had handed the money over I felt that Shona was really and truly mine. People came and went from the office and got used to seeing me in my chair with my white dog at my side.

The job involved phoning people and meeting them as they sat waiting in the office for a lesson and it all did wonders for my self-confidence. The phone was an instrument I had always regarded warily and whenever any serious phoning had to be done at home I had hitherto left it to Ken. Now, bit by bit, I was the master, the phone my servant. I was polite, friendly, but firm with cantankerous ladies who thought that Stuart existed solely to teach them and them alone how to drive a car. He was a marvellous instructor and in one instance coached a very pleasant Jewish lady who had sat fourteen tests and failed every one. After a fairly lengthy session with Stuart she sat the test again, passed without a hitch . . . and cried with joy.

When things were quiet I groomed Shona, played with her, and took her for walks through a little lane that ran

141

parallel to the office. Sometimes Margaret brought Judy, and mother and daughter romped happily though Judy was always the boss. They were wonderful dogs, very wise and interested in everything. If they heard the phut, phut of a two-stroke engine they rushed to the door to look out, thinking it was me passing though I was sitting in the office with them. Once Judy had almost killed herself by running over the road to investigate the occupant of an invalid car parked at the kerbside. Another time a buggy went toddling slowly along the road and Judy went haring after it, heedless of Margaret's calls. I think I can honestly say that Judy had always been devoted to me from puppyhood. She had spent a lot of time with Ken and me and her joy whenever she saw us was uproarious.

At ten minutes to five every night I packed myself, my chair, and Shona into the buggy and went to pick up Ken at his work just a short distance away.

Summer came round again bringing with it golden nights in which we went for long walks. Shona loved her life in the country and quite often followed her natural herding instincts by rounding up the cattle. Off she streaked over the fields, a mercurial blur, ears back, tail flowing behind, everything streamlined to give her speed. These were the times when her hearing became conveniently poor, the only times she defied us. She would gather the roaring young bullocks into a tight neat knot, running circles round them, silent and full of purpose, never nipping at heels or grabbing at swishing tails, just gently masterful till she got them all where she wanted them. Then, and only then, would she come slinking back to us, showing the whites of her eyes in apprehensive sidelong glances.

I think, if it wasn't for their independence, Samoyeds would make excellent sheepdogs. But they are a breed who like too much to 'go it alone', again a throwback to the days when they were working dogs. They are hopeless on a lead, always straining and tugging to get on ahead as if they are still pulling a sledge. Although we bought Shona a harness she still hauled grimly but in time we learned to put his habit to good use when we were out walking. When we came to a hill we popped the lead on to the harness and she would blithely pull me up a hill, taking the strain off Ken.

Penny, who had hated the pup so much at the beginning, was now one of her most affectionate friends. They sampled one another's food without malice, played hide and seek in the barn, and curled up together in the sun beside Jockey's cage. During the winter cat and dog had slept together in the kitchen with the cat snuggled into Shona's thick soft fur as she lay under the old kitchen cabinet.

With the coming of the warmer days Penny preferred the solitude of the cool dining room where she catnapped contentedly on the horsehair sofa. These were the times she did not welcome the attentions of the fun-loving young dog. One of Shona's favourite games was to go creeping into the dining room to sidle up to the cat just to check that she was fully asleep. Penny had a habit of sleeping with her long tail hanging over the edge of the sofa, and oh! the anticipation on that dog's face had to be seen to be believed. Suddenly she lowered her head and biffed Penny's rump into the air and while it was thus suspended she played 'headers' with the tail, tossing it about with her nose, this way and that with pure abandoned joy. Out flashed Penny's claws to grip Shona's black nose but she had the sense now to stay still till the hold was loosened. Sometimes I suspected that Penny secretly looked forward to this game because once or twice I saw a narrowed eye squinting open prior to the start of the 'headers'.

Jockey, too, enjoyed a game with Shona. Whenever she lay beside him with her face between her paws he could never resist a good peck at the black nose pressed up to the spars of his cage. In retaliation Shona licked the bird till he was soaked and quite often he gave her tongue a good pull to spite her for such treatment.

The pleasure that animals give! They can make you forget for a while the more serious and sorrowful issues of the human world. Our visits to Marjory became more frequent and there came a day when a report was sent out from the hospital. Marjory was in a coma, the family could be with her at any time of the night or day. Ken and I raced up one evening after work. Marjory's eyes were closed, her small dark head made hardly an impression on the pillow, her skin was waxen and her breathing so shallow it was difficult to believe she was breathing at all.

'She was talking in her sleep last night,' one of the other patients whispered tearfully. 'She said, "Yes, Dad, I'm coming, but I'll wait till my birthday."'

My scalp crept, Ken turned pale. Marjory's birthday was but two days away. We both knew then that Marjory was just waiting to join her father. In the depth of her twilight world she was between the living and the dead but she knew enough, was strong enough . . . to wait. It was an eerie sensation. Marjory always did know of things that were going on in other worlds, even at the height of her joy days there was an aura about her of an ephemeral being.

On the morning of her twenty-fifth birthday Mum phoned us to come to the hospital. Marjory was in an oxygen tent. Wrapped in that transparent sphere she looked to have already passed out of the world except for a pulse flickering erratically in her neck. All the family were there, gathered round the bed. I could hardly bear to look at poor Mum with her bowed shoulders and her dazed eyes. The ward was very quiet, everything seemed to be suspended in a time-lag . . . but yet the clock ticked the seconds away relentlessly. From somewhere at the top of the ward an old voice quavered, 'Oh love that wilt not let me go, I hide my weary soul in thee-e.'

The bedside locker was gay with birthday cards, arranged by a nurse but unseen by Marjory. 'Happy birthday and may you have many more.' The words leapt out in silent mockery. Yet it may have been that it was a happy birthday for Marjory. She had waited for this day to go to her father for it was certain there was no future for so young a life in this world.

The warmth of life was retreating from her limbs. Her hands were cold, fragile hands, lying on the counterpane. Once they had been very busy hands, now they lay quite still and peaceful. The clock ticked the leaden minutes away. The oxygen tent was taken away and now there was just a small oxygen mask over her face. Her life ebbed slowly away, just as the tide ebbs tranquilly from the shores of our earth. But I thought as I looked at her lying there, reminding me so much of Iona, the young girl who lay in the next bed to me in the days of my childhood and who had gone so gracefully and trustingly to that other world, that when the tide flows out from one shore it must surge on to another in distant reaches. Even as Marjory was slipping away from us she was slowly but surely floating out to meet her father and also the Father of all earth's children. Her face was calm in those moments, a ghost of a smile lifted the corners of her mouth. Perhaps she was already reaching out to take her father's hand to be led gently and without effort to a higher sphere.

The pulse in her neck did not stop beating suddenly. It just got weaker and weaker, slower and slower, till finally it just seemed to go out, like a candle that has burned so low it eventually drowns in its liquid remains. The staff nurse listened for a heartbeat but there was none. On the day of her twenty-fifth birthday Marjory Mabel Cameron had died. There were tears in the nurse's eyes as she removed the oxygen mask.

'I'm sorry, so very sorry,' she said helplessly. 'Smokey Joe has gone.' All down the length of the ward there came the sound of hushed weeping.

'Smokey Joe is dead! Smokey Joe is dead!' The words echoed through the ward in a genuine agony of sorrow for the young girl who had lain six weary months in the hospital with barely ever a word of complaint. She had gone through the winter days and into the summer and now it was June with life bursting from every eager bud.

Her three brothers stood round their mother in those

terrible minutes, John, Scott and Ken, silently ready to give Mum Cameron all the support she would need in the difficult days ahead. Ken put his arm round her shoulders and hugged her close and the minister who had been with us all afternoon, and who was such a faithful family friend, said a short but moving service at Marjory's bedside. He must have seen death many times yet there were tears in his eyes that day for he had known Marjory when her life had been exuberant and every minute sitting still was a minute wasted.

A few days later she was cremated and later her ashes were taken to Loch Garten and scattered at the same spot Dad's had been less than a year before. Great Aunt Agnes had been uneasy when Dad's ashes were brought to Loch Garten. She did not approve of the modern trend for cremation but mixed with her views were the Highlander's superstitious fears of the unknown. But she was resigning herself to the 'modern ways' of doing though she still stoutly maintained, 'Ach, I don't hold wi' it myself. When my time comes I'll go beside Neily beneath the daisies . . . and I'll die in my own bed forbye. You will no' catch me freezing to death in one o' they hospital mortuaries.'

Knowing Great Aunt Agnes we fully believed every word she said.

9. Marilla Mini

Just before Christmas 1967 we managed to scrape enough money together for a deposit on a little mini van. For some time now our lives had been made miserable by a Ministry god. This particular being had been watching us for some time. We had passed him once or twice on our way to work in the morning. He knew our route, our times of travel. In his own comfortable, Government-supplied car he pounced on us at every opportunity and ordered Ken out of the buggy. It was useless trying to explain our position to him. He was doing his job, that was all there was to it. Of course he was right. Every time I took Ken in the single-seater invalid car I was breaking the law but it would have been fine of me to leave him three miles from anywhere to make his own way to work while I waved my way off in Bertha.

We came to dread going anywhere together, always on the lookout for that ferrety-faced individual with his close-set eyes and his tight little mouth. He was a notorious troublemaker. Other ministry officials must have spotted dozens of invalid cars with passengers but there are other ways to look when the obvious hits you between the eyes. The ministry men as a whole were kindly, understanding people, just as anxious for disabled people to have better modes of transport as the disabled themselves. If they could not avoid ticking you off then it was done in a discreet and sympathetic manner, but not so Ferret Face. Ferret Face positively gloated whenever he sneaked up behind me and blasted his horn for me to stop so that he could have a lot of fun out of making me feel I had just crawled out from under a stone. On one occasion he had come alongside me in the road to glower, point at Ken, and utter tight-lipped profanities, before he forced me to the kerbside where I narrowly missed a woman wheeling a pram.

'Out!' he had bawled at Ken. 'This is government property you are breaking the law in! In case you are not aware of the fact I am empowered to take steps for this vehicle to be taken away from your wife!'

I, of course, did not remain meekly quiet on receiving this tirade, in fact I was inarticulate with wrath, but Ken went a step better. He did indeed hop speedily out of Bertha, his face white, his red hair bristling with rage. Over he beetled to Ferret Face's car and thumped it on the roof. 'And *this* is government property, too, in case you think I am ignorant of the fact!' Thump, thump. 'I could report you to the police for using a vehicle in a manner which is a danger to human life!'

Ferret Face almost collapsed with shock but Ken's words only deepened his ire. 'I will remain in this spot until I have seen you safely out of sight, young man! You will hear more of this I promise you – oh yes, the matter will not rest here!'

Poor Ken no doubt could have said a lot more but he was realizing that his hasty words had done nothing to help the situation and off he walked, up the street, while I could only sit helplessly and watch. Of course I picked him up the minute Ferret Face was out of sight but we remained in a state of trepidation for the rest of the day. By the next morning I knew I couldn't bear to await the outcome of the encounter and taking my courage in both hands I phoned the manager of the Invalid Car Section and reported myself. He listened sympathetically, gave me a gentle dressing down and told me not to get caught again! Ferret Face had not after all 'cliped' on me and I wondered if this had something to do with Ken's threat of reporting his road manners to the police.

We could not really afford a car. It was taking us all our time to gather a home together but we threw thrift to the wind and went to search out a second-hand vehicle with four wheels and two seats. Eventually we came upon a 1962 mini van. The car dealers saw us coming, of course. Greener than peas in a pod we were thrilled at the sight of a piece of scrap that was in the process of being overhauled and resprayed. Later we realized the van had been in an accident and was a near write-off when we saw it, but our vision did not go beyond the breathtaking assessment that the van was equipped with things we had only dreamed about in the four years we had been travelling together in Bertha. We were utter simpletons in the devious world of the smooth-talking car dealer but we took every word, every assurance, at its face value and waited impatiently for the delivery of the van. I had already christened it Marilla Mini and gleefully pictured myself behind the wheel. The little vehicle eventually arrived and we gazed at it in awed reverence. It was a dark blue shade and because the bodywork had just been resprayed it looked gleaming and new.

'Imagine actually having *two* seats,' said Ken in a joyous whisper.

'And a heater,' I added, thinking of freezing winters spent in Bertha.

The invalid car was now taken out of the shed supplied for it by The Ministry of Health and put to one side. In place of honour went Marilla Mini, out of the rain and wind so that nothing took away the miraculous beauty of the gleaming paintwork. We lavished it with care, polishing, dusting . . . and simply just touching it to make sure it was real. Everything that *real* cars boasted were there in the van and we gave not one thought to what lurked underneath the bonnet. We knew it was an engine with four spark plugs instead of one — another miracle!

Our thoughts did not wander further. It was enough that at long last we had a two-seater vehicle and we spent hours just sitting in it and talking about it. How lucky we were! No other couple in the world could possibly have felt luckier or happier than we did in those first wondrous days. The only thing we couldn't do was ride in it for I had still to pass the driving test and as Ken held no driving licence of any sort he couldn't sit beside me on the open road.

In the past I'd had various opportunities to try out my driving abilities, first in an old Ford belonging to Callum, more recently in Stuart's school cars. These times had been few and far between yet enough for me to know that I was perfectly at ease behind a driving wheel. Most of us are born to be naturally good at something. Driving was my forte. Since I had first taken to the road in shaky old Black Maria, my first invalid car, I had felt no fear of powered machines which in my position was just as well. Although I could not walk I had strength enough in my feet to operate all the usual pedals without the aid of hand controls, therefore I could get into any car and 'have a bash'.

My bedside cabinet was a jumble of highway codes and other informative pamphlets and I drove Ken mad repeating over and over the do's and don'ts of driving.

'Just see if I've got it right,' I said every night in bed. Forcing his bleary eyes to stay open he asked me questions about white lines, triangles and circles till we were both seeing them in front of our eyes. When he could stay awake no longer I employed the attention of Shona who made an alert and uncomplaining audience. I applied for the test and eventually received a date with a mixture of apprehension and eagerness.

'The end of January,' I told Stuart with a brave smile.

'Right,' he said, 'I'll take you out as often as I can. Don't worry, you're a natural.'

On the day of the test I felt anything but a 'natural' as I waited for the examiner to make his leisurely way out to the school mini. It was an automatic car and because I'd had to take whatever was available in the course of my lessons I had experience both of manual and automatic though I didn't like the latter. To me it wasn't real driving but it was as well I had become used to it because it was the only

school car available to me on the day of my test. Putting on
my nonchalant face I waited with outward composure for
the examiner to make his appearance. Inwardly I was a
seething mass of nerves, my heart raced, my bladder
screamed out to be emptied, the top of my head felt as if it
was about to blow off at any minute. I felt trapped because
my chair had been left behind in the school office. Across
my brain in large red letters the word 'toilet' seemed to have
been branded as my bladder grew fuller.

After an eternity of sweating the examiner strolled over to
the car. Why is it that official beings always look so calm
and assured even though they might just have stepped out
of a spaceship? Because when you meet certain ones at
certain times they appear to be anything except human.

'Don't forget to turn the ignition!' I screamed to myself. I
had heard stories about nerve-wracked driving pupils
sailing beautifully through the procedure of mirror adjusting, eyesight testing, signalling their intention of moving off
. . . only to discover that they had forgotten to switch on the
engine, or forgotten to take off the handbrake!

In beside me climbed the examiner, very silent and
purposeful, so businesslike with his neat suit, little sheafs of
forms, the eyes behind the glasses full of a patient
resignation that he was about to undergo a half hour of hell
with yet another learner . . . a disabled one at that!

The demands of my bladder receded into oblivion as I
swung into action. I felt detached from myself, a mere
onlooker as I swung in and out of streets, made a hill start, a
three-point turn, a reverse round a corner and an emergency
stop that nearly sent the examiner through the windscreen.
None of these procedures are in chronological order simply
because I don't remember what sort of order they were in at
the time. I kept my eye on the speedo needle throughout,
terrified I should go over the 30 m.p.h. limit, and over and
over I thought, 'You've failed! You've failed! He won't
forgive you for that emergency stop!'

The driving test in the buggy had been an entirely

different affair. It had been something of a hilarious farce with myself and the examiner in the starring roles. Because it was against the law to take passengers, even during a driving test, he gave me a verbal route to take and a list of all the things I had to do for the test. Off I set, uncertain of what was expected of me and trying desperately to keep all the instructions in my head, something I was usually hopeless at. I made the first right and left turns successfully but after that I forgot where I was supposed to go. Fortunately I was familiar with the various test routes and chose one at random, praying it was the one I had been told to take. I had no idea where the examiner was but chanting miserably towards a crossroads I saw his head peeping out of a shop doorway. After that I became so absorbed in wondering where his little dome would pop out of next I forgot the fact that I was sitting a driving test and went through all my procedures with mechanical ease. When I saw the examiner haring up a side street and into a close I almost forgot everything as I shrieked with utter and abandoned mirth and arrived back at the test centre without a care in the world. One half of me hoped that I had failed the test so that I would have the chance of taking part in another such pantomime in the future. But the examiner, panting a little with exertion, informed me that I had come through successfully and, sitting rather gingerly beside me on my little box-cum-stool, wrote out my certificate.

But I didn't feel like laughing that day of the test in the school mini with the examiner close beside me in regal flesh-and-blood aloofness. In a daze I realized we were back at the test centre and I was being asked questions on the highway code. The endless nights of pamphlet browsing did nothing to help me. My mind seemed to go completely blank yet I felt my lips opening and closing and actual sounds coming out in the Queen's English.

The efficient creature who had just recently caused several of my hairs to lose their pigment said calmly, 'I am very pleased to tell you that you have passed the driving test.'

I could find nothing to say and knew I was smiling like a complete idiot. On the opposite side of the road stood Stuart, sticking his thumbs up in the air then down. Comprehension dawned. I stuck my two thumbs joyfully into the air and yelled through the window, 'I passed! I passed!'

The examiner permitted himself a small dry smile and allowed me to recover my equilibrium before proceeding to give me some words of advice, then he handed me a pink slip and got out of the car.

Stuart found me kissing the piece of paper passionately. 'Well done,' he grinned, 'I told you there was nothing to worry about, you were born to the wheel.'

Words of praise indeed from my brother-in-law whose success partially came from the fact that he only handed out compliments if they had been well and truly earned. He ticked off his pupils when they needed ticking off, he praised when it was deserved, above all he was cool and calm and soothing in the most nerve-wracking situations. Rarely did he raise his voice and only then when he had been provoked to it by the most thick-headed of pupils. I think I always loved him for the utmost confidence he gave me and had in me. Whenever he got a new car he allowed me to drive it without hesitation. Quite often if he had to take a car to a garage for repair I came at his back to pick him up. Once, when he had just taken delivery of two brand new Avengers, we all went up north for the weekend. Stuart and Margaret and Judy were in one car, Ken, myself and Shona in the other. Another time he allowed me to drive his Dormobile but the clutch was so heavy he had to work it though I did the rest. The only car of his I ever refused to drive was a beautiful Citroën. He urged, coaxed, even bullied me to get in behind the driving wheel but I was too terrified I might get a scratch on the flawless paint.

When Ken heard my news he seized the chair and waltzed me round the living room while Shona, thinking we were playing some crazy game, leapt high in the air, finally landing with some surprise in my lap.

'And *that's* to you, you bloody old ferrety-faced official!' shouted Ken, putting his fingers to his nose in a rude gesture.

'My, that's grand, Christine,' said Mrs Murdoch over a cup of tea that evening. 'There won't be any holding you now. Fancy passing first time. Ay, you're a fine one wi' things on wheels an' no mistake.'

At first we went for cautious drives on the country roads round the farm. Despite having passed my test in an automatic there was no law then to say you had to stick to that type of vehicle though this was put into force not long after I had taken my test. But I was able to go from automatic to manual. My confidence grew and we went further afield till I no longer felt I was about to faint whilst waiting at traffic lights alongside monstrous buses. Oh the joy of that steering wheel after the rigours of continual combat with a tiller bar! We could never quite get over the utter luxury of having enough room for us both to sit in comfort with the heater blowing glorious warmth over our legs.

Shona sat happily in the back, able now to get up and stretch herself when she felt the need. There was also plenty of room for my chair; messages and coal carrying were no longer frustrating problems. The only thing I couldn't do was get my wheelchair into the van by myself as I could in Bertha. The only way was via the back doors which I couldn't shut after me but Ken solved this problem by making a handle which fitted through the existing back door lock. It was quite a performance getting the chair inside in this way. First I had to sit on the edge of the van floor, fold up my chair and get the front wheels hoisted in, then, praying that the chair wouldn't fall on its side, I crawled into the van, heaved the chair in, shut the doors with the new inside handle, after which I crawled the length of the van to manoeuvre myself somehow into the driving seat.

Getting myself and the chair outside again was an even more daunting task and in the end I just left my chair folded in the shed and drove away. If I had to go anywhere where I had to get myself out at the other end I just took Bertha and left the van in the shed.

Joy did not last long as far as Marilla Mini was concerned. The engine began giving trouble and we puttered through a snow-filled winter with our hearts in our mouths, never quite sure if we would make it home or get stuck miles from anywhere. We could hardly bear the thought of going back to Bertha. In the van we did not have to blow on the windscreen to keep it clear of ice, the heater did that for us. It was miraculous! It was unbelievable! But for the heater to blow the engine had to tick over and the engine was in no fit state to falter let alone tick. We had been sold a body shell, the rest was rubbish. We could not afford the required repairs so we reverted back to poor old neglected Bertha till we were able to save enough money to have the mini engine patched up.

Just in time, too! Ferret Face was on the rampage again. He had been utterly dismayed the first time he had espied us in Marilla Mini. With our noses in the air we had sailed past him then collapsed into joyous laughter. Back in Bertha we kept our noses well down, and everything else for that matter. It would never do to keep your head snootily high whilst sailing past a ministry official in an invalid car with a passenger at your side.

The first morning Marilla Mini was ready once more for the road we toddled past Ferret Face waiting for us in a side street. The look of sheer disappointment on his face made us scream with victorious glee and I dared to lift my thumb slyly to my nose in a way that suggested I might just be rubbing it or giving off a rude sign!

During that winter Ken had been doing a lot of serious thinking about the future and the acquiring of a house we could call our very own. Not me! I lived for each day that came to me! The only time I gave the future a thought was to look forward to some party or a camping spree. I hated the idea of leaving the cottage. We had lived in it for four years and had loved our time spent there. Within its walls we had known the unprecedented happiness of sharing our first home with each other, had known love, warmth and laughter almost every day.

'Why do we have to go?' I asked Ken tearfully.

'Because this can't last forever,' he explained patiently. 'You have to have security in life and owning your own place means security.'

'It can also mean whacking great mortgages,' I pointed out sulkily.

'It will be worth it, a means to an end. Someday we'll come back and live in the country . . . anyway, things are going to be different here. I have a feeling Mrs Murdoch will sell up and go and live with her daughter. We would have to get out of the cottage anyway.'

'It's terrible how things have to change,' I mourned. I was a romantic seeing life in an unrealistic light, never able to understand why people kept wanting to change ways of life that appeared ideal to me, but I was sensible enough to know that on the outside looking in you can never know all the reasons why people do the things they do.

Gradually I came round to Ken's way of thinking and, in the human way of things, actually began to look forward to moving, seeing the whole thing as just another adventure on the road through life.

Ken's old home had many empty rooms now that most of the family were gone. This would be the stepping stone between the cottage and a home of our own. In many ways it was entirely unsuitable for me with flights of stairs to the entrance and more flights inside to reach bedrooms and bathroom.

'Don't worry,' I told Ken flippantly. 'What's a wee thing like a few hundred stairs to a girl like me? I'll bum it . . . all the way to heaven if it means getting a house of our own. We'll be able to save money while we're at Mum's. I suppose it's worth making a few sacrifices.'

My brave words were only to reassure him because secretly I could hardly bear the thought of leaving our dear little cottage and the green fields of the country behind.

Mrs Murdoch was genuinely sorry when she heard our decision and told us she would never get such a nice young couple like us again. 'But ach,' she continued resignedly, 'you young yins must spread yer wings but the place will no' be the same withoot you. Good luck tae the pair o' you.'

We took our leave of the cottage in April 1968. The countryside was yielding tranquilly to the new young life that bedecked it with fat sticky buds and shy little banks of primroses hiding in the moss. The birds were soaring, singing, courting, filling the air with music, air that was so heady with the fragrance of spring that every time you breathed deeply it was like taking a draught of sweet wine. The cottage had never looked more beautiful with the sun streaming over the fresh wallpaper and poking accusing fingers at all the little labours of love we were leaving behind. We stood in the bare rooms, saying silent, tearful goodbyes to each one, remembering the days of our joy when we knew the cottage was to be ours and we had come breezing in to go charging through all the empty rooms, awed and thrilled that our first steps into marriage were taking us to a little love nest in the heart of the country. I sat in the dining room and looked out of the window. The daffodils in the glade were bowing golden heads into the wind and my young rowan tree, plucked by me from the dung midden and replanted in my garden, was throwing furls of bursting buds from its bare branches. My eyes filled with tears, daffodils and trees merged together in a watery blurr, abruptly I turned my chair, took Ken's hand, and left the room without a backward glance.

We did the flitting in the mini van. Miraculously we even managed to get our big bed settee into it, tying the doors back and anchoring the settee with ropes.

Penny was nowhere to be seen when we made our way over the gravel yard for the last time. She had been rather sulky for the last few days and we suspected she knew we were leaving her behind. This had been a sad decision for us, arrived at after much discussion on what would be best for the dear old cat who had lived all her life in the country. It was because of this that we made up our minds to leave her, knowing she would be lost and unhappy in a town environment. Mrs Murdoch promised to look after her and with this we had to be satisfied though there was a lump in my throat that I would hear no more the deep purrs of her welcome or feel her soft fur under my hands.

We were also leaving behind the tiny grave under the rowan tree where dear little Jockey was buried. He had died suddenly one winter's night, found by Ken the next morning at the bottom of his cage, his wolf whistles and cat calls silenced forever. We cried when we held his body in our hands, such a little body yet one that had filled our lives with fun and happiness. Reverently we put him in a box together with one of his favourite toys and laid him to rest. After he died we vowed we wouldn't get another budgie but we were lost without Jockey's gay chatterings so his scrubbed cage was resurrected and was now inhabited by Jockey II, a lovely blue little fellow who was already showing promise of a clowning acrobat ready to mimic all our whistles. On the last run to the manse he sat amidst carpets and boxes, giving cheek to Shona lying stretched out beside him.

Uneasily we settled into our new way of life. Mum was delighted to have us, giving us the run of the top part of the house. One of the rooms was turned into a sitting room and we slept in Marjory's old bedroom. Because of the difficulty getting up and down the stairs I left Stuart's driving school so I was at a loss as how best to fill my days. Gone was the freedom of the cottage and the walks in the country. I had to try and content myself with a more restricted way of life and began to feel something of the frustration of the Govan days creeping back. There was only one way to get down the long flight of steps, inside and outside. I took to my backside.

Sometimes the outer stairs were wet and I had to tie a large piece of polythene round myself whereupon I sallied forth looking like a sack of potatoes.

Shona settled into the Cameron household as if she had belonged all her life. She ousted poor blind old Minnie from the chair that had been her bed from puppyhood and gave the cats a dog's life, biffing resting rumps high in the air and daily giving each cat a good wash with her big pink tongue till they were dripping and bedraggled. But she also showed her respect for them in many ways, never having forgotten her early lessons on feline temperament.

Though we gave Mum our 'keep' money each week we were managing to put quite a little sum away for 'our house'. But as sure as fate every time we had gathered enough money to make us feel elated Marilla Mini broke down and had to have one big repair after the other.

'This is the limit,' I said to Ken. 'Do you think we'll ever have enough for a deposit on a house?'

'Some day we will, my lamb,' he said, trying to sound cheerful though I knew he was beginning to get despondent. 'We'll just have to be patient.'

Patience! I don't think I had any to spare in those days. I had used most of mine up in my childhood when each long frustrating day in hospital was a test of patience and endurance.

10. Doctor Pelvis

June was a hot month that year of 1968. Oh, to pop out of a cottage door and breathe in the summer but I had to be content with the overgrown 'garden' at the back of the Manse and count myself lucky to have somewhere to sit. Mum Cameron was the soul of kindness. She had to put up with a lot in her life but never seemed to lose her patience.

I was moody and temperamental, more so than ever now because as well as having no house in which to do as I pleased I also suspected that I was pregnant!

I told Ken one evening while he was struggling to glue the wings on to a model plane. No big fancy scene of falling into each other's arms, kissing, him ordering me to sit down and rest! I was never anything else but sitting down though I certainly never rested.

'When?' he asked tensely.

'Maybe never,' I said airily. 'I'm not sure yet but if it's the case then it will be next February. Don't let on to anyone yet.'

'We'll have to get a house,' babbled Ken. 'One without stairs! You'll never manage a baby with stairs!'

This sounded so funny we both laughed. 'If it has to be born without anything then I hope it will be born without stairs,' I said.

We stared at each other, suddenly taking in the meaning of the situation. Neither of us had ever worried away our early married years with longings for children. Even after my miscarriage I hadn't gone off my rocker with ideas that it was a sign I couldn't carry a baby. It was just something that happened. It happened to a lot of young women and it had happened to me but that was the end of it. But now we

160

were slightly overawed by the realization that inside me at that very moment a baby might be growing.

I bent to stroke Shona who was leaning against my wheels.

'Don't bend!' ordered Ken sharply and we both screeched with foolish mirth.

We went off to spend the Glasgow Fair fortnight with Great Aunt Agnes. Marilla Mini was behaving quite well at the time and it was wonderful bowling along the roads to the Highlands. No more crocodiles at my back champing to overtake. I overtook them and felt bubbles of triumphant joy rising in my throat.

At first Great Aunt Agnes would not come out in the van. 'Ach, no,' she protested, 'I don't go in much for fleein' aboot in cars. The roads are too busy wi' they tourists comin' in their droves to look at the osprey nestin' at the loch. Thon folk are no' right in the heid makin' such a fuss aboot a muckle bird ye never see anyway.'

Two days later she said somewhat indignantly, 'I thought I was tae come oot wi' ye for a drive!'

'Of course, Aunt Agnes,' I said merrily. 'Where would you like to go?'

'I'd like fine to visit Neily's grave. I've a feelin' I'll be joinin' him soon.'

She was right. On the day we left Croft na Geal she seemed sad. Her eyes were misty when she said goodbye, her words lacking in spirit.

'I don't know when I'll see ye again,' she said, her hand going up to brush away the strand of hair but again, stealthily wiping her eyes at the same time. 'Look after yourselves. I hope I see your mother in the autumn, Kenneth. The winter can be long and dreich and it's nice to have folks comin' aboot before it begins.'

She stood at the garden gate waving her white hanky in the air. In bygone days the hanky seemed like a gay little flag fluttering merrily in the wind. Now it looked like a symbol of defeat, a truce almost, and an odd pang of sadness went through me. Ken must have felt it too.

'She looks lonely, doesn't she,' he said quietly. 'Sort of old. I've never thought of Aunt Agnes as old before.'

We never saw her again because she died a few months later, found in her bed by the postman who became worried when he didn't see her about the croft. She got her wish. She died in her own bed and went to rest beneath the daises in a little graveyard not far from Croft na Geal, an old-fashioned place so far removed from the hustle and bustle of present-day times. There weren't many Aunt Agneses or places like the croft left in the modern world.

My pregnancy tests proved positive. We were happy and worried at the same time. The old Manse was no place for a wheelchair-bound mother-to-be and Ken was frantic trying to work out a solution to the problem. We had no deposit to put down on a house so there seemed no way out. I still 'bummed' up and down stairs much to everyone's dismay but my own. I felt exceedingly fit with no symptoms such as morning sickness to remind me of my condition. The baby was due at the beginning of March 1969 and we were overjoyed when Ken's firm offered to go security for a house mortgage. All we had to do now was find a house suitable for a disabled person.

After much weary searching we found one, a semi-detached bungalow in a 'desirable' suburban area. It was owned by an old lady who looked perfectly matched to a decor of biscuit-coloured wallpaper and brown varnish. But the decor was the least of our worries. If our offer was accepted we would soon change everything to suit ourselves. In a frenzy of impatience we waited till finally, after a bit of haggling about a hundred pounds the old lady was determined to extract from us for 'extras', we learned that the house was ours. It was unbelievable! We actually owned a house . . . except for the fact that we had to pay a hefty mortgage with interest. We who had begun married life just over four years before with nothing were now the proud

owners of four walls and a roof! Nothing could take away
those first hazy days of happiness . . . nothing that is till we
moved in at the beginning of December and realized the
fantastic amount of work and cash needed to make the place
presentable. But we were full of enthusiasm. Before we even
got the keys we swooped in on the garden, gazing around at
'our' land. Instantly I made tracks for the front garden to
examine the region by the front door, hoping to see a mass
of rose shoots arched becomingly round the entrance. But
there was only a rather sorry-looking hydrangea bush
sprouting out of the red, weed-strewn gravel and an
abundance of cotoneaster roots wedged around the steps.

'I'll get them out,' I told Ken with assurance, 'and in
their place I'll plant roses. I must have roses round the
door.' As soon as we got the keys Ken went to work in the
kitchen, coating it with white paint in an effort to smother a
sickly, public-toilet green.

I loved dabbling about with a paintbrush so my disappointment was intense when my doctor told me after a
routine check, 'No strenuous activities, my girl — and that
includes doing up the house. Your blood pressure is a bit
high.'

'Oh hell!' I groaned to Ken. 'What if I've to go into
hospital?'

I restricted my activities to knitting tiny garments for the
baby's wardrobe. The movements inside me were so strong
now there were nights when I got little sleep. 'Feel this . . .
and that,' I ordered Ken as strange lumps moved eerily
under my skin. With awe he felt the wonder of a growing
life popping this way and that.

When I went back to my doctor he smiled with
satisfaction. 'You've been obeying doctor's orders, your
blood pressure is down but go on taking it easy.'

So it was we were able to spend our first Christmas
together in our new home. We glowed with pride when we
sat back to admire our huge Christmas tree set in the
window of the 'lounge'. Round about was the debris of our

flitting, tea chests, boxes, piles of books, but we saw only the beauty of the twinkling tree.

Margaret and Stuart lived in a house but a street or two from ours and we all gathered there at the New Year with Kirsty, Callum, Sarah, and baby Linda. Margaret now had two little boys so we were quite a crowd. Callum had been marvellous at helping Ken to construct a concrete ramp at the back door of our bungalow so I was able to come and go as I pleased, exhilarated with the freedom after the restrictions imposed by the stairs at the old Manse.

Shona had long ago adapted herself to her new surroundings. She was happy to be wherever we were and delighted in the large garden at the back, bounding out each morning to sniff the frosty air and dig furtive holes to bury her bones. But no matter how careful she was a miniature mound of earth on her black nose always gave her away and she stood chastened while I washed her face and gave her a scolding. One of our fears in bringing her to suburbia had been the busy roads. In the country, freedom had been hers for the taking but we needn't have worried. With an in-built instinct she stayed demurely by our sides during a walk though whenever she passed Judy's house she could never resist breaking away from us to go racing up to the door. Judy came to visit us often and mother and daughter roared with delight as they chased each other round the garden.

Each morning Ken kissed me goodbye and set off to his office which was conveniently near the house. Before going away he set the fire in the little back sitting room which was the only room, other than the bedrooms, fit enough for habitation.

We had inherited a large black phone with the house. It was on a table by my bedside so that I could contact help if an emergency arose. Following doctor's orders I lazed in bed every morning with Shona snuggled up beside me, her downy head tucked lovingly under my chin. At midday I arose, did the housework and prepared a meal for Ken's return.

But despite all precautions my blood pressure soared and on one of my hospital check-ups I was informed that I would have to become an in-patient.

'Oh but I can't!' I yelped while my mind raced with a thousand and one reasons why I must remain in the outside world.

'Sorry but you'll have to,' said the nurse with a kind but firm smile. 'We'll expect you on Monday morning at ten.'

'It's for your own good, lamb,' said Ken later.

'But, what will you do?'

'Don't worry about me. I'll get my meals at Mum's then come straight to the hospital to see you every night.'

'What about Shona?' I mourned. 'She's going to be terribly lonely.'

'I'll try and get home at lunch times to feed her and let her out. Margaret's good. She'll look in and see that Shona isn't lonely.'

Monday loomed before me like a large black cloud. I felt sick at the thought of hospital but above all I dreaded how the other patients would react to a pregnant, chair-bound, young mother-to-be.

There had already been various reactions to my condition. The WOOPOS had had a field day.

'Will the baby be — normal?' had simpered one to Mum Cameron.

'Will she be able to carry?' another had asked during the early stages.

'Do you think she'll be able to have it — naturally?'

The last question had been asked by several WOOPOS until Mum could take no more. In a very genteel way she could really cut people down to size. 'So far Chris has done what comes naturally to us all,' she intoned politely, 'though in many ways I'd say she is more natural than any of us and she certainly doesn't go about worrying herself sick about other people's insides and I don't think she dwells enough on her own to let it get her down!'

The WOOPOS just did not realize that I was a perfectly

capable housewife who was able to perform the usual tasks around the house. Some looked at me with round eyes then at Ken with pity, obviously visualizing him coming home from a sweated day of labour to do all the household chores. Others heard me out when I stressed my competence in household management then told me benignly I had 'such spirit'.

Old ladies were the most maddening in an endearing old-fashioned way. 'How nice for you to be able to get out in the fresh air, dear,' they told me when perhaps I was sitting resting after having attacked most of the weeds in the garden. Others looked anxiously at the sky and murmured, 'Watch you don't catch cold, dear. There's some nasty black clouds up there.' They are of course oblivious to the fact that I wear only slacks and a jumper whilst they are adorned to the eyeballs in furs.

I will always remember one dear old lady who spoke to me while I waited for Ken outside a shop. At the time I was five months pregnant but very neat around the middle which was hidden away by a white furry jacket.

'Hello, my dear,' she greeted me gently, 'What's a lovely young girl like you doing in a wheelchair? You should be oot enjoyin' yourself and havin' lots o' boyfriends. You have the bonniest eyes I have ever seen.'

She kept her own strictly averted from my lower quarters as if the wasted sight that must surely follow my chair-bound condition was too terrible to contemplate.

She gazed into the window for a moment then said with slow deliberation, 'Whit happened if ye don't mind me asking?' For me it was a time-worn query and I had always rather enjoyed myself making up a list of different explanations, drawing on suitable ones to satiate the various appetites, gory details for the avid, gentle little snippets for the timid.

But this particular old dear had a kind, sweet face and I said simply, 'I took an illness when I was a little girl and haven't been able to walk since.'

'Ach, my, and smilin' through it all. You're a brave girl and yer mither must be proud of you. Here, buy a wee sweetie to yourself.'

She pressed something into my hand and when Ken came out of the shop he found me half-laughing, half-crying as I stared at the half crown in my hand, one of the most genuine gifts I had received in a long time.

It was the middle of January 1969 when I entered the big old-fashioned teaching hospital in the heart of Glasgow. I was whirled through a preparatory routine of getting undressed, being shaved in a lather of terror because in my ignorance I imagined this was a sign I was expected to give birth at any minute, examined by a kindly doctor whose face shall forever remain a blur, then being whizzed up to a ward by a cheerily efficient nurse.

I arrived in the middle of a rest hour with each bed screened and silent. In a way I was glad to get into bed without the whole ward witnessing my wheelchair entry but in another I was sorry because now there would be a slow recognition of my disability as eye after eye fell upon my neatly folded wheelchair at my bedside. I had quite a fight to keep my chair beside me. The nurse was all for whipping it away but I protested vehemently that my wheelchair at my side gave me a feeling of independence and with a rather snooty glance at the rusting wheels she relented, though told me it would have to be put out of sight during doctor's rounds. Doctors again! Everything in order so that they would not be offended in any way.

In *Blue Above the Chimneys*, the first half of my autobiography, I gave doctors the superior title of 'Gods' but I shall not do so here because I have learned they neither desire nor merit such elevation. They are human beings like the rest of us with the same faults and failings. I admire them for what they do, just as I admire a plumber for what he does. A doctor would not be a doctor if it was not his chosen profession or if he had not been chosen to enter that field. For I believe now that we are all chosen to fill various roles in life and if we cannot fill them to the best of our ability or in the way that we are meant to then we have obviously gone wrong somewhere.

I waited trembling for rest hour to end. It was heralded by a rattling of teacups and a surging of footsteps as the nurses swarmed into the ward to pull back curtains. Faced with my ward mates I was engulfed in homesickness and longed to see Ken's dear familiar face and to feel Shona's warm tongue on my hand.

'Tea, hen?' asked a hearty Glasgow voice and the ward maid looked at me kindly.

'Yes, please,' I faltered and took the cup from her. She didn't even notice my chair and passed on to the next bed. I relaxed a little and whilst sipping my tea I covertly sized up the occupant of the bed nearest me. She was no more than seventeen, fair and pretty. Her eye caught mine and she gave me a friendly grin.

'What are you in for?' she asked, getting down to brass tacks right away.

'High blood pressure,' I volunteered, hating the sound of the thing that had taken me from my familiar world.

'Same as me,' she said. All at once we were brought together by an invisible bond.

'When are you due?' she continued with friendly persistency.

'First of March.'

'Shake,' she grinned delightedly, stretching across the small gap that bridged us. 'That's when I'm having mine. It's a funny coincidence, isn't it?'

It wasn't a coincidence. It was God's doing. Looking back now I see that all the things I took to be chance were not so at all. Whenever my circumstances changed from the norm He provided something or someone to see me through.

After the first exchanges Laura and I compared belly sizes. Hers was double the size of mine which was firm and taut as a drum.

'I must have a lot of water,' she decided after discarding the notion that perhaps she was nurturing twins. 'They say it's easier when you have a lot of water.'

'Well, thanks a lot,' I hooted, inwardly cursing whoever 'they' were because I'd heard this belief before and if 'they' were speaking the truth then it looked as if I was in for a difficult time.

In the long days that followed Laura was my prop as well as my companion. Her blue eyes gave not a flicker of surprise when she found out about my chair.

'Some folk are born lazy,' she quipped cheekily, 'the rest of us have to walk and it's not easy with this load to cart around. I'll call you Billy Whizz. You scoot about in that chair as if you were at the races.'

Across the back of my chair she chalked the words, 'A Billy Whizz chair' together with a monstrous picture of a pregnant being haring around on a scooter.

As for the rest of the patients they were too engulfed in their own problems to concern themselves with mine. The inevitable questions were more routine than curious. Was it my first (the baby, not the chair)? Did I want a boy or a girl? Did I suffer from a lot of cramp having to sit all day with my belly lying on my knees? Was I a martyr to sickness, heartburn or both? When the cross-examinations were over with I soon merged in with the general scene of things and moaned, laughed and grumbled as loud as anyone.

The doctor assigned to my case was good-looking in an austere sort of way. In his middle fifties, he had the fresh complexion of a schoolboy, waving white hair and cool blue eyes. I shall call him Doctor Pelvis for reasons which will become apparent. With sickening accuracy he made a beeline straight for my legs instead of my belly. Metaphorically speaking, of course! This sort of thing so unfailingly happened to me I had come to expect it but I never became resigned to it. Whenever I had to visit medics for reasons ranging from bleeding gums to ingrowing toenails they blithely skipped over such minor nuisances and pounced instead on my legs. I'm sure they invoked more interest than the heftily insured limbs of famous stars though obviously for different reasons.

Doctor Pelvis was no exception. After a cursory examination of my 'swelling' his eyes travelled gloatingly down to my legs and after giving them a thorough going over he settled down to extract from me their long history and exact functions since birth. In no time at all his pals were swooping on me also, peering like lynxes at the scars on my knees, where once upon a time calcium had squeezed out like toothpaste from a tube, looking ogre-like at the long operation scar that stretched up from under my left knee to the base of my buttock. One even got out a tape measure and diligently made careful note of the length of the knife mark!

Despite these attentions the days dragged in monotonous routine. It was difficult to sleep owing to various distractions. Each night a nurse escorted the matron round the ward and they stopped at the foot of each bed to discuss the patients' wellbeing in virago-like whispers.

'Buzz, buzz, this is Mrs Smith, twenty-four years old, thirty-two weeks, chronic toxemia when admitted . . . buzz buzz . . .'

'And what is her condition now, nurse?'

'Better, urine output is . . . buzz, buzz.'

'Good, good . . . and now, this one . . .?'

Quite often someone would be in the throes of labour, bed screened, light shining through from a bulb that would have served well in a lighthouse, a doctor unsuccessfully tiptoeing on size ten shoes, heart-shivering moans from the patient, sounds that you felt sure *you* would never make when your turn came, which was a thing so unreal to you, you were sure your turn would never come anyway.

During the 'bad' nights Laura and I held giggling conversations, ate sweets and tried not to let the wrappings rustle lest we earn a visit from the nurse to see if we were perhaps starting labour. Then would come the exhausted drowsing into slumber which an army of doctors could not have kept at bay, after that the heavy deep sleep that you want to go on forever but which is robbed from you by the clattering of early bedpans and a thermometer shoved into your armpit and expected to stay there no matter how recently your relaxed muscles have come to life.

Each morning Laura's groans met my grumbling yawns. Every morning without fail there came a battlecry of sheer desperation from a lady who had been 'inside' several weeks and was finding her stay lacking in home comforts.

'Aw hell!' she roared boisterously, 'Here comes the nurse wi' her bloody wee trumpet! Whit the hell way are ye supposed tae get a rest I'd like tae know! If they're no' shavin' ye they're pokin' aboot yer belly! God, I wish I wis hame!'

The poor nurse, armed with the instrument for listening to a baby's heartbeat within the womb, unfailingly blushed crimson but bore down relentlessly on the unwilling mob who exposed their swollen bellies resignedly and asked vague but knowledgable-sounding questions about their babies' heads being 'engaged'.

Almost every morning the doctors came and smiled at everyone with reassuring calm. Sometimes one or other of us would have the screens whipped round, protruding tums would be exposed to be palpated. A nurse would get out a tape measure to ascertain the girth. Questions would be asked about bowel and bladder output, the latter being of the utmost importance. When you had to pay a visit to the lavatory the water had to be passed into a jug and the fluid ounces reported to a nurse.

Sometimes as I lay in bed in my misshapen birthday suit I felt strangely divorced from my tight little mountain. It was as if a foreign object from another planet was being examined with absorbed scientific interest. The doctors discussed certain aspects amongst themselves, nodded, and, somehow managing to distinguish your face from your belly, gave you reserved but reassuring smiles.

I, of course, was not within the norm. As my time drew nearer the doctors became interested in the agility of my lower limbs, wondering if they would be flexible enough to allow my infant's head to pop out of the birth canal. X-rays were taken and one day Doctor Pelvis bore down on me accompanied by several other doctors and a sprinkling of cherubic-looking students who looked as if they barely knew the facts of life, let alone the intimate make-up of the female body. The curtains were whipped round me and I was enclosed with half a dozen males and one rather embarrassed-looking nurse. My X-rays were produced and the lower half of my skeletal structure was embraced by several pairs of eyes. Several facts about my pelvis were pointed out to the students who peeped over the rim of the X-ray plate to see me squirming red-faced in the bed.

Doctor Pelvis tapped the picture of my pelvis and without looking at me said, 'Do you see your baby's head, Christine . . . perfectly in place . . . and the curve of the spine . . . legs, arms . . . here — and here.'

I looked and could make out nothing because I was looking for a baby, not the skeleton of one. But then I saw it, the round dome stuck between two looped bones that were mine, the spinal column, the tiny skeleton of a baby . . . my baby, growing inside me at that very moment with all the little bones padded by flesh and blood.

I felt wonder and awe. Creation was taking place inside me. All the lumps and humps that punched my flesh into odd shapes were arms and legs, the eerily strange knob that alternately explored my appendix and liver regions was actually a baby's head with eyes, nose, mouth and a brain.

'It's — amazing,' I stuttered stupidly.

'And that's not all, Christine,' boomed Doctor Pelvis for all the ward to hear. 'You have the most marvellous pelvis! Perfect! The best I've seen for a long time. Your pelvis was made for childbearing! You should have no trouble, none at all . . .'

I simply glowed with appreciation for my marvellous

pelvis but the rapture quickly faded when Doctor Pelvis continued, 'And now we'll just have a look at your legs to see how far they can stretch . . : must be prepared . . . eh?'

I was not prepared for his sudden attack, first on my bedclothes which he threw abruptly back, then on my nightdress which he whipped to my chin. The nurse was not prepared either and her attempts to cover both my nakedness and my embarrassment were in vain.

Doctor Pelvis seized one of my legs, ordered a hefty student to grab the other, and they both pulled. Mortification screamed from my soul and I hated every last person surrounding me in those moments.

'Fine — just fine,' pronounced Doctor Pelvis with cold satisfaction. 'We'll just leave you to start things off naturally . . . should have no bother . . . wonderful pelvis.'

Resentment flooded my being. A lot of the other patients with high blood pressure were induced into labour before the date their babies were due but it looked as if Doctor Pelvis was banking on nature to get things rolling for me. The entourage moved on to Laura's bed and I was left with the apologetic nurse who helped me to cover those parts of my body which I had, until recently, considered to be private.

My pelvis became a standing joke between Laura and me. When depression threw a shroud of gloom around us she would suddenly say, 'How's that smashing pelvis of yours?' and in the foolish wisecracks that followed we would gradually shake off our depression.

The ward had its fair share of Glasgow characters. One of these, a shrivelled little gnome of a woman with black circles under her eyes, was christened 'Bella Lugosi' by Laura. Bella Lugosi was determined that her offspring would be called 'Christine' if it turned out to be a girl.

'If it has your name and my looks it will dae all right for itself,' she informed me blithely. 'My man says I've got the looks o' a gypsy. He canny tame me. A born rover he calls me. He's right an' all. Every night I rove doon tae the pub fur a pint and a nip.'

Her 'man' was right about one thing. If she had nothing else she had the dark swarthy colouring of a Romany but there the resemblance ended. Of course, her tan skin tone might have had something to do with her continual smoking. No matter how often she was ticked off by the nurses, she gave them the 'V' sign behind their backs and continued to belch smoke like a dragon. Her 'man', a surprisingly good-looking creature, smuggled in cans of beer and 'nips' to her so that she lived in a perpetual haze of alcohol and nicotine which stained her fingers and the skin round her lips. When the nurses grew really severe about her smoking she humped herself under the bedclothes, to all intents and purposes appearing to be sound asleep except for the occasional clouds of smoke that wafted out from various openings in the blankets.

Another lady, who looked more like a grandmother than a 'lady in waiting,' spent the day talking to herself and glaring at Laura and me if we laughed for any reason. The lady had waited twenty years to reach her present condition and now at the age of forty-five was suddenly terrified at the idea of having a baby. The whole thing had literally 'gone to her head'. She was suspicious of everyone, thought the whole ward was talking about her and laughing at her. It was really very sad but also rather frightening because you were never quite sure what she would be up to next. One night she hopped out of bed and had a set-to with her neighbour who had been snoring peacefully. She accused the poor bewildered soul of laughing at her in her sleep which really was the limit. Soon afterwards she was taken away screaming to some unknown destination but arrived back some weeks later, restored in mind, and gave birth to a lovely baby girl.

A young 'lady of the streets' was a regular 'customer' in the hospital and was well known by all the nursing staff. She had been admitted with slight bleeding and a leg sporting a toe-to-thigh plaster. After a few days of lying in bed, polishing her nails, cursing loudly at the doctors, and generally creating a most unusual diversion in the hospital routine, she signed herself out, hobbling out of the ward dressed to the nines in an imitation leopard-skin jacket and a mini skirt. This was short enough to reveal her knickers, being several inches higher at the front as a result of her 'bun in the oven'.

I christened another patient 'Phil Silvers' because she looked exactly like him with a wig on. She and her pal were WOOPOS. One day I heard them in the toilet together obviously talking about me.

'Ye wonder how she'll manage,' came in Phil Silvers's masculine tones.

'I mean, it's bad enough wi' a' yer faculties, Annie.'

'Ay, mind she's an able enough lookin' lassie but a wean and a wheelchair wid be too much even fur me.'

'Dae ye ever wonder how they dae it, Annie? Get preggers I mean.'

'Same as you and me, Celia.'

'Och ay, but ye know whit I mean, able tae move their legs and that . . . fur a man . . . *you* know.'

'Ay, but she moves hers, she uses them tae pull her along in her chair . . . anyway, nae doot she can move other things as well.'

I remained stolidly at the wash basin because I just had to see their faces as they vacated the 'cludge'. I was well rewarded. Phil Silvers's heavy jaw receded into one of her three chins, Annie's beady eyes flickered rapidly but she was the first to recover her equilibrium. 'I wis jist sayin' tae Celia here, "It must be difficult fur that wee lassie tae manage intae these narrow lavvies in her chair", Zat no' right, Celia?'

'Ay, but I told Annie yer good at movin' yer legs and that,' gabbled Celia with a distinct lack of poise.

They departed leaving me in a giggling heap over the wash basin. They had been right about one thing. It *was* difficult for me to manage into the 'lavvies'. When the nurses saw how independent I was they rarely offered me assistance and I told no one that my chair was too broad to get into the narrow toilets and that I had to get down on my hands and knees and crawl in, my belly scraping along the floor as I did so. It was a very antiquated hospital with few modern amenities, especially for a wheelchair. Amenities or no I was thankful that at least I was allowed to get up out of my bed to go to the toilet at all because others with high blood pressure had to remain *in situ*.

The first of March came and went with nothing to indicate that it had been the day I longed for with all my heart. Doctor Pelvis came and manipulated his fingers round my abdomen till I felt as if it had been punched for weeks. 'Your baby's a bit small yet,' he told me off-handedly, 'I think we'd better leave it for a while.'

'It's because I have no water,' I wanted to scream at him but instead I covered my tum and lay gloomily back on the pillows. Ken had been a faithful visitor for seven weeks and the strain of rushing about from one place to another was beginning to tell on him.

'No joy yet?' he asked at visiting, eyeing the mound under the blankets with something akin to desperation.

I plied him with questions about Shona. I had missed her more than I believed was possible and longed to know again the exquisite joy of burying my face into her soft white coat.

'She's lonely,' said Ken, holding tightly on to my hand. 'I go home at lunch time and she nearly eats me alive. When I go away again she just lies with her nose in her paws looking at me.'

'Oh, I wish I could see her,' I sighed. 'Why can't they allow dogs into hospitals? She's cleaner than some humans could ever be.' I had a photo of Ken and Shona at my bedside, one taken at the farm when Shona was a little snowball of a pup. Each night I kissed the tip of her black nose then gave Ken similar treatment.

'That you at it again, sexy?' Laura would giggle bringing me back to reality.

On the third of March Laura was taken 'upstairs' and the next day I heard she had given birth to a little son. I missed her cheery companionship and sank into an abyss of lonely self-pity. My blood pressure soared, I wasn't allowed to get up any more to the toilet and was finally given an injection that put me out for almost a day and a night. When I awoke the curtains were round me and the sounds of the ward filtered into my fuzzy brain.

'How's your pelvis?' came a familiar voice, then Laura was inside the curtains. She was pale, thin, but smiling. Warily she lowered herself into my chair, claiming it was softer than the hospital chairs, and proceeded to give me some details about her baby's birth, though for a girl of her age she showed remarkable restraint, sparing me the less glamorous aspects.

Some of the stories I had heard had been truly hair-raising, especially to a 'first' like myself. During my early days in hospital I had been utterly alarmed by tales on the dangers of high blood pressure.

'You can take fits,' said one, her face agloat with pleasure.

'Ay, I knew somebody that took a fit and died,' relished another.

'Aw, that's nothing,' triumphed a third. 'I heard ye can go aff yer heid wi' it! I knew a lassie that ended up in the nut hoose . . . mind — it doesny happen often . . .,' she finished consolingly when a strangled sound escaped my dry lips.

A few days later Laura went home and I lay in bed feeling abandoned and ill. The doctors descended, looked fleetingly at my blotched face, then applied their attention to my tum.

'Your baby's a nice size now,' one told me with satisfaction.

'I think it's time to give it a little encouragement,' said Doctor Pelvis. 'Tomorrow morning we will take you upstairs.'

The look he threw me when he passed away from my bed

was rather peeved. His predictions about the baby arriving 'any minute' had not come to fruition and I had the feeling he blamed me entirely. I was angry at him. He had let me go too long over my time. I was sure of it. If I had been a private patient things would have been different. Friends of ours had two children and each one had been induced to arrive exactly on the date specified . . . delivered by Doctor Pelvis privately!

I looked forward to going 'upstairs' with an enthusiasm that took the other patients aback. 'You're no' goin' oot for a picnic,' they told me but nothing could take away the joy I felt in knowing that things were starting to move after eight weeks in hospital. Ken was glad and worried at the same time and that night we hardly knew what to say to each other, so taken up were we with our emotions.

Next morning the students descended on the ward as usual, armed with stethoscopes, syringes, and sphygmomanometers for taking blood pressure. Patients were allocated to different students and for several weeks now I had been the subject for a tall, fair-haired, young hopeful who regularly dropped his stethoscope when he came up to my bed and blushed to the roots of his hair because Laura had been inclined to laugh at him.

He had taken my blood pressure with unnerving lack of skill, patted rather than prodded my belly with cold, unsure fingers, and had drawn blood from my arm to the accompaniment of an unending stream of apologies for hurting me. Whenever he squeezed the little bulb attached to the sphygmomanometer an audible 'Pamp! Pamp!' had come from Laura's bed making him blush redder than ever and spill his stethoscope all over my bed. His attempts to get the uncooperative tubes back into his pocket were hilarious but despite Laura I somehow always managed not to burst out laughing in his face. Over the weeks I had grown fond of him and he had endeared himself to me further by remarking that my appearance was very like that of a dark-haired glamour girl whose sylph-like figure writhed on the front cover of a magazine lying on my bed. The compliment had cheered me and for the rest of the day I had stared at the picture in the magazine and had bored Laura silly by my vain self-appraisals in the mirror.

Now I said goodbye to The Stethoscope Student. He said he was sorry to lose me but would come and see me after the birth of the baby.

At 11 a.m. on 11 March I was taken upstairs and induced into labour, a horrible procedure. Doctor Pelvis 'ruptured my membranes' and a nurse had stood ready with a jug into which only a small amount of amniotic fluid dribbled. On the way back to the ward I told myself happily that it would be all over by this time tomorrow. But I was wrong. Only a few miserable back pains reminded me that my membranes had been ruptured but a nurse sat at my bedside all night, taking my temperature and listening with her little 'trumpet' for changes in the baby's heartbeat which were beginning to speed up. Towards morning I was given an enema which I had dreaded more than anything. I rumbled and boomed into the bedpan and held my breath in anguish to listen for any comments outwith the curtains but the ward was used to such sounds and slept on undisturbed.

Morning came and with it a trolley to whisk me up to the labour ward. There I was put on a drip to induce contractions and stepped over the threshold into a world of utter hell. When the day of agony was only halfway through a doctor came to rupture some more of my membranes and I gathered from the subtle exchanges between him and the nurse that the job hadn't been done properly the first time.

It isn't smugness that makes me say I didn't once scream, shout or cry. It is the truth. Da was in there beside me, making me grit my teeth even while I thought my body was being ripped apart. All I said over and over was, 'Oh God, oh dear God,' which, though I wasn't aware of it at the time, meant that my trust in God was quite explicit. A dear little nurse sat beside me bathing my brow and giving me ice to suck. She was quite a plain-looking girl but to me she was an angel of mercy and appeared beautiful.

Time didn't pass, it seemed to have stood still, holding me in a pain-filled void. When Ken suddenly appeared at my side I asked stupidly,

'What are you doing here? It's still morning.'

'It's evening, my lamb,' he told me gently and stood helplessly looking at me.

'Rub her back,' a nurse directed him but instead he had to hold a bowl for me while I was sick.

'I'll stay, I'll stay with you all night,' he said in despair but I told him to go and for once was actually glad to see his dear familiar figure walk out of the ward, his copper head sunk gloomily into his chest.

The hours passed in a jumble of agony. Women who say that childbirth is the most wonderful experience of their lives must either be superhuman or indifferent to pain or perhaps among the lucky few who really don't have much pain. Though I was given morphine, and later another injection that gave me odd fantasies, I was still aware of agony piling upon agony and still I felt no desire to 'bear down'.

Then quite suddenly I yelled, 'Nurse! Nurse! I want to push!'

There was a rush to my bedside and a great display of delight from the nurses who had been asking me for hours if I had felt the need to 'push'. Hastily I was deposited on to a trolley and taken to the delivery room where two young nurses gave me constant and expert advice. I was instructed how to use the machine containing 'twilight sleep' and clamped the mask over my nose and mouth hoping to be transported into an idyllic world but for all the good it did me I might as well have breathed in farmyard manure. The other drugs had long ago lost their effect and when my baby was born at 6.45 a.m. on Thursday, the thirteenth of March, I was able to struggle up to witness its entry into the world.

The drama of giving birth to a new life in that quiet delivery room with the two masked nurses in attendance is something I will never forget. I watched as the birth cord was cut. There was no sound from the tiny blue-tinted mite on the table. A nurse whisked it to a little suction machine which cleared all the air passages. There was a short bawl then silence. The baby had fallen asleep after filling its lungs with air. It had arrived into the world sound asleep, giving me no help at all in getting it out safely, and now it had fallen tranquilly back into slumber. The nurse wrapped it in a blanket and brought it over to me, dumping it into my free arm. The other still had needles attached to it through which dripped a clear fluid.

'A lovely wee daughter,' smiled the nurse. 'Seven pounds, thirteen ounces, a good weight.'

Baby Evelyn opened her blue eyes and looked straight at me with a puzzled frown creasing her brow — and she smiled. It wasn't wind. How could a newborn baby have wind? It was a smile, especially for her brand new mother. Everything was in its proper order, fingers, feet, little spaghetti arms that boxed vigorously at the air.

'We'll take her to the nursery now,' said one nurse.

'Would you like me to phone your husband?' asked the other.

I nodded, feeling guilty that I hadn't thought about it and excited at the idea of Ken receiving the news he had awaited so long.

Doctor Pelvis had not appeared once since the start of my labour but I didn't care. Another doctor came and stitched me up, an unpleasant experience but nothing to what had gone before.

'Cup o' tea, hen?' a ward maid asked cheerily and I lay back to drink the best 'cuppy' I have ever tasted.

Ken arrived at 8.30 a.m., bringing with him a huge box of chocolates. The curtains were pulled discreetly round the bed leaving us to look at one another rather shyly. Strange how that can happen between two people who are so close to

181

one another. Seconds later we were ourselves again, talking, laughing, amazed at ourselves for having produced between us a real live baby. Now that it was over all I wanted was for us to go home together and I grew rather dismal as Ken got up to go.

'Never mind, lamb,' he said, squeezing my hand. 'It won't be long before we're all together.'

I stared at him as I experienced a sudden rush of apprehension. 'It used to be just you and me. Now there will be four of us including Shona, and it − the baby − is only a stranger yet.'

He smirked wickedly. 'Not for long, babies have a habit of making themselves known. Enjoy the rest while you can.'

But I was too exhausted to sleep and was ready to greet the stream of visitors who arrived that evening. Margaret had been a faithful visitor and now gave me a sisterly hug, Ken's brother John, also a regular presence at my bedside, shook hands heartily and looked embarrassed, Mum Cameron declared herself delighted to be a granny for the second time (the first to John's little daughter) and added wistfully, 'If only Dad could have been here. How proud he would be.'

Her words made me think of Dad and Marjory and my own dear Mam. How happy she would have been to see her grandchild. She would have held it in her arms and called it 'lamb' as she had called all children.

I cried a little that night thinking of Mam. Since her death I had felt her spirit close to me many times. Tonight she was closer than ever and I held her memory to me, finding comfort in the knowledge that, unlike mortals, she could be with me at all times.

Faithful to his promise the Stethoscope Student came to see me, still blushing and nervous and having trouble with his stethoscope which wormed inch by inch out of his pocket with every long step he made along the ward. Beaming down at me he rained congratulations upon me together with his stethoscope; it seemed to have a life of its own as it sprang out of his pocket, unwound itself and settled, with what seemed to be the utmost satisfaction, over my bare arm.

'One day,' said the Stethoscope Student grimly, 'I will master these stupid tubes.' So saying he plucked the offending object from my arm, treated me to another warm smile and retreated down the ward, stuffing the unruly tubes back into his pocket.

Fortunately for him his visit did not coincide with that of Laura. She came bearing a gift of a beautiful pink cot blanket. 'How's that smashing pelvis of yours?' she grinned cheekily.

'Still hanging together,' I laughed. 'Just.'

A week after the birth the doctors were not willing to let me go home.

'How will you manage?' they asked while the young ward sister, knowing this was a sore point with me, smiled behind their backs.

'Better than I can here,' I answered smartly. 'I want to get out of here before my little girl starts school.'

Impudent of me I know, but I'd had enough of doctors telling me what to do. They gave me sour looks then grudgingly told me I could go home the next day. I knew that I would find my own way of managing a baby at home. At the hospital all the baby accoutrements were designed only to be managed by able-bods. The high trolley cots were beyond my stretch and when feeding time came I had to depend on the nurses to lift Evelyn out. The babies had to be changed in their cots, an operation entirely outwith my capabilities. One day I lost my temper and went whizzing into the nursery, holding my soiled, wailing infant.

'How am I supposed to reach these cots?' I demanded of the nurses. 'I have to wait ages for one of you to come and help. I want to be independent.'

Sister heard of my problem and told me that I could change the baby on the bed on the condition that I draw the curtains round me so that the other patients couldn't see what was going on. The other patients laughed when they heard this because they had goaded me to make my protests in the first place but I had to follow orders and draw the curtains round my baby and myself.

From the beginning I didn't treat her like a fragile piece of glass because I soon realized that my tiny daughter was tougher than she appeared. My fellow patients stared when first they saw me throw her over my left shoulder and go trundling about with her. 'Walking' my chair came in extremely useful because it left my two arms free to attend to all a baby's needs. Sitting was extremely painful for me because of the stitches in my tail but these were removed on the morning I was to go home. Then came the struggle into clothes that were a size too small; a moment of frustration when I discovered that Ken had forgotten to bring me pink knickers to go with my slip; a glow of pride when my cherubuc-looking child, wrapped in her pink blanket, was carried by a nurse round the ward in which I had spent eight long weeks.

A friend drove us home. It was strange and wonderful to be back in the outside world. We arrived at our gate and Ken rushed indoors to shut Shona into a room in order that we might all get inside without being knocked over. But she heard my chair creaking up the path to the ramp at the back door. She let out a roar that was a mixture of frustration, desperation and sheer abandoned joy. Once inside the little back sitting room I received a quick impression of a huge fire leaping up the chimney, a spring-like show of pink and blue hyacinths on the windowsill, a welter of cards on the mantelpiece, before a silver-white blurr streaked towards me. She bounded straight on to my knee and buried her head under my chin. The tears welled in my eyes and I cried . . . I cried and Shona cried! Her face was wet with the water spilling out of her black-rimmed eyes. Nonsense? No. Shona cried that day and the friend who had brought me home said to Ken in the hall, 'If you had told me I wouldn't have believed you but I saw – that dog actually cried!'

Shona was a big dog now. The weight of her pressed me

into my chair. Her paws were round my neck and my arms were round her. She smelled of warmth and of earth. On her nose was a miniature mountain of brown soil and I stopped crying and laughed instead.

A small sound came from the carrycot and Shona put her head on one side to listen. She was enthralled when she discovered the baby. There was no jealousy, only curiosity. She appointed herself chief babywatcher, spending long hours lying beside pram or cot. She had a busy time keeping me in sight and guarding Evelyn because from the day I came out of hospital she never let me out of her vision. She was making sure that I would not get away so easily again.

The garden glowed with daffodils that first spring in our new home and the weather grew warmer. Now I had to think of a way to get Evelyn out in her pram into the fresh air. The ramp at the back door was quite steep and I always negotiated myself up backwards. Going down was no problem — I just whizzed, using my feet for brakes at the bottom. One sunny April morning I left Evelyn in her cot and took the empty pram to the back door. I must have presented a strange sight, pushing a pram with one hand, guiding my chair with the other, somehow edging, slithering, braking, to the foot of the ramp. In days gone by I might have hesitated, wondering what the neighbours might be thinking, but now I didn't care. A small human life was dependent on me and she was more important than foolish pride.

When I regained my breath I went back up the ramp to fetch the baby, holding her in one arm while I guided my chair with the other, using my feet to turn corners. Soon she was lying in her pram breathing in the sweet air and Shona, who had hovered at my side during the whole tricky operation, settled down to be her guard dog. I prayed no rain would come that morning because it would have been impossible to get both pram and baby up the ramp but the skies stayed clear. Evelyn had been fed and changed so I knew she would sleep for hours. When Ken came home at lunch time he brought her back indoors so that I could feed and change her before putting her back out again.

This procedure went on for the rest of the summer and I was kept busy with a million and one things, even managing to get the garden into some semblance of order though I never got round to planting roses at the front door. Sometimes I fed the baby outside and changed her in her pram so from the start she became an outdoor girl. She grew chubby and smoothly tanned. So different from when she had been born with her skin flaking off owing to postnatal maturity. This was because she had arrived a fortnight overdue. So much for Doctor Pelvis telling me I had got my dates wrong!

By the time she was three months old she was lifting her head from the pillows to gaze in fascination at the trees. Also at this time she kept rolling on to her front and trying to get her knees up under her. At three and a half months she was rolling over the lawn and had cut three teeth. At five months she rolled under furniture and suspended herself shakily on all fours and at six months and three weeks she was crawling like a little crab. It was an amazing sight to see so small a creature getting about in this fashion. Other mothers with babies of the same age still managed to keep them in angelic pinks and blues, but our daughter was a tomboy in jumpers and cat suits with holes in the knees. She now had five teeth and gnawed everything in sight including Shona's tail. She loved the big white dog. Shona was wonderful with her and let her play with her soft ears and her bushy tail but we were careful never to let the baby take too much advantage of the dog's gentle nature. Often baby and dog would fall asleep together on the floor, Evelyn's head buried in Shona's soft flanks.

One day we lost Evelyn. We searched the house high and low, we even raked through the bushes in the garden. For a whole hour we looked everywhere and eventually found her underneath the couch, fast asleep against Shona who no doubt had retreated under the settee to get a bit of peace from the baby's too-frequent attentions. Life was full of such small adventures at that time.

The problem of transport was with us again. On my return from hospital we had sold Marilla Mini for scrap. It was back to Bertha again but we were unable to go out as a family. Frustrated we went to look at another mini van, knew we couldn't really afford it, but bought it on impulse and the whole family was mobile once more.

Shona had been a born traveller and so now was Evelyn. She made sounds like a car revving up and cried when she was removed from the van. Ken and I were beginning to realize that the gentle little daughter we had visualized before birth was fast growing into a regular tomboy with a very decided mind of her own.

11. I Remember . . .

Thinking about it now it seems to me that March was the month when all the really momentous events took place in my life. I had made my arrival into the world in March, Ken and I were married in March, Evelyn was born on 13 March and she took her first steps almost a year after she was born. This happened when Ken was in hospital for an operation to bypass the ulcer that had bothered him for years. Wee Sadie came to stay with me then. We had lost touch with many members of the club but never had we lost touch with Wee Sadie who was a regular visitor to our house. She was wonderful with the baby who giggled with glee when Wee Sadie's rich deep voice boomed out from her small frame.

When Ken came home, thin, pale, but relieved that his ordeal was over, Evelyn wobbled towards him and screamed, 'Ken!' She called us both by our Christian names and we liked it so much we never thought it was wrong. To this day she still calls us Chris and Ken.

We all watched the tiny tottering baby make a beeline for Ken but before she reached him she landed with a soft thump on her bottom.

'See what happens when I'm here,' chuckled Wee Sadie. 'She watches me falling about and thinks it's the bloody right way to walk!'

It was good to have Ken home again. I had worried about the operation and as a result was rather run down, so while he was off work recuperating we invested in a frame tent and took Evelyn camping for the first time in her life. The first night we camped at Kilmelford and the rain which had been with us for most of the journey was blown away by a fresh breeze coming in from the sea.

'Oh, it's lovely to smell the salt air,' I cried delightedly. 'It's ages since we camped! It feels so good to have the freedom again!' Evelyn, screeching with delight, half crawled, half walked on the springy turf, not minding in the least when she landed flat on her face amidst a pile of ancient sheep's droppings. Shona was in ecstasy and went racing towards the water, barking cheekily at the gulls perched on the rocks.

I sat back to admire the blue and orange tent. 'It will be great to sleep in the inner bit with no creepies in with us.'

'We've certainly come a long way from our bivouac days,' said Ken.

'And the buggy days,' I added, gazing at the grey van.

Ken's eyes grew reminiscent. 'Ay, and yet we had some of the happiest times of our lives in the buggy — Arran, Skye, all over the north, countless times to Loch Eck. You fairly covered the miles steering old Bertha. No wonder you have arms on you like a boxer.'

'Cheeky bugger,' I smiled and went to get Evelyn into pyjamas. She never batted an eyelid when Ken wrapped her in a woolly blanket and tucked her into her sleeping bag and she lay chuckling and talking to herself till she fell asleep.

'A born camper,' said Ken. 'She must take it after her mother.'

We were thrilled with our large roomy tent. It was wonderful to be able to get in and out without crawling around in 'Kismet' shoes. In the old days, in bad weather, we had to cook crouched up on a bedroll, huddled over a primus stove. Now we had a table and a folding chair for Ken.

Thoughtful as always, Ken put a hot water bottle into my bed and I snuggled in beside it. He shone the torch on Evelyn. She was like a little cocoon in her blankets, her flushed face was contented. Her first night in camp was a complete success and though it rained for most of the holiday we all enjoyed every minute.

When we got home we took Shona to the vet because her mouth was giving her trouble. She kept pawing it and we decided that she must have a bad tooth. When we got her to the vet Shona slid quietly under my chair, her refuge in times of uncertainty. Everyone in the waiting room admired her and commented on her obedience. All round us there came yelps, snarls, barks, whines, but Shona made no sound under my chair.

On the vet's table she shivered and looked pitifully hangdog while the vet gently explored her mouth. He probed around her mouth for some time but as yet no warning bells rang in my mind, no premonition of the heart-rending days to come.

'She must be in terrible pain,' said the vet at last. 'There's a very nasty ulcer at the back of her mouth. I'll give her an injection and some pills for you to crush into her food. Come back and see me next week.'

Kirsty, Callum and the children, unable to take any more of the housing scheme way of life, were taking the ultimate step and emigrating to Australia in the middle of September. Kirsty adored Evelyn and had offered to look after her during our holiday in the last fortnight in August, after which she and her family were coming to stay at our house before their departure to the other side of the world.

On the second visit to the vet we all got safely into the waiting room. It was a few minutes before we realized that Shona had disappeared and Ken found her outside, waiting patiently beside the van. She had slipped outside, not relishing another interview on the vet's table. But there she landed a short time later and it was then he told us he wanted another opinion and that he was going to arrange for her to be seen at the vet hospital on the outskirts of Glasgow.

Ken asked the vet if we ought to postpone our holiday but the young man shook his head. 'No need for that. It will be some time before we can get Shona up to the hospital. Go away and enjoy yourselves. I'll give you some pills to give

Shona. Don't worry too much just now. It may be nothing serious but I'd just like to make sure.'

Two days later we left Evelyn in Kirsty's care and went to camp beside the waters of Loch Fyne. It was a perfect spot with a tumbling river rushing down to the sea and blue mountains on the far shore. Dusk spread a soft blanket over the land and we lit a fire near the burn to make tangy tea and to cook sausages. The smoke curled lazily into the air and drifted without haste over the sea. Peace was all around us.

Shona was sitting on the edge of a grassy hillock, the proud outlines of her body etched against the background of misty blue waters. Her head was nobly arched, her ears pricked forward as they always were in the country when every sound and smell was a glorious challenge to her senses. Her coat glinted silver in the firelight and her ever-mobile tail flicked with pleasure. She was so whole, so beautiful, too healthy-looking for there to be much wrong with her. I convinced myself of this even while fear made me catch my breath on a tear. She sensed my thoughts and turned to strip her jaws in a smile which was followed by a yelp of pain. The sound sent a shiver through me. These yelps were becoming more frequent now, the smiles showing less and less.

But she was up now, forgetting the pain, looking at us then back out to sea, her tail wagging in circles. A seal had popped its head out of the water and was staring at us. Shona had sat down again but her body was taut with curiosity and excitement. We watched the shiny black head of the seal bobbing leisurely along, leav ng a little V-shaped wake on the glassy surface of the sea.

The scene was one of complete tranquillity. For a split second the whole of time was suspended. The fire crackled and hissed, a heron glided low over the water, the river gurgled and laughed over the stones, Shona sat like a silver statue, the seal stopped for a moment to stare at us quizzically. Everywhere there was serenity, in the gleaming water rattling the pebbles on the shore, in the smell of wood smoke and salt, in the single haunting cry of the lone bird, in the swift tense appraisal of the two animals.

Then the seal let out a short muffled bark. Shona jumped up to step back two paces, amazement on her face. 'She thinks it's another dog,' chuckled Ken.

Shona could contain herself no longer. She went bounding towards the shore, her barks ringing joyfully in the air. The seal was in no hurry to go, waiting till Shona paddled for a few feet into the water before it disappeared in a flurry of wavelets.

We lazed at Loch Fyne for seven days then packed up and went to spend the remainder of our holiday by our beloved Loch Eck where we renewed old acquaintances. Shona was hailed by all who knew her. In the past I'd had many offers from rugged forestry workers wanting to buy my dog. My gentle faithful Shona loved all humans, shaking hands with them, smiling at them but always she came back to me to lie quietly by my chair.

'Ay, she's your dog, all right,' I was told, 'She'll no' go far from your side.'

It was to be the last holiday we ever had with Shona. When we got home we were thrown into one of the busiest Septembers I can ever remember. Everything seemed to be happening at once. Our house was a jumble of relatives and friends coming to say their goodbyes to Kirsty and Callum.

Word had come from the vet hospital. I was to take Shona there the day before my big sister was due to start the journey to Australia. Callum came with me to the hospital and I was glad of his company because we had to leave Shona for a few hours in order that a biopsy be carried out under anaesthetic. I went back at two in the afternoon, alone in Bertha because Callum had to borrow the van to see to last-minute affairs. I left Evelyn with Kirsty and raced the miles away to the hospital.

The sights and sounds of the place were to become familiar to me in the next few months. The grounds were spacious, all sorts of animal noises could be heard from various buildings. I entered by a side door where a ramp made easy access to the reception area. When I saw a kennel maid coming towards me carrying a limp white bundle I almost cried. Somehow I hadn't expected Shona still to be under the effects of the anaesthetic and the sight of her lying so helplessly in the girl's arms came as a shock. But her eyes were slightly open. When she saw me they widened in recognition and her tail wagged feebly.

There is nothing so heart-rending as a helpless animal, especially when the animal happened to be my beloved dog. The young vet told me that the biopsy had been done and that I was to phone in a few days for the results. 'I can't tell you very much at this stage,' he explained tactfully. 'We had a good look inside her mouth and she has a terrible sore ulcerated mass on her upper right jaw. Give her soft food, it must be painful for her to eat.'

'Will — will it be all right?' I whispered.

'We can only wait and see, even if it turns out to be something more than an ulcer I'm sure we'll be able to treat her.'

I led the way out to Bertha and helped the kennel girl settle Shona on the cushion-padded shelf behind the driving seat. I drove away in a daze, behind me Shona whined and nuzzled her face under my hair, her tongue came out and licked the salt tears away from my cheeks. When we got home Callum carried her indoors and laid her on a soft rug in the bedroom and there she stayed for the rest of the day.

The remainder of that day was strangely unreal for me. My sister was going away to the other side of the globe and my dog had an unnamed illness that filled me with foreboding.

Evelyn was still in the land of dreams when Ken and I arose at 5 a.m. next morning to see Kirsty and her family off. For Kirsty to have got this far had been a touch and go affair. She wanted to start a new life yet she could hardly bear to leave Scotland and her family behind. She had panicked and told Callum that on no account could she leave her sisters behind, nothing could make her get on that plane for Australia. Callum had coaxed, pleaded and finally bullied, till now she was ready to go, very pretty in her new rig-out but her green eyes clouded with mixed emotions.

Sarah and little Linda were filled with excitement but when the taxi came they ran to it crying. Callum put his strong arms around me and kissed me, shook hands with Ken and went outside leaving me alone with Kirsty. She said goodbye quickly. Delayed partings were too much of a strain on our feelings. For a moment, as she kissed me on the cheek, pictures of our early Govan days flashed through my mind. They seemed so far off now, things that had happened in another world. Yet for a moment they were tangible, not just phantoms of the memory, half-remembered places and incidents. For a split second I saw Kirsty as she had been in those days, slim, pigtailed, always more lady-like than me, the big sister who had been good to me in a hundred different ways, a comfort when things had gone badly in my child's world, the world of tenements, back courts, Mam, Da, brothers and sisters . . .

I remember, I remember the place where I was born,
With the chimney stacks and the court-backs,
And the play clothes dirty and torn.
I remember, I remember, my brothers and sisters at play,
And the Elder Park and the Parkie's bark,
When he chased us all away . . .
I remember, I remember a voice that called us 'lamb',
I hear it still inside my head,
The voice of our own Mam . . .

Margaret had said her goodbyes the night before so now it was only Kirsty and me, gripping hands briefly, fleeting kisses, so light they might have been imagined, the feathery touch of her long auburn hair against my cheek, the perfume, of warmth, reality, of new clothes and the tang of fresh lipstick.

'I remember . . . ' my voice broke on a half-sob.

'I know, Chris, so do I,' she whispered, the gleam of tears drowning out the green of her eyes. 'Look after yourself and my dear little Evelyn. You're in good hands with Ken, he's a great guy. I'll miss him too and I'll be thinking of you all — and Shona. She'll be all right, Chris, don't worry too much.'

With that she was gone. We waved them off in the cold light of morning and as Kirsty's face looked from the taxi window I wondered if I would ever see her again.

We went back inside, to our early morning house with the ashes grey in the hearth and the living room smelling of stale smoke from the night before. We sat miserably, staring before us, then the door opened and Shona came padding through. 'Well, it's decided to get up,' smiled Ken and stooped to hug her. She was still groggy and we decided to take her for a walk to waken her up. The morning was calm, the air cold and fresh. Shona's toes scuffed the pavements but she was in good spirits and lifted her black nose to sniff the dewy air.

A few days later we received a postcard from Kirsty telling us they had arrived safely in Australia, the weather was warm, the plane journey had been uneventful . . . and already she was homesick for Scotland. I phoned the hospital for the results of Shona's biopsy, lifting the receiver with mixed feelings, half of me wanting to know the results, the other half rebelling against it. The vet's voice seemed to come from a very long distance when he told me that the biopsy had shown a sporous type of carcinoma, cancer of the right cheek and upper jaw.

'Oh God, no!' my inner self screamed but I knew I was going to ask the vet some calm and sensible questions. Whenever I was shattered inside another part of me took over, forcing me not to give way, not to show my true feelings. The voice droned on. They wanted to try out some new treatment. It would be quite expensive and would involve many trips to the hospital. Would I be willing to go through with it?

Quietly I said, 'Please do what you can. I'll bring Shona whenever you want.'

I put the phone down and burst into tears, Evelyn put her little baby arms around me and told me 'don't cry', Shona came over to bury her soft muzzle into my lap. It always distressed her to hear sounds of grief.

'Don't worry, Chris,' Ken told me later, 'We'll manage somehow. The main thing is that Shona gets better.' I knew he was referring to our shaky financial state. We had put all we had into the house and there was very little left over but we still had the van and I was prepared to sell it if need be.

When I took Shona to the vet hospital for the first part of her treatment she was nervous and stayed close to my chair, every so often looking back at the buggy as if she would like to fly straight back into it. She remembered the hospital, a place that meant strangers and separation from all that was familiar, but obediently she followed me inside. When the kennel girl came to take her away she refused to go and for the first time in years a lead was slipped round her thick ruff. She was led away, looking back at me, reproach in her brown eyes.

'Where Shona go?' asked Evelyn but I couldn't answer and fled outside as fast as my wheels and Evelyn's little legs would allow. At eighteen months old she was a hardy little blighter and I had my hands full with her. She was strong-willed, stubborn, restless, unable to amuse herself with toys but always wanting to be on the go. But she was also sunny and sweet-tempered, as yet unaware that I was different from any other mum because I played the rough sort of games that she adored. What I was really seeing was myself growing up all over again, a rough-and-tumble, never still for a minute, but I had been blessed with an active imagination from the start. As yet Evelyn had none. She always loved to be surrounded by things animate and could make little of things that did not move under their own steam. Shona had been her companion from the start but now there was no white loving bundle to meet us, the house was empty and silent, the gift she had brought me in welcome the day before, a little roll of paper, lay crumpled and forgotten in a corner.

Evelyn grew fretful and wearied of her own company and I was delighted when I phoned the hospital three days later and was told that I could collect Shona that afternoon. The first part of the treatment was over but I would have to take her back at the beginning of the following week.

Oh, how joyfully I fled to the hospital! Evelyn remembered her surroundings and lisped happily, 'See Shona now.' A door opened at the end of the corridor and a white streak came rushing towards us. Never shall I forget the utter rapture of that welcome. She threw herself at me, a white blur, her tail wagging so hard it took her rump with it backwards and forwards. She was howling as she ran, her mouth pursed into a tight ball, her 'woo, woos' rising to a crescendo and echoing in the passageways. She knocked Evelyn over and Evelyn sat where she was, chuckling with glee, then she hurled herself into my lap, her body trembling, pressed so hard against me I could hardly breathe.

The kennel girl came rushing up. 'Hey, steady on, Shona,' she laughed. But Shona was not to be cheated of her moments of ecstasy. She lifted her nose to the ceiling and roared with happiness. A crowd of students stopped in their tracks and laughed as the sound hit the roof and bounced from the walls.

'How has she been?' I asked the girl through a mouthful of fur.

'The best patient we've had for a long time. She let me handle her without a murmur and after examinations went straight back to her pen without being led. She was terribly sad though, just curled up in a corner all day with her nose in her paws. I couldn't believe it when I heard her just now . . . look at her − she's smiling.'

For the first time in weeks Shona had stripped her jaws so hard her gums were showing. I looked at the smile and warmth flooded every corner of my heart. 'She's going to get better,' I told myself and took her home.

That night our house became alive again. Shona was there, padding in and out of all the rooms as if she couldn't believe her luck. While she had been absent I had pictured her in her daytime bed, under the kitchen cabinet, and at night I had imagined her white form lying on the rug beside my bed. Now she was here, warm and real, her brown eyes following our every movement. She was so much better that she enjoyed a tumble with us all on the floor. Crawling about on all fours we wrestled with her as we had done when she was a tiny pup.

For a time the treatment appeared to be successful. She was away from us for three or four days out of seven and the house was quiet, waiting for her return. Each time I went to collect her my heart sang and her greetings were rapturous.

But gradually the tumour took hold again, the regression had only been temporary. The vets decided to try radio-therapy on her and she was taken to one of the big Glasgow infirmaries to use the same sort of facilities as humans. But now her illness showed in the slimness of her body, her soft white muzzle became sharper. It was heart-rending watching her try to take food from a plate. Sometimes she gave up the struggle and left the food untouched. Eventually I fed her by hand, pushing pieces of soft meat and fish into her mouth.

I always phoned before going to collect her from the hospital and one day in early December I lifted the receiver and was put through to the vet. He was genuinely sorry when he told me there was nothing more they could do for my dog and offered to keep her at the hospital and put her to sleep. But my whole being cried out in anguished rebellion. Never see Shona again? Leave her without a goodbye? I couldn't do it!

'I'll come for her,' I said quietly. 'I'll get my own vet to put her to sleep when I think it's time.'

I don't remember clearly how I felt that day. I had expected the news for some time but now I couldn't grasp it. I knew I was only prolonging the agony by having Shona home for a little while but what else could I do? Shona was mine, loved by me for so long now. It wasn't right to let my most beloved friend leave the world without a farewell.

At the hospital the kennel girl saw me before I got out of Bertha and kindly she told me to wait while she fetched Shona. The dear white shadow came bounding towards me, her thin little face expressing her devotion. I held her to me, breathing in the scent of her warm ears, feeling her heart pounding under my hands. Somehow I felt I had let her down, my prayers, my love, the painful treatment she had undergone, had all been for nothing. The girl handed me a letter I was to give to my own vet. I was to keep it till I was ready to have Shona put to sleep.

'I'm sorry,' mumbled the girl, her eyes shiny with tears. 'She's such a lovely dog, she's been so good . . .', she fondled Shona's soft ears for a moment, 'Goodbye, Shona,' she whispered and hurried away, leaving me desolated, my final link with hope broken.

Ken and I cried together that night, unashamedly, and Shona came to us, whining softly, burrowing her muzzle into our entwined arms.

From then on every movement she made became precious. Some days she felt good and sat behind a clump of shrubs in the garden watching the birds. She thought herself to be hidden from them but of course she wasn't. She was very naive about such things. The birds taunted her unmercifully, strutting in beady-eyed confidence close to the shrubs but always ready to take wing when she finally rushed out at them. Each night in bed I stared at her white figure stretched out on the rug beside me, remembering the times we had had together, how she had always given me assurance in crowded places because people were so busy looking at her beauty they didn't bother to look at me. She had given us pure love, pure loyalty, pure joy, and for that bounty of treasure had asked little in return except to be loved too as a part of the family circle.

She had always been a good dog in the garden. Except for her occasional digging sprees in the uncultivated parts she had left flower borders strictly alone. Now she dug a hole for herself in a little border beneath the ramp at the back door and spent most of her days curled up in it, a miserable ball of white fur, her black nose buried in her tail, only her eyes looking unseeingly at the world. It was as if she was already glimpsing something beyond. How silently, how patiently, animals suffer. They ask only solitude that they might pass with dignity their pain-filled days.

When two of her back teeth fell out I knew the time was near. Now an agonizing decision had to be made. We who loved her had decided that the time was come to take her life but how to go about it was another matter. To let her be taken away and put to sleep in a strange place, not knowing why none of us was beside her? Or have it done at home where she would not feel afraid and where we could be with her in her last moments? Silly human sentiment? Oh no! She was one of the family, for four and a half years she had shared our lives, it was only right we should share hers till the very last. We settled on the latter choice and on the fourteenth of December 1970 I phoned the vet. Ken took an afternoon off work . . . and we waited, wordlessly.

The afternoon dragged, there was no sign of the vet, the phone rang and we were told he had been called out on an emergency. It was a cruel reprieve and meant another sleepless night, looking at Shona lying on the rug beside the bed, unsuspecting, unaware that her life hung on such a delicate thread.

She was at the front door next day when the vet arrived. She had taken to sitting on the step, watching the world go by, wagging her tail when the neighbours spoke to her. They all loved the big white dog with the friendly grin and the willing paw of friendship. When the vet's car drew up at the gate she ran to meet him, wagging her tail in welcome.

Oh, bitter irony! Running to meet he who had the task of taking away her life.

When he came indoors and began rummaging in his bag she sensed that this was not the usual type of visitor and ran under a chair. He was a young man and couldn't hide how upset he felt. That was good. He hadn't become immune to such things. He told us he was going to give her an injection that would make her feel sleepy then he would examine her mouth to see if anything further could be done. He, like us, could hardly believe that a dog so beautiful and whole-looking could possibly be so ill. My heart leapt with foolish hope. I got out of my chair and sitting on the couch I told Shona to jump up beside me. Obedient to the last she did as she was told, the injection took effect, her eyes grew blue and misty.

The vet looked into her mouth and shook his head. 'I'm sorry, it's too far gone. I thought that perhaps an operation . . .,' he shook his head again, 'I'll give her a bigger dose and it will be over. Don't worry, she will never know and she won't feel a thing.'

I held her as she was given the final injection. Her limbs twitched, her downy head grew heavy in my lap, very soon she was dead in my arms. I cry as I write this and remember that time. The tears pour down my face now, as they did then. I cry because she was the best friend I ever had. Human friends come and go, full of petty differences and jealousies. Shona had given only unstinting affection. When she sensed our sorrowful moods she was always there to give quiet comfort, when we were happy then so was she, throwing herself into our glad times with a love of life that was so infectious you felt like throwing out your arms and embracing the world to your rapturous heart.

Now the vet carried Shona's lifeless body out to his car and like a child without rein on its emotions I wanted to go after him and wrest her from his arms. Evelyn cried from her cot where Ken had put her because he didn't want her to witness Shona's departure. At just a year and nine months old Evelyn had lost the companion of her babyhood and it was going to be hard explaining to her that Shona would never come back.

Ken came back from helping the vet get Shona into his car and putting his arms round me he whispered, 'I loved her but she was yours . . . from the start she was yours . . .'

I remembered then a fragile, newly born pup struggling to get at one of Judy's teats in a search for nourishment.

> I watched you being born,
> Knew you right from the start,
> I was there when you died
> And it broke my heart . . .

Though she was gone she was everywhere. At night I still folded my chair at my bedside in order to give Shona room to stretch out beside me, several times Ken went to the back door to let her in only to arrest the impulse when he was halfway through the kitchen, Evelyn searched the house high and low every day. Once, she toddled to the cupboard, took out Shona's dish and holding it out to me asked me to put food into it to 'bring Shona home'.

Two days before Christmas a knock came to the door. When I opened it Stuart and Margaret were there with young Stuart dancing excitedly in the background. They said nothing as they followed me into the living room but a gleam of mystery shone in Stuart's eyes. Suddenly he opened his coat. A tiny white head peeped cheekily out, a shiny black nose snuffled the air, fluffy white ears tinged with biscuit flopped over a downy, silver-tipped ruff.

'Shona's home!' screamed Evelyn joyfully.

'Merry Christmas, darling,' said Stuart. 'You'll never forget Shona but this might help you to get over losing her.'

I took the tiny bundle in my arms and buried my wet face into its soft fur, smelling the fragrance of milk and warmth, feeling the slap of a little tongue sweeping over my salt-wet cheeks. My heart was so full I couldn't speak, all I could do was cry helplessly and Stuart said, 'It's been worth all the trouble to see your face. We sent to England for her and I got up at five this morning to meet the train. It took a bit of doing to get a pup in time for Christmas. We phoned everywhere . . . even to Wales — but the pups either hadn't been born or were too young to be sold. The last number we rang was the lucky one — they had two pups left and one of them was meant for you.'

A moment to thank God for a sister like Margaret and a brother-in-law like Stuart! With their shining faces they were utterly beautiful in those minutes of selfless giving and I have never forgotten them for what they did for me then. They left me tactfully alone, the pup in my arms, the tears coursing down my swollen face.

When Ken came home from work he didn't notice the minute white figure lying under a chair. Then she stretched and yawned, a squeaky yawn that made her tongue curl at the end and her whiskers bristle forward.

'What the . . .?' laughed Ken and stopped in amazement leaving me to explain everything midst tears and laughter. We all looked at the pup who was cheekily pulling at a corner of the rug. One of her ears had not yet strengthened enough to allow it to stand up and she looked an extremely comical pup with one ear up, the other down.

'We'll call her Crumples,' grinned Ken but by the end of the week the ear had straightened and she was a perfect little Samoyed.

Photographs of Shona have looked down on me all through the writing of this story. She was alive when I started it, now she is gone. Yet her pictures have somehow kept me going, made me write when I least felt like it.

Soon after Christmas we had to sell our van to meet the expenses incurred during Shona's treatment but when the spring came we bought a Mark I Cortina estate car and went off to Lock Eck. Somehow Shona was there, in the beaches and woods she had loved so well. I could see her in my mind's eye, waiting for us to throw stones into the water, barking, brown eyes aglow with the joy of living, ecstasy in every whisker, every wag of her tail, each movement an expression of her fun-loving personality.

Now there is Tania, the lovable clown, who when she first saw the sea thought it was a continuation of dry land and went plunging in to 'walk on water' for a few feet before she sank like a stone only to resurface seconds later, her face a study of canine indignation. When first we took her camping she wouldn't behave in the big tent so we put her into a bivouac on her own, tied her in and went to bed. Next morning we all screamed with laughter at sight of a 'walking' tent with a black nose poking through one of the air vents. She had pulled out all the tent pegs and, quite unconcerned about it all, went about her business with the tent draped around her!

She is the complete opposite of Shona except for her appearance. In the beginning I often called her Shona by mistake and she would look about for another dog. Tania has no finesse, none of the sense of delicacy that made Shona turn away at meal times so that we wouldn't think she wanted to watch us. Tania stares openly with watering mouth. Where Shona would go miles to find a patch of long grass in which to 'perform', Tania is quite happy with a couple of weeds. Nevertheless, she is completely loveable. She has a habit of passionately kissing and nibbling human ears and of getting into bed between Ken and me in the middle of the night. Sometimes in the early dawn we waken blearily and wonder where all the blankets have gone and there is Tania, lying on her back on a heap of bedding, her face blissful, her mouth grinning as she snores immodestly. She enjoys a long lie and gets quite indignant if she is turned out of the door too early in the morning.

In those early days she and Evelyn got up to all sorts of mischief together. They helped one another dig holes in the garden till it began to resemble the moon's surface. Tania pinched Evelyn's sweeties and great battles arose between them. Tania also had a great weakness for chewing plastic toys and eating newspapers. Quite often it was possible to read yesterday's headlines in a little mound lying behind the dandelions in the garden!

To this day they both fight jealously for my affections and if Evelyn dares to come near me when I'm having a Sunday lie-in Tania is up like a shot, singing in her throat with worry in case she gets left out . . .

Sometimes it is very poignant to remember; at others it can be so happy you want to share your thoughts with others, just little things that take you back over the years and bring a tear or a smile.

Epilogue

When Evelyn was just about a year old I experienced the old restless yearnings to write but I didn't want to go back to the tales of girls in a boarding school dormitory, giggling with excitement at the absolute daring of having a midnight feast by torchlight. I suppose it took me a long time to mature in my writings but I was a bit of a late starter in many things. I had been too busy catching up on the kind of things that should have happened to me as a teenager but didn't.

I think I wasn't just surprised when Ken said to me, 'Why don't you write about yourself? Your own story?' I was highly sceptical about the whole idea.

'Who would want to read about *me*?' I scoffed.

'I would for a start,' he said in his quiet reasonable way. 'You and your sisters have had Callum, Stuart and me in tears of laughter about the goings-on in your Govan days . . . then you could go on to write about your experiences as a disabled child and adult. If it was ever published it could be an inspiration to disabled folk and would let the able-bodied see how you all manage.' He said the last word laughingly because it was a joke between us the way people often said to me, 'My, it's great how ye manage,' but I dismissed his suggestion rather rudely and went into a muse.

A week later I thought his idea was marvellous and could hardly wait to start my notes. Once I started to write the 'book' I simply couldn't stop. It went on and on, finally ending up a great tome with about forty chapters. It took me two years, off and on, but it was almost finished in 1971, the year we decided to move away from suburbia and go to live in Argyll. Our house was lovely by this time. Ken had torn the place apart, putting in new fixtures in all the rooms and building a beautiful stone fireplace in the front room. We had installed central heating, carpeted and redecorated the entire house but in the four years we had been in suburbia we had been forced to live a life of almost total seclusion simply because we couldn't afford to entertain. We were up to our ears in debt, saw no way out . . . except to go and live in the country.

We knew we would sell the house for a good profit and so we set about finding a place in our dear Argyll. Eventually we came upon a grand old semi-villa on the shores of the Holy Loch. It was being sold as two flats and had been converted as such with a separate entrance at the back to the top flat. In a state of great excitement we asked Mum Cameron to come with us and live in the top flat. She had never been happy since selling the old Manse and going to live in a busy thoroughfare. She jumped at the chance. We put our respective houses up for sale, and made an offer for the semi-villa — and waited.

By January 1972 our house was sold, Mum Cameron spent a further two nerve-wracking months waiting for her flat to be bought but by April of that year we said goodbye to the city life and went to live by the Holy Loch. It was wonderful. Everything that we could have dreamed of. The lower flat had roses round the living room window, big fat pink roses. There were none round the door but I told myself I would soon change all that. The front of the house faced south to the sun with the waters of the Holy Loch a mere few yards away from the front garden.

Ken commuted back and forth to Glasgow, staying there all week and coming home on Wednesdays and at weekends. I missed him terribly and had to cope with the entire running of the house. The evenings were the worst when Evelyn was in bed and there was no Ken to talk to. It was then that I took up oil painting. One weekend Ken came home bringing a huge set of oil paints. I was bitten. It seemed as if I would never stop wanting to paint pictures.

Like my writing it was a solitary apprenticeship. I had no one to show me what to do, only Ken to criticize. It was the best way. I had no one to copy so my style was entirely individual. At this time, too, I resurrected my 'tome' and sent it off to a publisher. They kept it for a long time but eventually it came back with a marvellous letter of encouragement. They had found it 'lively and readable' but much too long for a book of its type. I was advised to break it up into smaller sections and then a publisher might be interested.

I put it away to the back of the wardrobe and forgot about it. Life in the country was so new, so full of exciting things to see and do. Once again we had bought a house that needed to be completely modernized and for the first year, till all the messy jobs were completed, we thumped about on bare floorboards and didn't give a damn. Our house-warming party was an unrivalled success on the bare boards. No need to worry about spilled drinks and fag ash. A quick sweep with a broom and the house was done. Sometimes I think the trappings of fancy carpets and all the trimmings just give us unnecessary extra work but it is in the nature of the human beast to want these luxuries and within a year we had them. With the extra money from the sale of the suburban house we replumbed, rewired, redecorated and carpeted the entire house.

After a year and a half Ken got a job in a local boatyard and we were in seventh heaven. Mum Cameron had soon established herself into the kirk, the OAPs and the Guild. She had a string of friends and led a full and busy life. Evelyn started school in the next village and she too settled in.

While Ken was still working in Glasgow Tania gave birth to a litter of ten Samoyed pups and Mum and I had a busy and hilarious time helping her to bring them up. Mum claimed one of the pups, little Wendy, the first of the litter to waddle upstairs into the upper flat! Before we left suburbia poor dear Judy was killed in the street outside her house. A wise old dog who from the beginning had had marvellous road sense killed at her own kerbside by a blind old dear who claimed she hadn't seen a snow white dog sitting peacefully by the pavement! I mourned with Margaret and Stuart, they who had risen at five o'clock on a pre-Christmas morning to go to the station to collect my Tania. They saw her pups and no doubt one of them would have been theirs but they, too, had decided to emigrate to Australia.

We had been at Holy Loch just over two years when they went. They had sold their house and were living with Stuart's father in the north for about a month before their departure date. We went up there to say goodbye. Dear Margaret. I can see her that last night, laughing, fooling around as we played a final game of gin rummy. Margaret could have made a cat laugh, I'm sure. It was the finale of many nights of fun with her and Stuart. Even as I giggled with the others I cried inside. First Kirsty, now Margaret, my two dear sisters, one already twelve thousand miles away, the other on the brink of the journey.

In the cold light of morning we said our farewells, everyone trying to be normal till the last moment when we all broke down, Stuart with tears in his eyes, Margaret, never as demonstrative as Kirsty, falling into my arms, our tears spilling, hands touching, hugging and sniffing, remembering, wondering many things but most of all wondering, 'Will we ever meet again?'

Then the moment of wrenching away from the grasp of dear and loving arms, getting into the car, looking back at beloved faces, waving till we could see them no more from eyes that were blurred with tears that poured relentlessly mile after mile.

Wee Sadie died two years after we left suburbia. She went into the operating theatre and never woke up from the anaesthetic. She had never managed to come to see us at the Holy Loch because of bad health. She had spent almost two years in hospital while I was still in Glasgow and every week

I had gone to see her, taking Evelyn who was just a toddler.

Wee Sadie was heart-broken when we told her we were coming to live in the country but she did her best to hide it. I had made the usual sounds of appeasement, assuring her that she could come to see us, perhaps spend a holiday with us. She had smiled, nodded, and knew she would never share our lives in the way it had been in the old days. I knew she had died before anyone told me. For such a small person she had a very strong character and it came through to me days before I heard the news. She filled my thoughts constantly and I could see her, toddling about on her sticks, her dark head thrown back to allow her deep hearty laugh to ring out. She had been the most constant of our friends from our days in the Disabled Drivers' Association.

I was in the living room when the phone went in the hall. Ken went to answer it and I could hear nothing but the murmur of his voice. When he came back I said, 'Wee Sadie's dead, isn't she?'

The idea for my first novel came to me slowly when we had been at the Holy Loch for two years. It was to be set on an imaginary Hebridean island which as yet had no name. But all the characters were fixed in my mind, the dramas, the romances, the humour. I titled it 'The McKenzies of Laigmhor' but Ken didn't like it.

'Call the island "Rhanna", he told me, 'And call the book *Rhanna*, short and sweet. People will remember it better.'

I sulked but as always came round to his reasonable way of thinking. 'Rhanna, Rhanna!' The name spun round in my head. I loved it. Now I set to work with a will. I rushed to get all my housework done in the mornings that I might have a few free hours to write before Evelyn arrived home from school. Out in the front garden in the sun, indoors in the front room during rain, I wrote and wrote and *Rhanna* took shape, with all its loves, hates, tears and laughter. Because I had so little time for reading my writing was not in any way influenced by other writers. It was all my own, from beginning to end, a pure creation, and — because I was writing to please no one but myself, as it were — utterly natural. I gave no thought to the notion that one day it might come under public scrutiny. Only other people had their books published. Such luck could never be mine. At the back of my mind I longed to be published. With incredulous eyes I gazed at the blurbs on book jackets. I sighed over the great names of the big publishing houses, never dreaming that one day I, of all people, would get a work accepted by one of them.

From the time I could write I had written stories and poems. Along the path of my life the writing bug had cropped up relentlessly. It had been pushed aside, squashed, sometimes forgotten, but always it popped up again to itch at me. Write! Write! Write! I was born to write and now I was writing like fury till at last *Rhanna* was finished and Ken was reading it, amazed at how my style had matured, astounded that I had written such drama, such love scenes.

'Get it off to a publisher,' he ordered, and without ado he wrapped it up and Mary, my dear half-sister with whom I had never lost touch, posted it for me during one of her summer visits. She kissed the package for luck and I settled down to await the results. I say settled but I should have said teetered — on the brink of a volcanic mixture of seething impatience.

Six months elapsed before I heard from the publisher. He loved it, he wanted it! But he couldn't afford to publish a novel. He had held on to it in the hope that he could see his way to publishing it, but alas! He was not in a position to do so and regretfully he was sending the manuscript back to me. Undeterred I sent it off immediately to another Scottish publisher, and it came back. It went the rounds for almost two years and meanwhile I sat and wrote another novel, a very modern murder mystery that just seemed to roll off my pen without effort. I didn't send it anywhere but 'kept it up my sleeve' for the future.

During this time an Edinburgh publishing house was offering an award scheme for works of fiction and non-fiction by Scottish authors. At Ken's urging I went to the wardrobe, brought my 'tome' out of its mothballs and rewrote the first section of it. Then I sent it off. In time it was sent back with a kind little letter. I got very few outright rejections; mostly there was a note of encouragement that wished me luck with some other firm.

By 1977 I was growing rather despondent over my novel, but Ken would not let me give up. 'You'll have to try further afield,' he told me. 'Try the London publishers.'

I sent it to the wrong one, a firm that dealt mainly with text books and the like. The name of this firm had begun with an 'A' so I decided to do the thing in alphabetical order and looked in my *Writers' and Artists' Yearbook* for a firm whose name began with 'B'. One took my fancy, again the manuscript was parcelled and, as always, sent with a certificate of posting. This was on 31 October 1977. Weeks went by and I heard nothing, not even the usual acknowledgement. Even Ken was depressed by this. We assumed the parcel to have gone astray because he phoned up the publishers and was told that no manuscript such as Ken described had been sent to that address. I sank into despair. Being the greenhorn I was I had not made a carbon copy of the book. It was a one-off and it was lost. I would never be able to write it again. We informed the Post Office who promised to look into the matter and I told Ken, 'if they can't trace it then that's me finished with writing. My nerves can't take the strain of all the waiting . . . and now this.'

The Watchnight service on the Christmas Eve of that year was particularly beautiful. Ken and I were not churchgoers but always tried to attend the services at Christmas. I had never found God in any church I had ever been in. They were usually cold places, rather austere and forbidding. I am sure God never meant us to worship Him in places like these. No doubt they were all right in the past when whole families had to attend Sunday worship. The churches might have needed all that space then but not in the present age. Far better a small cosy intimate place where a feeling of unity existed. I had come through many phases in my search for God. For a time I forgot about Him altogether and it was during this time that I had a terrible fear of dying. I didn't like to hear people talking about death. It was so final, so cruel to those that were left. I kept my fears to myself but often I would come out in a sweat at the idea of dying.

I think I really began to find God when I came to live in Argyll. I found Him in the solitude of wide places, by rushing rivers and wild beautiful glens. It seemed He was everywhere in the countryside but also He was very much in the humbler dwellings, in little crofts and cottages where people were attuned to the earth and had never become entangled in the materialistic snares of modern living. Gradually my fears left me and peace came to me instead. After the Watchnight service of 1977 I was lying in bed just thinking about the beauty of the Mass of Christ, thinking about the service, about a lot of pleasant things. Quite suddenly a voice broke into thoughts inside my head and I knew it was Jesus talking to me. The voice said very plainly, 'Peace be with you, Christine. Don't let go of your goals in life. Write, keep on writing . . .' the voice began to tail off.

At that moment I felt the most glorious sensation of serenity washing into my soul. God existed. He had spoken to me, directly into my mind His voice had spoken and I fell asleep like a contented child.

I am no Holy Willie. You will never hear me spouting off about my beliefs or trying to cram them down other people's throats. It is enough that I *know*. He is there and that is all that matters. Looking back I see that God has been very good to Ken and me. Everything we ever wanted had come to us, slowly but surely . . . We wanted a house of our own. We got it. We were both determined that one day we should come back to live in the country — perhaps retire there. We got our wish while we were still young. True, we worked hard to get it but unless you are going in the right direction God won't give you a helping push to get there.

I wanted to be a writer, to get a book published — and I

got that too! On 26 January 1978 I received a postcard from Blond & Briggs, a London publisher. They apologized for taking so long to get in touch with me, the reason being that they had changed their address and things had been chaotic for a time. They were very interested in the manuscript and asked me to bear with them a little longer. They would let me have a decision soon. I was enthralled. The manuscript was not missing after all! And there was hope that it would get published.

A month later I got a letter from the publishers together with a reader's report which was excellent. The letter asked me to wait till the third partner in the firm came back from America when they would give me a firm decision about *Rhanna*. Two days later the phone went. It was the third partner speaking from London. He told me he was hardly off the plane before my manuscript was shoved into his hand for his perusal. He was pleased to tell me they were accepting it. Had I time for a good long chat with him? I managed to mumble in the affirmative. My head was swimming with disbelieving joy. His voice went on. They were sending me three contracts. Did that suit me?

'Yes, oh, yes,' I gasped. I think I babbled a bit. I don't remember clearly. He went on to assure me that the days of beating my head against the thick wall surrounding the world of publishing were over. I thanked him with reasonably intelligible words, put down the phone and just sat for a minute in the hall with my thumbs in my mouth, staring unseeingly through the glass door to the sea beyond. Then I phoned Ken at his work and told him the news, bubbling over with animation so that he hardly knew what I was talking about.

'I always told you you would do it,' he said with quiet jubilation. 'Congratulations, my lamb.'

It was a wonderful year. The publishers found out I could paint and asked me to design the jacket for *Rhanna*. Ken sketched out an idea and I set to work putting it on canvas. Ken had already drawn out maps of my imaginary isle and these were to be used in the endpapers of the book. I had to have the manuscript retyped professionally because it was grubby with continual handling and it was typed in single spacing. When a proof of the jacket arrived Ken and I were so thrilled he seized my chair and charged with me all over the house. During April I started to write my second book about Rhanna in longhand and finished it before the summer was out.

We went away to the island of Mull that summer for a fortnight leaving Tania and Jockey, now twelve years old, with Mum. We had a glorious holiday and returned refreshed. We had been at the Holy Loch four and a half years now but had decided to move to a cottage in a beautiful glen not far away. The Holy Loch was lovely but not quiet enough for us. We found the noise from the Polaris base in the Loch annoying. To write I had to have even more peace than there was on these shores and in the September of that year we moved to our present home. The access is excellent for a wheelchair, the peace and solitude entirely beautiful.

It was from here that we went to Glasgow on 15 November 1978 for the launching of *Rhanna*, staying at the Albany Hotel in Glasgow. I had expected the interviews with the press but hadn't bargained for going to the BBC broadcasting studios in Queen Margaret Drive, nor had I expected to be interviewed for BBC Television. Ken had made the arrangements from a telephone box in the glen as we didn't have a phone in the cottage and didn't intend getting one. He had spoken with the publicity agent arranged by Blond & Briggs who had told him about the forthcoming publicity coverage. Wisely Ken didn't tell me about the radio or TV interviews or I would never have gone to Glasgow. As it was it came as such a surprise I had no time to feel nervous and came over reasonably well on the two mediums. If someone had told me back in my Govan days that one day I, Christine Marion Fraser, chief of the snot-nosed urchin clan, would in years to come get a book

published and appear on TV I wouldn't have believed them.
Ken was with me in Glasgow, just there, quietly giving me
his support the way he had done since our first meeting.

It was during that time in Glasgow that we met a
gentleman I shall call 'the author's friend'. Ken told him
about my tome lying gathering dust at the back of the
wardrobe. He told me to send it to him. I did this after
Christmas and at the end of January 1979 I got a letter
telling me it was to be published. Ken's quiet rapture at this
news was perhaps even greater than mine. He had suggested
I write my own story. When I showed waning faith in it he
remained optimistic, telling me that he knew it would be
published one day. And so it came to be. The first volume of
my autobiography, *Blue Above the Chimneys*, came to the
public eye in May 1980. God has indeed been good to me.
When I was very young I made up my mind I was going to
be so great a writer the world would know about me. Now I
am content to write to the best of my ability. If my books
please then I am happy. Reaction to them has been good, I
get many letters from people telling me how much they have
enjoyed them.

It is a strange feeling to be recognized in public places as
an author. Not so long ago I went with Ken to a Corries'
concert. Uppermost in my mind was the notion of getting
their autographs. At the interval we were in the foyer when
several people came up to me wanting *my* autograph. While
my mind went into a blind panic outwardly I remained calm
and complied gratefully to the requests, my shaky hand
somehow managing to get my name down on proffered bits
of paper.

I smile when people say to me, 'Oh my, I've always
fancied writing a book,' and I tell them, 'Why don't you?
No use talking about it, get it done!' What I don't tell
them is that they might have to experience many years of
patience and frustration whilst pushing their book from one
publisher to another. One would-be writer came to me and
said, 'I feel a book is about to be born . . . you know . . . like

I am pregnant and about to give birth!' I had to hide a smile. The comparison was so ludicrous. If I felt that I was giving birth every time I wrote I would never pen another word — it would be too painful!

On the whole people are delighted about my books but I tell them I would never have got where I am without the encouragement of my wonderful husband. He has coaxed, persuaded, berated me when I have been at the lowest ebb waiting to see if a manuscript was going to be accepted or rejected. Evelyn is very proud in a quiet unassuming way. She makes me little bookmarkers and homemade cards of congratulation when the news is good from a publisher. I have kept them all for to me they are more precious than the most elaborate could ever be. She is eleven now, a fine, straight, healthy child who loves fishing, swimming, cycling. I have outsmarted those WOOPOS who, before she was born, would ask Mum Cameron,

'Will it be normal, do you think?'

'Will it be able to walk like a normal child?'

If by chance Evelyn had contracted some disabling illness it would have been assumed that I had passed mine on to her. Before I was even married I knew my illness wasn't hereditary, just something that happened to one in a million children. If an able-bodied mum had borne a child who later became handicapped, then of course it wasn't caused through a genetic weakness but owed itself to a misfortune stroke of ill fate! The WOOPOS are few and far between, thank goodness. The rest of us are too busy getting on with our lives to spare the time to sniffle our noses into the affairs of other people's bodily functions.

Evelyn is by no means perfectly sweet. She has been rather difficult to bring up owing to her taking from me a lot of stubbornness but there is also a lot of Ken in her and she is mostly even-tempered and of a sunny disposition. She is still a tomboy although she is beginning to take a slight interest in her appearance and makes the effort to change out of torn denims into something decent when visitors come. We have tried to bring her up with a good sense of values though this hasn't been easy with the influences of a modern world that shouts 'Give! Give! Give! Take! Take! Take! And don't bother to work too hard or to say "thank you" for that which you get.'

We have taught Evelyn to say 'please' and 'thank you!' We encourage her to write letters of appreciation to those who give her gifts. We have quite a battle over it but in the end she gives in and sits down to write her thank-you letters. She is kind to old people, adores animals, loves reading. She hates the word 'cripple'. She says the very word itself is crippled and ought to be banned from modern language. I don't think she has suffered through having a disabled mother. We get on well together, so much so she sometimes treats me like one of her pals. We fight like cat and dog occasionally because I am a disciplinarian and will battle with her till she does what I think is the right thing for a child of her age to do, yet she respects me for sticking to my guns. Ken is a bit of a softie with her but if he goes into one of his rare tempers she is so taken aback she scrambles to obey him without argument. She has a marvellous sense of humour and we have laughed together till she rolls off her seat. She is used to the sight of wheelchairs, crutches and sticks. Her young mind has been conditioned to recognize them as just another part of life.

On the whole I think children of today are terrific. They are open-minded, frank, and never bat an eye at things their elders might think unusual. Naturally they are curious and I used to flinch when a big pair of wondering eyes stared at me. The present generation don't stare nearly as much. They ask outright what is wrong with your legs and once told they accept the whole thing philosophically. If only parents didn't indulge them so much, rob them of their ingenuity with too much ready-made entertainment, then they would be the most visionary of small human beings.

Tania is still with us and though she is now ten she acts like a big daft puppy at times. Jockey II died of old age before we left the shores of the Holy Loch but now there is Jockey III, a lovely green and yellow budgie who has an amazing vocabulary, all spoken in a Glasgow accent.

Little things spring to mind as I write these last few pages. Recently Ken and I were in our local supermarket when a lady came up to me and said smilingly, 'I don't know if he's your boyfriend or your husband but he's very attentive to you.'

'Oh, he's my husband,' I told her with a laugh.

Her face sparkled and she said eagerly, 'You look so much in love I thought you must be sweethearts!'

This after sixteen years of marriage! Although Ken and I giggled with delight under cover of a display of tinned goods we were thrilled. It's these little incidents that make life the sweet thing it is for us. People, just the good, ordinary, kind-hearted people, are what life is all about. The rich, the grand, the elevated are in the minority. The everyday people, the characters, are the sort that makes my world go round, the world of books, filled with the kind of beings that might live in the next house, the next glen, the island over the sea!

I still don't have roses round the door. Our house faces north. The sun streams in from the east, the south, the west, but the north side is sunless except in high summer. However, there is still hope. Recently I cut an article from a newspaper listing the different kinds of rambling roses that will grow on a north wall. Till then my rose bowers must be symbolic of our lives, the big fat juicy buds symbolizing the good times just ready to burst into flowers; the thorns convey the dark rough spells that we have encountered along the way . . . all of them draped round the doorway of life.

I come to the close of this book at the start of the International Year of the Disabled. I hope at the end of it the attitudes of the able-bodied towards the disabled might be broadened a good deal. We are part of the populated world, a big part of it, and that is all we really want to be.

Do not regard us as an abnormal, individual race who must get about our business as best we can. Include us, consider us, for as I have already said, 'Tomorrow it might be you'.

Recently we had a visit from the secretary of the Glasgow Disabled Drivers' Association. He has been the secretary for twenty-six years, an intelligent, marvellous individual despite the fact he lives life from a wheelchair. His wife came with him, an able-bodied young woman who has been around disabled people for most of her life. She enjoys their company, she looks beyond the wheelchairs and the crutches to the people they support. She has an instinct for knowing what is right and what is wrong for them. To me she is the epitome of everything I would like to see in the attitudes of all able-bodied towards the disabled. She has accepted that we are all alike in the eyes of God.

I no longer have my little invalid car. Despite the inadequacies of the little three wheelers I will always have a soft spot for them. Without mine I would never have known independence or been able to explore the beautiful Highlands of Scotland. Ken and I would never have met and there would have been no Evelyn. I look back on my life and I have no regrets. I am what I am, I have learned to use my capabilities to their full extent and I appreciate a God who gave me the strength to find them out.

What way to end a story that as yet has no end?

Coming Home to Argyll

Dear Argyll, land of purple mountains.
Of trees whose every shade of green
bring tears to seeing eyes.
Where life abounds from every rushing stream.

Land of sea lochs and peaceful lapping shores.
Of mists and suns that smile on sleeping bens
And storms against which grass and trees bend low.
And amber rivers cascade helplessly in fertile glens.

Argyll, where it would not seem out of place,
to hear a lone piper, high on some unseen height,
play splendid tunes that stir the hearing soul.
And crying hearts relive again what once was Scotia's
 might.
A land where guardian mountains tower in awesome
 mastery.
Of inland lochs where sombre beauty lies
in dark green depths and changing face.
And winging curlews startle hushed glens with lonely cries.

Argyll; where seals lie lazily on sun-warmed stones.
And otters play on rolling crested seas.
Where heather grows in fragrant massed array.
And winds sing soulfully through swaying trees.

Oh sweet Argyll! With every turning road,
my seeking soul and wayward heart comes home.
With every passing mile my searching eyes find beauty,
and tell my heart there is no further need to roam.

Rhanna
Christine Marion Fraser

A rich, romantic, Scottish saga set
on the Hebridean island of Rhanna

Rhanna

The poignant story of life on the rugged and tranquil island
of Rhanna, and of the close-knit community for whom it
is home.

Rhanna at War

Rhanna's lonely beauty is no protection against the horrors
of war. But Shona Mackenzie, home on leave, discovers
that the fiercest battles are those between lovers.

Children of Rhanna

The four island children, inseparable since childhood, find
that growing up also means growing apart.

Return to Rhanna

Shona and Niall Mackenzie come home to find Rhanna
unspoilt by the onslaught of tourism. But then tragedy
strikes at the heart of their marriage.

Song of Rhanna

Ruth is happily married to Lorn. But the return to Rhanna
of her now famous friend Rachel threatens Ruth's
happiness.

'Full-blooded romance, a strong, authentic setting'
Scotsman

FONTANA PAPERBACKS

Fontana Paperbacks: Non-fiction

Fontana is a leading paperback publisher of non-fiction. Below are some recent titles.

- ☐ THE LIVING PLANET David Attenborough £8.95
- ☐ SCOTLAND'S STORY Tom Steel £4.95
- ☐ HOW TO SHOOT AN AMATEUR NATURALIST Gerald Durrell £2.25
- ☐ THE ENGLISHWOMAN'S HOUSE
                    Alvilde Lees-Milne and Derry Moore £7.95
- ☐ BRINGING UP CHILDREN ON YOUR OWN Liz McNeill Taylor £2.50
- ☐ WITNESS TO WAR Charles Clements £2.95
- ☐ IT AIN'T NECESSARILY SO Larry Adler £2.95
- ☐ BACK TO BASICS Mike Nathenson £2.95
- ☐ POPPY PARADE Arthur Marshall (ed.) £2.50
- ☐ LEITH'S COOKBOOK
                    Prudence Leith and Caroline Waldegrave £5.95
- ☐ HELP YOUR CHILD WITH MATHS Alan T. Graham £2.95
- ☐ TEACH YOUR CHILD TO READ Peter Young and Colin Tyre £2.95
- ☐ BEDSIDE SEX Richard Huggett £2.95
- ☐ GLEN BAXTER, HIS LIFE Glen Baxter £4.95
- ☐ LIFE'S RICH PAGEANT Arthur Marshall £2.50
- ☐ H FOR 'ENRY Henry Cooper £3.50
- ☐ THE SUPERWOMAN SYNDROME Marjorie Hansen Shaevitz £2.50
- ☐ THE HOUSE OF MITFORD Jonathan and Catherine Guinness £5.95
- ☐ ARLOTT ON CRICKET David Rayvern Allen (ed.) £3.50
- ☐ THE QUALITY OF MERCY William Shawcross £3.95
- ☐ AGATHA CHRISTIE Janet Morgan £3.50

You can buy Fontana paperbacks at your local bookshop or newsagent. Or you can order them from Fontana Paperbacks, Cash Sales Department, Box 29, Douglas, Isle of Man. Please send a cheque, postal or money order (not currency) worth the purchase price plus 15p per book for postage (maximum postage required is £3).

NAME (Block letters) _____

ADDRESS _____

_____

_____